A Darker Truth

"My tomb . . ." Asvoria reached out her hands as she approached the statue next to the mauseolum.

Suddenly, there was a sharp crack, and a sheen like silvery metal erupted from thin air. Asvoria fell backward onto the path . . . Snarling, she picked up a rock and hurled it at the tomb. It collided with the magical barrier, sending sparks flaming down from the impact. "I'll just have to wait," she mused, tapping her chin with a long, elegant finger.

"Your little friends will be so busy looking for my sword that they won't see danger stalking them. They already turn their back from the evil within their midst, ignoring all in order to seek me out."

Asvoria smiled. "Yes, all I have to do is wait. Wait for them to seek and find a darker truth than they ever imagined . . ."

THE NEW ADVENTURES

SPELLBINDER QUARTET

Volume 1

TEMPLE OF THE DRAGONSLAYER

TIM WAGGONER

Volume 2

THE DYING KINGDOM

STEPHEN D. SULLIVAN

Volume 3

THE DRAGON WELL

DAN WILLIS

Volume 4

RETURN OF THE SORCERESS

TIM WAGGONER

DRAGON QUARTET

Volume 5

DRAGON SWORD

REE SOESBEE

Volume 6

DRAGON DAY

STAN BROWN

(March 2005)

Volume 7

DRAGON KNIGHT

DAN WILLIS

(May 2005)

Volume 8

DRAGON SPELL

JEFF SAMPSON

(July 2005)

THE NEW
ADVENTURES
VOLUME
5

DRAGON SWORD

REE SOESBEE

COVER & INTERIOR ART
Vinod Rams

MIRROR
STONE

DRAGON SWORD

©2005 Wizards of the Coast, Inc.

Distributed in the United States by Holtzbrinck Publishing. Distributed in Canada by Fenn Ltd.

Distributed to the hobby, toy, and comic trade in the United States and Canada by regional distributors.

Distributed worldwide by Wizards of the Coast, Inc. and regional distributors.

Printed in the U.S.A.

Art by Vinod Rams
Cartography by Dennis Kauth
First Printing: January 2005
Library of Congress Catalog Card Number: 2004113597

9 8 7 6 5 4 3 2 1

US ISBN: 0-7869-3578-2
ISBN-13: 978-0-7869-3578-9
605-17639-001-EN

U.S., CANADA,
ASIA, PACIFIC, & LATIN AMERICA
Wizards of the Coast, Inc.
P.O. Box 707
Renton, WA 98057-0707
+1-800-324-6496

EUROPEAN HEADQUARTERS
Wizards of the Coast, Belgium
T Hofveld 6d
1702 Groot-Bijgaarden
Belgium
+322 457 3350

Visit our web site at **www.mirrorstonebooks.com**

For Kevin.
And there are about a million reasons why.

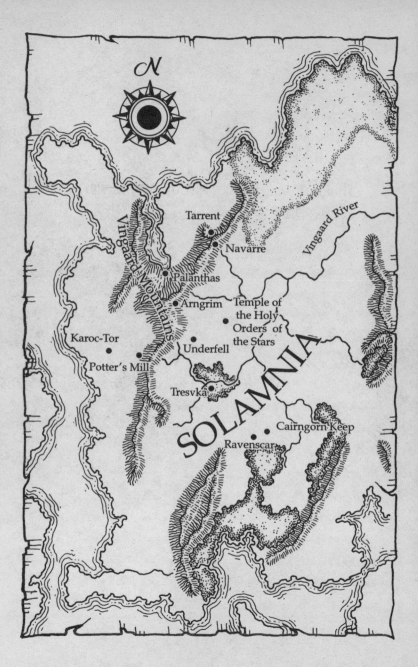

Contents

PROLOGUE. 1780 P.C. 1

1. Blood of the Future...7

2. Secret Maps and Secret Pacts...............................19

3. A Forgotten Path 33

4. Dreams of Glory 45

5. Tongues of Stone 53

6. Into the Earth 63

7. Broken Stone..75

8. The Cost of Knowledge 81

9. Through the Darkness to the Light.........................93

10. Freedom and Truth...101

11. A Portal Opened 109

12. Long Forgotten Lies..117

13. Protections 131

14. The Last Priest of Asvoria 135

15. The Tomb of a Fallen Queen...............................147

16. Blood and Promises..159

17. Betrayal 173

18. A Little Misdirection 183

19. The Darkness Beyond.......................................197

20. Echoes of Salvation, Shards of Pain 209

21. Bitter Revenge..219

22. The Price..225

23. Splintered Nightmare 229

24. Falling Into Darkness.......................................235

25. Maddoc's Lie 241

1780 P.C.

The earth around Cairngorn Keep was damp and dark. Boots crushed the soil as the soldiers marched relentlessly toward the high black gates. In the sky, a silver moon shimmered, waiting to be joined by its fellow moons as the night advanced.

A woman stood before the keep's gates. Her own army had long since fled, and her enemies swarmed across the field. Yet even standing alone before hundreds of soldiers, she did not show fear.

Three monstrous red dragons flew against the dark clouds. They swooped down, one by one, their raucous cries like the caws of crows over the battlefield.

The woman lifted her chin, her jet-black hair swinging in a long coil down her back. Her clawed hands tore through the air. Blue fire flung from her fingertips again and again, cutting through the army marching toward her. One by one, the soldiers fell, until only a handful remained.

They ran for their lives.

"Fools!" she cried out. "You cannot stand against Asvoria! Not today . . ." Sparks of magic swarmed around her like fireflies in the night sky. Today her magic was stronger than ever, hoarded and ready for her final victory. As she watched the soldiers' retreating forms, she laughed, a terrible sound that echoed through the skies.

But one man defied her.

One man did not flee.

He forced himself through the fire of her magic, toward the gate. On his armor, the sigil of a bronze dragon shone, its head raised in a fierce roar.

"Asvoria," he said. "You have lost all. The kingdom is broken beneath you, and your rule even now fades. Your army is defeated, and already the cities of this land celebrate your death."

The brave man wore a simple black helmet, black armor, and bore a sword that was darkened with battle. Beneath the helmet's visor, his eyes were dark with sorrow and weary with pain. "I can no longer allow your tyranny to grind us all to dust."

"Poor Captain Viranesh," Asvoria greeted him mockingly. "This is not my end. On the contrary, it is the beginning of a new life for me. A new beginning—and one in which you can still play a part." Her amethyst eyes flashed. On her breast, a necklace hung; the medallion brilliant as the sun at noon. "You say my power is fading, but you are wrong. I am stronger than I have ever been! The defeat of my soldiers means nothing, no more than the scattering of a thousand ants. When I ascend, I will have no need for any pitiful armies. My magic will overwhelm you all, and still I will reign. When the three moons rise and join together . . . I will become what I was meant to be!"

The man shook his head, lifting his sword and taking a battle-stance. "You are wrong, my dear."

Asvoria laughed once more, her hands forming strange patterns in the air. Her magic swept forward, the green and yellow wave swelling like an ocean's tide . . . but when the surge subsided, the captain still walked across the keep's bridge, advancing step by step toward her.

Stunned, Asvoria staggered backward. Her face contorted viciously, hands clawing at the air as she spoke a phrase of power. A crack of dark thunder broke the heavens.

Still Viranesh advanced.

"It cannot be . . ." she whispered, the first touch of fear illuminating her shining eyes. She tossed her ebony hair. "Are you here to kill me, Captain?"

"I am here," he said slowly, "to prevent your ascension. To destroy the woman I love before she becomes an abomination."

Viranesh raised his sword and saluted. On his breast, the bronze dragon seemed to roar out the grief that he felt but could not utter.

"You, of all people," Asvoria said. "Of all those in my kingdom, you believe that you can destroy me—with what? With your *love?*" She sneered. "What we had once is dead."

The sorceress reached to her side, unsheathing her own slender sword. The silver steel rang as it came free of its bonds, and green lightning flickered down the blade. A malachite stone shimmered in its handle, and emerald shards embedded within the sword's blade twinkled like envious eyes.

"Recognize this, Captain?" Asvoria hissed. "It is the blade Aegis, the most powerful weapon any human has ever known. With this alone, I could reconquer my kingdom and bring fear to those who have defied me.

"But more," she continued, the blade flashing in her hands, "When I have ascended, then I will walk the skies." Her eyes glittered with the fire of her conviction.

"Yes," he replied quietly. "I know what you plan. And it will never succeed. No one has ever transformed permanently from human to dragon. It cannot be done."

"Simply because something has not ever been accomplished does not mean that it is impossible," she crowed, lifting one hand from the blade. Her skin shimmered, small scales coating it, like the fine tracings of a spider web. "You see? Already, it begins."

The captain stepped forward, but Asvoria gripped the Aegis once more, steeling it against him. "A new reign, Viranesh. A new kingdom, ruled by a queen who spans both dragon and mortal kind. A reign I shall christen, I think, with your death." She raised the Aegis in a strong, overhand stroke.

Viranesh swung his sword, and the dark blade rang against Asvoria's shining green steel.

"It's over, Asvoria," Viranesh said. "You cannot defeat me without your most powerful magic, and you can't afford to use it, not now. If you do, you won't have enough for the ascension." He glanced up at the sky.

Lunitari, red as blood, began to crowd the silver moon. The black moon waited, hidden against the darkness, for the final moments of the confluence.

"You underestimate the Aegis, my *dear*," Asvoria spat.

She swept her sword toward his legs. Viranesh stepped far to the right to avoid its sharp bite. And Asvoria over-extended.

Viranesh chose his moment quickly, jabbing the hilt of his weapon against Asvoria's unprotected stomach. She screamed, more in fury than in pain, and staggered back into the keep.

Viranesh pursued her through the narrow doorway, and the green fire of the Aegis crashed against the captain's black sword. Asvoria fought unflinching, but Viranesh's prowess with the sword proved legendary. He pressed her deeper into the keep with each swing of his blade, down long corridors of gilded mahogany, and up winding stairs. Finally, in a small room filled with tapestries, Asvoria found herself backed into a corner, unable to retreat more. She wielded the Aegis as though the sword had its own mind. But it was not enough.

Viranesh's sword cut her, slashing a thin red line along Asvoria's midsection. She pressed her hand to the wound.

Staring at the red blood upon her hand, she said, "Well, Viranesh, my dear, it seems I do bleed after all." Her eyes glowed in the light of the Aegis's sickly flame.

"End this," Viranesh whispered, his sword inches from her throat.

Behind him, the three moons of Krynn shone through a tall window. The silver light of Solinari had narrowed to a crescent as its ebony brother moved across the sky. Only a few moments more . . .

"Never," she hissed. "Even after my death, I will still seek my destiny. You can only slow my ascent. It cannot be stopped."

"Then you leave me no choice." With a muffled cry, Viranesh plunged his dark sword into Asvoria's chest.

Asvoria fell backward, her blood soaking the magnificent tapestry behind her. The Aegis's dying fire was captured in the thin slivers of her pupils, defiant even at the end of all things.

"I am . . . I will be . . ."—she choked, one fist clenched around the Aegis and the other scrabbling desperately at the tapestry's thick material—"the Dragon Queen . . ."

"I'm sorry that it came to this, my lady." Viranesh fell to his knees as the three moons became one. "I'm so sorry." Tears ran down his cheeks, but he refused to turn away.

Asvoria lifted the Aegis with both hands, bringing it up with all of her strength into Viranesh's chest.

He died there, her sword piercing his heart.

With her last breath, Asvoria began to chant, holding the tapestry to her chest and letting her blood deluge its bright colors. Her last magic . . . her last spell. She had saved her power for her ascension—now she must use it to create a new beginning—one that would take place when the moons conjoined once more.

The spell was rough, half-wild with pain and with splintered dreams, but it would be enough . . . enough to hold her soul. The threads of the woven fabric shimmered with a strange green light, and the tapestry fell away as her eyes closed.

She would never die.

1   Blood of the Future

Thousands of years later, in the same dark keep, Davyn lowered his knife, the rage on his face slowly ebbing away as he regained control. He pointed with the blade toward the old man who sat on the nearby bed.

"Nearra is *not* dead," Davyn said bitterly. "Never say that again."

Maddoc met the boy's steely gaze and said nothing, the lines in his aged face showing weary solemnity. His black robes were unruffled despite wear, and he bore their depth like a dethroned king.

"I said she was lost, Davyn, not dead." The old wizard sighed lightly, keeping his eyes locked on his adopted son. "But the difference is small."

Davyn's sandy brown hair was unruly, his eyes were fierce. "It isn't true."

Standing in front of him, Catriona said, "Davyn, we aren't getting anywhere by fighting. We need Maddoc—we need his knowledge—or we'll lose any chance we have of finding her and bringing her back."

Behind Catriona, a small kender hopped up and down on the

tips of his toes, his purple wizard's cape fluffing out like half of an indigo toadstool.

"You tell him, Cat!" Sindri chirped.

"Hush, Sindri, you're not helping." Catriona rolled her green eyes and turned back to Davyn. "I know you're worried about Nearra. We're all worried about Nearra." Catriona was much taller than Davyn, and held him back with arms woven of solid muscle. "But attacking Maddoc is not going to get her back."

"Why not?" Davyn asked. "This is his fault in the first place."

Another voice hissed from the shadows at the far side of the room. "Blame is a waste of time."

Catriona glanced back at the slender elf leaning against the corner wall, and nodded. "Elidor's right. Blame doesn't get Nearra back. It just means we sit in this keep, arguing among ourselves and getting absolutely nothing done to save her. Is that what you want, Davyn? To waste all of our energy yelling at Maddoc, and have none left to fight for Nearra when she needs us? We're going to find her, Davyn."

Davyn sheathed his long knife and shrugged off Catriona's hold. "I know." He stared out the window at the grounds of Cairngorn Keep, watching as the pounding rain soaked the bare earth below. "But I don't have to like it."

The kender joined Davyn by the window, ducking underneath Cat's arm as she tried to grasp his collar. Tugging on the ranger's belt and grinning, Sindri said, "I know you hate him, Davyn. I'd hate him, too, if he'd pretended to be my father and had ruined my life."

Catriona grimaced, and Elidor stifled a groan.

Sindri didn't seem to notice. "But Maddoc knows magic. And he knows Asvoria. We've got to work with him." Sindri climbed up onto the windowsill, staring at Davyn. "Don't worry, though.

If he makes one wrong move—boom!—we'll take him apart."

The kender's sturdy assurances brought a faint smile to Davyn's face, despite their lack of tact, and the ranger nodded. "All right, Sindri. All right."

Sindri beamed.

Maddoc rolled his eyes, lifting his bound hands. "Do you really think I'm going to do much, trussed up like this?" The old wizard wiggled his fingers. "Couldn't you just—"

"No," Davyn and Elidor chorused.

Maddoc sighed. "Even if I could move my hands, I have no magic. Asvoria burned it from me. I could not even power the smallest cantrip."

"He's lying." Davyn whirled to face the old wizard. "I'll agree to let him live for now—but I still say he can't be trusted. It's his fault Asvoria's returned—his fault that Nearra's soul is trapped. This was his plan."

Maddoc replied patiently, "My plan was far more elaborate, Davyn. You should know that. But now there is no hope of it ever succeeding. Why beleaguer the point, Son?"

"Don't call me *Son*," Davyn snarled. "I'm not your son. And you have magic, I'm sure of it. You're just hiding it—and until I know why, I'll never trust you, not a single moment. No matter what bonds hold you or what promises you make."

Maddoc sighed, and looked away.

Elidor drew a small knife from his belt, cleaning his fingers with the blade. "You're wasting what patience we have, Maddoc," he said quietly. Long blonde hair brushed against his shoulders and catlike eyes glinted with the same steel color of his knife's blade. "Tell us what we need to know about Asvoria."

"Asvoria," the old wizard muttered. "Yes, Asvoria. Ancient sorceress, tyrannical queen, phenomenal magic-user and to all historical accounts, a classic beauty . . ." Sensing his audience's impatience, Maddoc spoke more quickly, "She trapped her spirit within an ancient tapestry. I discovered it and used it to restore her."

"In Nearra," Davyn spat the words like a curse.

Maddoc merely nodded, showing no sign of remorse. "And it worked. Asvoria has returned."

Sindri whistled from the windowsill. "Weren't you afraid?"

Maddoc shot a scathing glance at the kender. "No. Why should I be? Asvoria and I are of like minds. I assumed she would understand—not see me as a threat." He looked down at his empty hands. "I thought I could control her. Merge our magics—take the world and split it between us."

The revulsion on Catriona's face was echoed in her words. "The world is not yours to take or to split."

Maddoc ignored her. "Nearra's soul should have tempered Asvoria's greed and anger. I considered every option. I made allowances . . . "

"So what are we going to do now?" The elf looked up from his knife, eyes slitted dangerously.

"Well." Sindri pursed his lips and reached inside his cloak to pull forth a gleaming amulet. "I suppose we're going to have to use this."

"Put that away, you fool kender!" Maddoc shouted. "You don't know what it can do!"

"Fool?" Sindri harrumphed. "I'll have you know that my family is descended from a great wizard, renowned for his magical prowess through the lands of the kender! We're practically famous!"

"Famous, but obviously short-lived." Maddoc sneered. "Now put that away before she senses it."

Chagrined, the kender tucked the amulet back into his brown cloak. "She can do that?"

"It is not beyond Asvoria. Her two main goals now will be to reestablish her power—to consolidate what she has lost, and to rebuild her kingdom."

"What will she need to do that?" Davyn asked, his eyebrows knitting. Catriona leaned against the foot of the bed, her eyes focused on Maddoc's every move.

"The Daystar"—Maddoc gestured toward the kender's medallion—"and the Aegis."

For a long moment, the four others exchanged confused glances. The room was bathed in light as a strike of lightning lit the window and ignited Maddoc's stoic face. The marble walls shone for a flickering moment.

"The Aegis?" Catriona asked at last, her patience breaking. "What's the Aegis?"

Maddoc did not reply, staring down at his hands. Elidor kicked the bed, shaking the dark-robed wizard.

"What is the Aegis?" Elidor repeated, his white teeth shining in a near-feral snarl. The elf's Kagonesti blood showed most when he was upset or angry, and now it revealed itself in an almost wolfish grin of ferocity. "Talk, wizard."

Maddoc lifted his bound hands to his eyes, rubbing them wearily. "The Aegis, sometimes known as the Dragon Sword, is the most dangerous weapon that Asvoria possesses. Where the Daystar is a primarily defensive weapon, able to reverse enchantments and levy only minor offensive powers, the Aegis is a sword of tremendous power. Its force rivals the power of a hundred dragons. The last time its full power was called upon, Asvoria scattered an army with a single stroke."

Catriona's eyes flew wide, but Sindri was first to speak. The kender leaped from the windowsill and climbed onto the bed beside Maddoc. "That's amazing! It really can do that? What's it made of? Who forged it? Where did she get it? Where is it now?"

The barrage of questions came like elven arrows, leaping one after the other from the excited kender's mouth.

"Slow down, Sindri," Davyn said grudgingly. "Maddoc has to answer the first question before you can ask more."

But Maddoc shook his head, his expression dim and reserved. "No, I will not say any more. It is dangerous information to have. More dangerous, still, to give out to those who will not respect it."

Davyn pushed past Catriona and gripped the frame of the bed, white-knuckled. "You'll tell us, or I'll kill you."

Maddoc began to laugh. His humorless laughter was low and broken, rolling from his throat like rocks in an avalanche. The wizard lifted his bound wrists next to his face.

"Kill me?" Maddoc chortled. "There is little more you could do to me in this world, Davyn, than Asvoria has done. I am a broken man, with no magic and no further ambition. Death—even death granted to me by my own son—would be a blessing." Maddoc pushed himself from the bed, striding forward without fear to face his adopted son. "Kill me, then, Davyn, and finish it. Lose Nearra, and everything you fight for, but gain your *revenge*." The word was spat from Maddoc's clenched jaw, his eyes as dark as his black robes.

Before he could help himself, Davyn staggered back a step, the lessons of his past too firmly ingrained in his soul.

Catriona leaped between them again, her red hair a tempest against her pale skin. "Stop this!" she shouted, and Maddoc and Davyn were forced apart. "We will rescue Nearra, but not like this." Wheeling on Maddoc, Catriona shoved him in the chest with her finger, eyes blazing. "Answer the questions. Now."

Maddoc nodded, relenting. "The Aegis is a sword forged by the gods themselves, long before the Cataclysm. It is like no other weapon in the world. Some say that the Goddess Takhisis wielded it, before she was cast down by Paladine. Other legends say her first High Priest forged it in the fires of the broken earth, before cities rose in the Vingaard Mountains."

"Legends." Davyn scowled. "Is there anything you are certain of?"

"I am certain that Asvoria wielded the sword during her first reign. I am certain Asvoria will try to find it, and with it, she will become as powerful as she was before—during the height of her kingdom, and the strength of her tyranny.

"As for the Aegis, I know what the sword is said to be capable of performing. It enhances strength and agility, erases fatigue. The longer you have the sword, the more it is able to increase your power. But the Aegis is also like a drug; once you have used it, you are addicted to it forever after. Asvoria feels that she *must* have the weapon or her rise to power may fail."

"Ooh," Sindri said. "Is it made all of magic? I mean, does the blade glow, or turn into a tiger, or strike people with lighting?" A flash of light outside the window echoed the kender's words.

Maddoc smiled sardonically. "It has power over lightning, yes. But that is not its main ability. The Aegis was created at the same time, and with the same magic, as the Daystar. The Daystar can cancel magic potency, while the Aegis protects its wielder from offensive magics—but only so long as the wielder has conviction. If the user's conviction fails, then the sword loses its power."

"Asvoria's got enough conviction to enslave nations," Elidor said quietly. "If that's all she needs, then she'll never fall, as long as she has the sword."

"We can't let her get it." Sindri bounced upon the bed, his black hair flouncing against his back with emphasis. "We have to stop her. We have the Daystar, that's something."

"With the Aegis, she could easily retake the Daystar, and then conquer much of Krynn." Maddoc said quietly to the kender, showing an uncharacteristic gentleness. "You would have no chance against her."

"We must find it first, then," Elidor murmured, resheathing his knife.

"Yes, where can we find it?" Sindri asked.

Maddoc hung his head. "I have been asking myself the same question for many years. Only a few months ago, I came across a legend that claims the sword was buried with her bones, interred in her tomb at Navarre. But I do not know if this legend can be believed."

"Where's Navarre?" Sindri asked eagerly.

Maddoc sat down on the edge of the bed once more, with a soft sigh. "Navarre was once a summer home to Asvoria, one of her favorite places. It is mentioned in several texts. When she was buried, the small palace became her tomb—and its location was removed from every map, every text, and every memory. Her body was taken from Cairngorn Keep after her death, and hidden there by her most loyal servants for the day that she would return. All those who knew the location of Navarre were killed—by Asvoria's servants, who then took their own lives to protect her secrets. It is said that the palace was buried under tons of rubble to keep her possessions safe from tomb-robbers, in the hope that she would rise and return once more."

"Well, she did, and that's your fault, but do you know *where* it is?" bounced the kender.

"No." Maddoc said a bit too quickly. He looked down at his bound hands.

"You're lying!" Davyn snapped.

Maddoc set his jaw and looked up. "The location of Navarre is an ancient mystery—one that I could never break. A few months ago, I learned of a group of explorers who *had* penetrated its depths. They entered Navarre and were all killed, all but one. The fool reached Asvoria's tomb but he dared not enter alone. So he placed a spell around its entrance, and vowed to return. I compelled the man to tell me how to disarm the shield-spell. But he . . . he died before he told me the exact location of the palace. And now, even if I were to find the palace now, the spell would be much too strong and in this shape,"—he raised his bound hands once more—"it would be suicide for me to try to retrieve the sword."

"But not for us," Catriona said firmly. "You could try to lead us to Navarre."

"I will not. It would be madness."

"No matter." Davyn broke in. "We don't need the wizard. I know someone else who can help us." Heads turned toward him, and Elidor's face darkened with concern. Davyn continued, "There is a bard in Ravenscar—a mapmaker. He's got maps of every inch of Krynn. If he doesn't have a map showing Navarre, then one doesn't exist."

"How do you know this man, Davyn?" Catriona asked.

The ranger shrugged. "He pays well for maps of untraveled country. I sold him some maps a few years ago. His name is Godwin Elfbearer. I'd say he's our best bet."

"I told you. Every map that showed Navarre's location has been destroyed," Maddoc said quietly. "It's a waste of time."

"Maybe you think it is. To me, it looks more like our only hope." Davyn said, turning on his heel to face Catriona. "Are you in?"

Catriona grinned. "Of course."

The others nodded, and Sindri leaped from the bed to the floor. "This is exciting. There must be tons of information in Asvoria's tomb. Spell books, lost alchemist's texts, a hundred magic items forgotten to all but the ancient scholars! Can we start out right now, Cat? Can we?"

The beautiful warrior shook her head. "No, Sindri. We're all tired, and we'll need to restock our equipment and our food. And

. . . we need to decide: what will we do with Maddoc?"

"He'll come with us, of course!" Sindri smiled. "He knows Asvoria better than anyone in the world. He knows how to disarm the tomb spell. And he's the only one who knows what the Aegis looks like—what if she's got other magic swords, huh? How will we know which one is the Aegis?" Sindri's eyes were pleading as he looked back and forth among his friends.

Davyn shook his head roughly. "No. I don't trust him. Who knows if this tomb even exists? It might be another trick."

Catriona and Elidor considered in silence before Cat spoke at last. "I'm going to say we can't leave him here, Davyn. Maddoc's no real threat to us now. He's got no magic left, and Asvoria's as likely to kill him as she is to destroy us. We're the only people standing between him and death at Asvoria's hands. And if he does have some information from his research that can help us once we're in the tomb, we can't turn our back on that."

Davyn turned to Elidor. "You can't agree with them," he said. "You, of all people, know what Maddoc's done, how he's tried to kill us at every turn—what he did to Nearra. Do you think we should trust him?"

Exasperated, Davyn kicked at a stool, skittering the light wooden object across the floor. "We can do it ourselves. We just need him to write out what he knows, and then we can . . . we can . . . "

"Turn him over to the authorities?" Elidor murmured. "Do you really think anyone will believe us? 'Hello, sir, this black wizard kidnapped our friend and released the soul of a pre-Cataclysm sorceress into her body. Will you hold him for us?'" Sarcasm dripped from Elidor's words.

Davyn scowled. "But—take him with us?"

"There's no other choice." Elidor nodded to Catriona. "And if he betrays us, I relish the fact that it's going to be my dagger in his back, the instant it happens."

If the threat made Maddoc uncomfortable, he did not show it. He sat upon the bed in his black robes, his sharp face registering neither emotion nor interest. Davyn shot him an icy look. "I don't have to like it," Davyn said, turning toward the door and throwing it open. "And I don't have to pretend that I do." He strode through the door, slamming it behind him and vanishing into the dark stone corridors.

Catriona, Sindri, and Elidor gazed at one another. "Should we go after him?" Cat said.

"No," Elidor replied. "Let him walk it off. He understands that it's our only option."

Elidor turned away from the door and reached for his pack. "He won't do it for us. He will do it . . . for Nearra."

2 Secret Maps and Secret Pacts

As dawn's first light touched Ravenscar, Davyn, Elidor, and Catriona hurried down a muddy street. The sun shone through the fog, washing a rosy glow over the otherwise ramshackle town.

"There's the shop." Davyn pointed. It was a small, wooden building, an attachment to a much larger market. If Davyn hadn't pointed out the small window by the thin door, Catriona would have missed it completely.

She squinted at the nondescript doorway. "I'd thought it would be . . . I don't know . . ."

"Cleaner?" Elidor finished for her, swiping a fingerful of dust off the shop window.

"Maybe." Cat smiled nervously. "I guess I expected harps or something."

Davyn snorted. "Godwin is a bard, but he's not a musician. You two have a lot to learn."

A hawker somewhere in the fog called out, "Mutton! Get your mutton! Wake up right in the morning!"

Catriona paid him no mind as she pushed open the shop door, with Davyn and Elidor right behind her.

"Hello?" she called, peering into the dim space. The shop was a strangely cramped little place, filled with piles upon piles of books stacked in haphazard zigzags. A long table in the center of the main room was covered with sheets of paper, ink bottles, and thin, tapered quills. A candle flickered on the table, and a pair of watery blue eyes glared back at Catriona from between two high stacks of books.

"Don't need any," the proprietor snapped. He was a tiny man, with white hair and crumpled clothing, the pockets of his once-fine coat stained with dried ink.

Before Catriona could say anything, the small gnome hopped off his chair, and waddled toward the trio, shaking his fingers. "Did you hear me, girl? I don't need any. No mutton, no milk, no papers. Now, get out."

The gnome shooed them aside as one might a stray dog, his ink-stained fingers fluttering through the air.

Davyn couldn't help a faint smile. "Mr. Elfbearer, my name is Davyn, I sold you some maps of the southern forest, east of Tresvka—"

"I remember you," the white-haired little man said irritably. "Your mapmaking skills were atrocious. Your waterways looked like worms."

Davyn grimaced, but he continued. "I'm not selling any maps today. We're here to buy."

The gnome stopped still, his long ears seeming to perk forward. "Buy?"

"Yes, buy," Catriona said, stepping closer. "We're looking for—"

The little gnome interrupted her, waving his arms grandly and tottering to the door. "Come in, come in, yes, yes, of course!" He bustled the three of them in, fluffing his sash and trying to straighten his white nest of hair. "Maps, maps. I'm Godwin

Elfbearer, you know, minstrel at large and mapmaker extraordinaire. Welcome to my shop, welcome, welcome!"

The gnome climbed a footstool at the base of a bookshelf and began rifling through a stack of papers high above. "Are you interested in the ancient city of Palanthas?" he asked. "The Bay of Branchala? The Gates of Paladine? The lands to the east—"

"Actually," Davyn cut the little man off, "we're interested in a place known as Navarre."

The gnome started, nearly tipping off the footstool. Elidor and Cat leaped forward, to steady him. "Did you say—" He choked, trying to catch his breath. "Navarre?"

"You've heard of it?" Catriona asked. She, Davyn, and Elidor exchanged glances.

"Heard of it . . . heard of it. Oh, yes, I've heard of it." Godwin crept down from his stool, his face a chalky color that matched his unkempt hair. "You don't want to go there, my lady. No, not at all."

"We do, actually." Davyn cocked an eyebrow. "What can you tell us of it?"

"The last person that asked me for the maps of Navarre . . . ," The gnome rubbed his arm unconsciously, and Cat saw a faint, trailing scar across the man's wrist. "Well, he wasn't pleasant. No, no, no reason to go to Navarre. No reason at all. How about some nice maps of the apple orchards near Solanthus?"

"Navarre," Davyn said, pressing his fists to the table. "We want Navarre. Nothing else. And we have little time."

Cat stepped smoothly between Davyn and Godwin. "Please. It's very important."

Something in Catriona's eyes muted the gnome's protests, and the little man sighed. "I can't talk you out of this?"

Elidor shook his head sternly.

The gnome's button face wrinkled with worry. "Even if I told

DRAGON SWORD

you about the terrible evils—the horrible monsters that protect the tombs there—the unknown terrors . . . ?" Godwin sighed, looking from face to face. "No, no. I see you're used to such things."

"Please," Cat said again.

"Navarre. Navarre." Godwin's shoulders slumped. Quietly, he walked to the back of the shop, pushing aside tall piles of books and wedging himself through crannies too small for humans to follow. They could still hear his voice murmuring as he passed through the stacks. "Dark places, dear me, dear me."

He returned a few moments later, blowing the dust from an iron box the size of a small tool kit. A heavy lock clanged against the latch as Godwin set the chest on the table. Godwin brushed his shaking hands over the lid. "What do you know of Navarre, adventurers?"

"It's a tomb," Elidor volunteered, repeating what Maddoc had told them. "A very ancient and dangerous tomb."

"Yes, yes, that's right." As they continued, Godwin walked across the room, drawing down the shades over the front shop window and locking the door. He peered out cautiously as he turned the sign on the door to "closed."

He turned back to face the group, scowling. "A tomb, but more than a tomb. It is a sacred place, still inhabited by the spirits of those still loyal. Enchanted. *Dangerous*. For centuries, it lay beneath the Vingaard Mountains to the north, undisturbed. Then, about five decades ago, a ranger fell through an opening in the rocks above, and found himself trapped in the darkness of Navarre."

"He really is a bard, after all," Elidor whispered to Catriona.

Godwin climbed once more on his stool and leaned over the table. "The ranger's companions found him—luckily, before he starved to death—but they returned to Ravenscar speaking of dark spirits, shadows that moved and fought, and tunnels collapsing under the weight of a thousand years. I purchased copies of their maps from their widows, you know. Years later."

The gnome felt though his pockets nervously as he spoke, at last extracting a ring of small brass keys. "I was young when I bought these maps—and that should tell you something, madam." A mild chuckle punctuated the bard's uneasiness, but the shaking of his hands was caused by more than age.

"Did you ever speak to the men who went into the caverns of Navarre?" Davyn asked.

"What?" the gnome looked up sharply, drawn out of his musing. "Oh. Oh, yes. Yes, I did. They told such tales—tales of enchantments, dangers. Beasts. Their maps only showed the location of the site; when they went back, to search inside . . . well, as I said. Their widows were only too happy to have a bit of extra money. The caverns are no mere catacomb, no lost goldmine with treasures waiting to be plundered. I doubt there is treasure at all to be found in that dark and lonely place—only death awaits there. Death, and miles of cursed stone."

Godwin turned the key halfway in the lock, and listened for the cautious click of a trap disengaging before he nodded and turned the key fully. "Navarre was once a small but ornate palace—said to be one of the most beautiful places in the world." He pulled out a mahogany scroll case, opening it and drawing out the rolled contents with a gentle hand. It held an ancient, hand-drawn map, which Godwin placed on the table with great care. The vellum was old and browned; the paints upon it dim, having lost much of their glory to time. It depicted a magnificent palace, small, but ornate, whose golden doors were flung open before a twisting fountain of water flowing down the wall of a high mountain. "Navarre was not always beneath the mountain. Once, it stood against the side of a cliff, by a forest that stretched for miles through the hillside. But with the Cataclysm, it was fully condemned—buried beneath stone and sorrow. It is said that a queen was buried there—and in sorrow, all mapmakers removed its location from their charts."

"Asvoria," Elidor said through clenched teeth. "Not sorrow, Godwin, but fear."

"So do you think the palace itself is intact?" Cat interrupted, her finger tracing the gilt edges of the manor on the page.

"Parts of it still stand, yes, or so the mapmakers said. But they had only seen a few rooms. Later, they returned planning to go in farther, but . . . only the ranger came home alive. Legend says that the queen's bones were interred in her palace before it was buried—that her servants, slaves of all races, were buried with her in that terrible place. The explorers saw bones there, scattered throughout the caverns. Bones of those who died, they told me, clawing at the rocks as they were sealed in with their mistress."

"That sounds like Asvoria," Cat said under her breath.

Godwin drew out another scroll-tube from the chest, unrolling the page inside—this one significantly newer. "The opening to the caverns where the ranger fell is the only known way into Navarre. That opening is roughly here." His stubby finger wavered over a map of the northern Vingaard Mountains, near the eastern shores of the Bay of Branchala.

Elidor's face grew grim. "I know that area." His eyes followed Godwin's fingers. "I've traveled it, though that was several decades ago. The land may have changed." He looked up. "But I believe I could find the opening, given some time and a copy of this map."

Catriona caught something in Elidor's face, a hesitancy that was unlike the self-confident elf. Elidor's smile faded, replaced by a quiet thoughtfulness. She started to ask, but caught herself—

whatever it was, Elidor would not wish to speak about it here, in front of Davyn and the shopkeeper.

"Well . . . that's good," she said instead, trying to infect Elidor with her smile. "At least we won't waste time wandering lost in uncharted mountains."

Elidor nodded, allowing himself a faint chuckle.

"How deep are the caves?" Davyn asked. "Do you have a map of the tomb itself?"

"Only this." Godwin drew the last paper from the small chest, unrolling it from its scroll case and flattening it on the table. It was hardly more than a torn scrap, drawn as though copied from someone's sleeve. "It is a map they made when they first entered the caverns."

"You don't have a newer one?" Davyn took the paper and studied it intensely.

"I am lucky to have this one." Godwin shuddered, collecting the papers on the table and rolling them gingerly back into their cases.

Davyn reached into his pocket. "We would like a copy of the mountain map, and one of the tunnels. If you can spare the time to re-draw it, that is. We can pay you generously for your time." He dropped three steel coins on the table, and the gnome perked up again.

"Oh, of course, of course." Godwin's fingers hovered for a moment over the coins as he relaxed. "A copy, I can make you a copy in just a few hours. Very precise. Very exact."

"I'm certain it will be." Elidor smiled. "We'll be counting on it."

"My mother was a prophetess, you know." Sindri said from his perch on the bed. "She used to foretell wonderful things. All sorts of adventures. I haven't gone on all of them yet, but I used to keep a journal, a list of all the things I needed to do when I grew up. I don't remember if she mentioned Navarre. I don't have the journal anymore, you see. I think my cousin Phadri took it. You never can tell where these things will end up . . ."

Maddoc and Sindri were sitting in the room in Cairngorn Keep, waiting for Davyn, Elidor, and Catriona to return. The wizard stood near the window, looking out over the city of Ravenscar.

"Are you hungry?" The kender perked up, lifting his head sharply. "We could—oh, but no. We can't." Sindri's grin faded. "I keep forgetting that you're under house arrest. And I'm the warden." Sindri put his chin in his hands.

The old wizard sighed, folding his hands within the rough-cut sleeves of his faded black robes. "I don't need a guard. Where would I go?"

"I know that," Sindri replied. "But Catriona and Davyn made me promise. And they told me that if I didn't keep my promise, they wouldn't let me go to Navarre. Not that I think they could keep me away, not with my powers. They're going to need a wizard, and you're no good anymore . . . oh, I mean . . ." Sindri put his hands over his mouth and sat up. "Oh, Maddoc, I'm sorry. I didn't mean to say that."

Maddoc's gray face was haggard, his eyes lusterless and quiet. "No, kender, it's true. Without my magic, I am next to nothing. Even my most faithful servants, even Oddvar, have abandoned me, now that my magic holds no sway over them. No, I have only my knowledge. If that makes me useful enough to stay alive, then I must rely upon it."

"I know what you mean." Sindri perked up again. "I know what it's like to have others doubt your magic. Magic is power, you know. Life. And speaking of magic, I loved those pictures you had in the Gallery of Despair. You remember? The ones that people stare at." Sindri bugged out his eyes and swept his fingers in spirals before his face. "And their minds go all gooey? Those were the greatest! I could have stood there for just days and days, but Catriona made me leave. I wish I could have stayed. Here, look."

The kender fumbled in his pouches and drew out a chicken's foot and three blue stones. "No, that's not it," he muttered, pulling out more junk. "Oh, look at this!" Sindri held aloft a strange blue stick, twisted as though by an unknown fire. "This is a thorngurn root. I'm learning a new spell, Maddoc. It's going to make me a legend among wizards. They'll have to let me take the Test of High Sorcery after this. They'll have no choice! I also think it will be very useful in Navarre and—"

"Kender don't have the ability to use magic," Maddoc broke in. "It is a distinct lack within their species; perhaps some curse placed upon them by the gods of creation. And likely better for the world that they don't have it—I'm not certain society would survive it if they did." Maddoc strode to Sindri's side and snatched the thorngurn root.

"Hey!" Sindri cried out, swiping uselessly at Maddoc's hand. "That's mine. I do know magic. It's just different from yours, that's all."

Maddoc let the root fall loosely from his hand. It bounced on the bed.

Sindri picked it up, clutching it to his chest and scooting forward to face the wizard. "I could bring a fireball down on your head right now! I could level mountains, if I had a little time. You just watch me." Sindri set his jaw and glared at Maddoc.

He pushed out his small hand, pointing fiercely at a bowl on a nearby table. The bowl lifted from its place, hovering a foot above the small table.

Maddoc's hand struck like a snake, capturing the kender's wrist. He jerked back Sindri's robes, pinching the first finger and holding the ring he found there between finger and thumb.

"Parlor tricks, Sindri. Nothing more." The bowl fell to the table, shattering with a crash as the kender's concentration broke and the ring lost its power.

"That isn't magic," Maddoc continued, releasing the kender's hand and stalking back to the window. "That is nothing. Magic— true magic—is so much more than this. It is an extension of the soul, a movement within the sphere of the universe. To *will* and to *do*. How could you know it? Unless you have tasted the power of magic, you can only pretend.

"Magic is a buoy of color and light in a world of gray and darkness. Those people who live without it are more than blind—they see, but they do not *know*." The dark wizard reached his hand over the city, engulfing the wave of humanity in the streets beneath them. "They live, they die, and no one cares. But a wizard—a wizard is more than mere flesh. A wizard is intellect. *Will*."

As Maddoc spoke, Sindri's eyes grew round and his mouth hung open in a small O. Maddoc didn't pay him any mind, speaking as though he defended himself before judge and jury, his passion clear in the movements of his wide-flung arms and his resonant, clear voice.

"You seek magic, Sindri. But do you know what you are looking for? Your trinkets and toys are nothing compared to your will. They are tokens, chains, manacles that hold you back. Use them, yes, but when the moment comes and you feel true *will*, then you shall see that they are no more than crutches holding you back and imprisoning the strength that lies within you. Magic . . ." his voice took on a dream-like quality.

"How sad," Maddoc whispered, clenching his fist. "To never know that feeling, that rush of power. But how much more so"— the old wizard rounded on Sindri, his voice a terrible growl—"to have known it—and have lost it forever."

Wringing his hand around his bruised wrist, Sindri whispered softly, "I'm . . . I'm sorry."

"Do you know what is now denied me? The song of the universe around us—the power and glory of the gods—the knowledge of all that has been and will be. Gone . . . gone." The last word was a gasp, and Maddoc threw back his head.

"Maddoc—I . . ." Sindri struggled for words. His face contorted with sudden understanding. "That must be horrible. I've always had magic, maybe not like yours, but powerful in its own way, and if I lost it, I would . . . I would . . ." There was nothing terrible enough, even to a kender, that would express the feeling of loss. "After I take the Test of High Sorcery, I'll help you get your magic back. You'll see." Defiantly, Sindri shook his head, and his long black hair wavered with conviction.

Maddoc looked down at the kender, running his finger through his stiff beard. "Impossible. A kender could never pass the Test."

"You could help me." The words were halting at first, followed by a rush like a river after the dam has burst. "You could teach me what you know so I'll pass the Test, and I could use my magic to help you. It would be like a trade, but in advance. And if I get your magic back, then you could go—and that would be all right, because I'd have learned already."

Maddoc looked back down at Sindri's hopeful, eager face. "Your companions will not like it. You, learning magic from a wizard of the black robes?" He shook his head. "They won't trust you. As they don't trust me."

Sindri chirped, "Well, you did release an ancient sorceress who stole our friend's body and is going to try to take over the world."

Maddoc's hands clenched into fists.

Sindri took a step back, raising chubby palms in defense. "Hey, now, I'm just telling the truth as I know it. You shouldn't complain just because you got caught. So you're a dark wizard. All right. I get that. So, how's this for an idea?" Taking a deep breath, Sindri said, "We don't tell them."

His words were met by a raised eyebrow, and silence. For a moment, Sindri thought Maddoc would laugh at him, but instead his aged jaw remained clenched, his eyes steely and thoughtful. Sindri gulped, sticking out his chest and flipping back his long, unbound hair. He waited for the wizard's response, the seconds ticking past as Maddoc regarded him with an unblinking stare.

"Well?" Sindri asked.

"You must be joking."

"I'm not," protested Sindri. "You could teach me, and I could use the magic to help you. That's between you and me. Davyn and Cat don't have to find out. I won't tell them why I'm doing it."

"You can't even resist telling them what you ate for lunch," Maddoc retorted. "You don't seriously think you could keep this a secret?"

"I could!"

Ignoring Sindri, Maddoc continued, "I can hear them now, accusing me of corrupting you with dark magic." He snorted, shaking his head. "Davyn's already threatened me at the edge of a blade. Do you think I want to prove him right and lose what little protection I have?"

"No, no. It wouldn't be like that. They might even be pleased. The information you're giving us about the Aegis is useful. This would be more useful. I'd use it to fight Asvoria, you know, and that's what we all want—Davyn, Cat, Elidor—they can't argue with that."

Maddoc turned back to the window and its view of Ravenscar. "It is still too great a risk," he said at last. "You do not understand the temptation of dark magic. You are naïve, young, far too concerned with your friends to be able to control the awesome powers you would be facing." He gripped the windowsill firmly, staring down at the people in the city below. "So few apprentice wizards survive the Test, and you will have far less time than most who study magic. You may not be able to control the power . . ."

Sindri all but leaped at the faint opportunity in Maddoc's voice. "I will. I know I will. My mother's prophecies, you know. She foretold that I would be a great wizard. I could do it on my own, of course, but it makes for a much better story if you help me. And I know you will."

Maddoc's mouth twisted into a reluctant smile, and he briefly nodded. "But remember, Sindri," he said, placing one gnarled hand on the proud kender's shoulder.

"This was entirely your idea . . ."

3 A Forgotten Path

"The horses are getting skittish." Davyn reined in his black steed, patting the creature's neck as it breathed in heavy, whiffling snorts. The ranger peered into the woodlands at the base of the Vingaard Mountains, trying to catch a glimpse of any movement. "There may be wolves."

The days of travel had been mostly uneventful and swift, thanks to these horses from Maddoc's stables. But now, for the first time, Davyn sounded concerned.

"I told you we should have taken the main road," Sindri called from the rear of the party. He was perched high on the crup of Elidor's saddle, craning his neck to see around the elf. "There are undoubtedly entire packs of predators following us right now. Hordes! I bet there's even a wyvern or something!"

"Be quiet, Sindri." Elidor looked down, a faint smile marking his lips. "Or we'll leave you here to find out."

Sindri glared at Elidor with irritation, but he fell silent. He watched Davyn glancing through the underbrush, saw Elidor's mild irritation, and noted Catriona's eyes—strangely, hovering on Maddoc.

33

For a moment, Sindri wondered if this delay was of the wizard's manufacture, but the old man sat on his steed, a line tied from the horse's reins to Catriona's saddle. Maddoc's hands were bound to the pommel. His eyes were closed, his body sitting with grace upon the gray pony, uncaring as to the danger that stalked them in the forest.

Beneath her, Catriona's war-steed skittered to the side. Cat patted the horse's shoulder, calming her easily.

Davyn swung to the ground, pausing to study the forest floor for a moment before heading into the brush. "This is the shortest route to Navarre. If we had taken the road, we'd have to go days east of the caverns before we can head north. We save more than a week by riding through raw forest."

The woods around them were deep and lush, filled with thick evergreens and the wide-bodied trees of the deep forest. The brush itself was thick, covering the ground with tangled bushes and high clusters of weeds. The path they followed was one of the few clear areas—an obvious passageway through the woods.

Davyn picked up a handful of sandy earth, letting it trickle through his fingers slowly. "I'd say wolves, but the few tracks I see are much deeper than normal wolves. Not broad enough for worgs, though, and the larger wolf-types live farther south, where the cold suits them." The ranger's keen eye picked up a tuft of blackish fur deep within the thorns.

"What's this?" he asked quietly, reaching through the bramble to draw it out as Sindri craned his neck to see. Davyn held the scruff of fur aloft against the late afternoon sunlight, rubbing it between his fingers to test its thickness and length.

"Davyn looks worried. Doesn't he look worried? Ooof!" Sindri grunted as Elidor elbowed him. "I'm just saying!"

Catriona's horse suddenly skittered sideways, jerking the reins from her grasp. She grabbed the bridle, seizing control again before the animal could panic the others. Her horse raised its head, whiffling loudly and stomping a hoof against the ground. It sniffed the air again.

"Whatever it is," she said, looking over her shoulder. "It's close."

"Davyn," Elidor said, his hand on the pommel of a long knife at his side. "We should make camp. If animals are stalking us, we'll be better prepared against them with a fire and shelter."

"I can make shelter!" Sindri began to climb down off the horse. Elidor grabbed at the kender's trailing cloak, but missed, and Sindri landed on the ground and trotted eagerly to Davyn's side. "I can! We kender live in grass huts, you remember? I can make a lean-to. We can put the horses in it, and then the fire outside it, and take watch in shifts."

"He's right," Davyn said, straightening and drawing his horse's head down to scratch the worried animal's muzzle. The ranger pointed down the path ahead of them. "There's a larger area ahead, and I see a large pine tree. We should hurry, there's only a little light left."

Together they worked against the dying light. After tying up the horses, Davyn and Catriona carried large branches to the clearing, and Sindri worked them together with long strips of twine and leather cord. Elidor began a small campfire in the center of the clearing, his knife resting, unsheathed, by his side. Even Maddoc helped as best he could with his hands bound, stacking stones loosely around the edges of Elidor's fire.

By the time the darkness settled through the forest, the lean-to was finished, and Sindri bustled back and forth beneath it, trying to ensure that the four horses had as much cover as he could arrange. It wasn't much, but at least it would prevent predators from surrounding them.

The edge of the sun slipped beneath the horizon, golden rays vanishing through the forest. The shadows of the trees clung to the earth, spreading out to cover every inch of the ground. The brush and bramble were swallowed by it like a rising tide, and the moon's gentle glow was cut off by the thick canopy of pine. Only the light of flame kept the darkness at bay, licking greedily at the twigs Elidor fed to it as he lay beside the small fire pit.

From inside the shelter, Sindri saw Catriona standing just outside the circle of firelight, her hand running along the hilt of her sword. Her chain mail glinted, flickering like stars in the darkness as it caught the reflection of the fire's spark. Her eyes flickered over to the horses, then back out into the shadows beyond the campsite. "It's all right." She soothed her steed, patting the animal's muzzle gently.

"The horses smell something," Davyn said softly. "There's no room for my bow here. The trees are too close—by the time I had a clear shot, they'd already be upon us."

"They?" Sindri asked, twisting his head from side to side and shaking his arms as though to prepare for spell casting. "Who are 'they,' Davyn?"

"Here." Elidor tossed Davyn a long sword in its faded sheath. "Use this." In answer to the ranger's quirked eyebrow, Elidor said only, "A souvenir of Cairngorn Keep."

Elidor seemed the most concerned, unsheathing four knives and placing them in a straight line before him on the stones. "I know these forests, and Davyn does right to concern himself. There are beasts in these woods the like of which you will see nowhere else on Krynn. Terrible things that roam in the night."

"You say you know these woods," Maddoc said, his craggy face shadowed and grim. "How well do you know them, elf?"

Elidor did not look at him. His Kagonesti heritage showed clearly by the flickering firelight, and the light picked up every dark curve and tanned line of his profile. Elidor shrugged, placing a fifth knife by the others. "Well enough," was all he chose to answer.

Sindri suddenly tensed. "Did you hear that?"

"What is it?" Cat whispered.

"I don't see anything," Davyn replied, scanning the forest beyond the dim glow of their fire.

Long minutes passed as Sindri listened, his ears picking up every nuance of the forest around them.

Elidor sat by the fire, his eyes half-closed in silent meditation. Though he seemed lost in thought, Sindri knew that any motion or sound from the forest would cause the elf to fly into action with horrifying speed.

The fire flickered, and guttered out. Elidor quickly fed it more twigs, placing them between the small logs and blowing on the coals to start the flame once more.

A cold breeze blew through the trees. The limbs overhead creaked and groaned in the night as though they bore a terrible weight.

Sindri gulped, as the sounds came again. "More than one . . . I hear their feet, padding on the needles. They must be . . . somewhere . . . beneath the trees." His voice broke, and he cleared his throat, swallowing hard.

Sindri could hear himself breathing, his breath misting on air that turned suddenly cold.

Davyn nodded, falling to one knee and raising the sword to a guard stance. Catriona unsheathed her own weapon as Sindri turned slowly in a circle, his eyes trying to pick out any movement through the trees.

Sindri looked up, his eyes better in the darkness than those of the others. Only Elidor shared the gift of such sight, but the elf's eyes were blinded by the fire he tended.

"There," Sindri whispered, pointing up into the trees where a black shadow moved stealthily against the upper limbs. "Davyn! Catriona! Above us!"

But it was too late.

The creature dropped from the trees onto them with a terrible, piercing howl.

Like a large panther, the dappled animal moved softly, its feet leaving no mark and making hardly a sound. It had four thick paws with sharp claws, able to grasp and clutch the limbs of trees. It seemed the color of smoke and blended with the shadows beneath the trees. Its head and face were covered in black scales while the rest of its body, from neck to the tail, was wrapped in a dark gray fur. The wide tail was covered with long, dangerous-looking spikes.

Davyn slashed at the animal, throwing the creature back with a poisonous hiss. "It's a varanus lynx!" Davyn yelled. "Be careful, its bite is acidic!"

Another one plunged through the branches behind Catriona.

"Cat, look out!" Sindri cried from the shelter.

She spun around to face the lynx, her sword raised. The creature's black, glassy eyes reflected the faint hint of firelight. Its face was elongated and sleek almost like a lizard. The massive jaw snapped at Catriona with enough force to break bones, revealing rows of sturdy teeth.

She twisted, letting the lynx rush past her. But as she moved, she was forced to step beside the beast's writhing tail. The tail struck just inches from her foot, breaking the earth and sinking its massive spikes deep into the ground.

Darting from the shelter to hide behind a nearby tree, Sindri watched another beast hurl itself from the tree limbs toward Davyn. Davyn struck against the beast's ribs with his sword, but it landed on the ground with sure, safe feet.

It snarled, long threads of drool dripping from its reptilian jaw. It circled Davyn warily, staying just beyond the reach of the ranger's sword. Davyn drew a long dagger from his belt.

There was a rustle from above, and Sindri glanced upward to see sharp claws descending toward him. "Ah!" Sindri threw himself to one side to avoid the attack. Even as he rolled away, he heard a shirring sound, and saw two knives sink into the lynx's shoulder.

The beast howled in pain and turned away from Sindri, lashing out instead toward Elidor, but the elf already had two more knives in his hands.

Sindri crawled quickly toward the fire and the old wizard who stood there, wary of the hanging limbs of the trees. Maddoc helped Sindri to his feet, gripping the kender's purple cloak with his bound hands.

"Untie me," Maddoc said, shaking Sindri's shoulder. "I'm useless this way. Your friends need help." He thrust his bound wrists before the kender's face.

"You swear you won't try to escape?"

Maddoc's thin lips forced a smile. "We have a deal already, small one. And a deal with a wizard is a deal that cannot be broken."

Quickly, Sindri made his decision. The kender pulled a small knife from his pocket and cut the wizard's bonds. Maddoc took the blade from Sindri, concealing it beneath the sleeve of his robes and glancing back up at the combat.

Cat shifted, her sword cleaving the head from one varanus lynx's shoulders even as another dropped from above toward her. Only an instinctive dodge saved her from its slashing claws, but the lynx fell within a foot of her. The beast's lizard-like tongue lashed out, dripping acidic poison onto her hand. Her leather glove steamed, and Cat tore it off, dropping it to the ground before the acid ate its way to her flesh.

Sindri saw Davyn grin. With the swing of his sword, he forced the smoke-gray creatures slowly toward Elidor and the fire. Two more daggers flew from Elidor's swift hands and sliced one creature's tendons. It went down with a howl of agony, the beast's legs literally giving way beneath its weight.

The rest of the creatures had dropped from the treetops, pacing the camp. Cat fought two alone, while Elidor and Davyn worked in concert to destroy the creatures. Sindri bit his fingers, watching as Elidor depleted his store of knives. There were so many of the creatures, and they seemed to shrug off most wounds with ease. Even with Elidor's help, Davyn was badly outnumbered—five to one.

One of the beasts moved behind the ranger. Davyn didn't appear to see it. It crouched, lashing its tail and preparing to pounce.

Desperately, Sindri held his hands out toward the crouching lizard-cat, stuttering any magic words that came to mind. The ring on his finger glowed. The beast leaped, but suddenly it stopped with a sudden jerk.

"I did it!" Sindri crowed in triumph, then gasped and yelped as the ring's power began to fade. He struggled to press his will farther, concentrating on his own magic to supplement the ring's ability. As he did, something moved within Sindri's soul. It was wild, uncontrollable, and strange—but it gripped the ring's power and threw the beast back into the air.

Jerked back and forth like a marionette by Sindri's magic, the lynx yowled, trying desperately to regain control of its actions.

"I'm losing it!" Sindri yelled, watching as Davyn spun to face the beast. But even as the ranger's sword pierced the lynx, Sindri felt magic surge in his veins, blowing him off his feet. He landed heavily, skidding against the ground with the heavy force of the magical explosion. He slid across the campsite, face first.

Gasping, Sindri lifted his head from the ground. He spat out a mouthful of dirt, and saw another lynx pacing before Maddoc. Its mighty jaw widened in a feral half-smile.

Maddoc stepped a pace backward by instinct. He raised his hands as though to cast a spell before he realized what he was doing. The beast crouched, ready to spring. Maddoc cursed beneath his breath. The knife in his hand wavered, unfamiliar. The lynx leaped forward.

Maddoc tried to avoid the creature, but to no avail. The force of it slammed him to the ground, sharp claws tearing into his shoulders. The beast's weight pressed him, immobile, beneath it.

"Help! Help!" Sindri cried. He glanced around the campsite. Cat was battling two beasts at once, her sword making quick stabs in their flesh. Elidor was rushing to draw one of his knives from a fallen creature. But Davyn stood stock still on the far side of the campsite, weapons frozen and lowered, and a thoughtful look in his deep brown eyes.

"Davyn!" Sindri called. "We need you!"

But Davyn made no move to come closer, simply watching as the wizard struggled.

Maddoc drove Sindri's small knife into the beast's leg; wounding it deeply enough that it lost its balance and the aged man was able to roll from underneath it. The creature lashed forward again, once more clawing Maddoc. Blood ran down the wizard's arm, coloring his black robes with scarlet.

Maddoc clutched his wounded shoulder, a growl in his throat. The knife was lost, still buried in the beast's leg. He did not raise his hand to call to his magic, nor did he mutter words of any spell. Instead, he faced the lizard-creature with sober resignation and a terrible hatred.

"Maddoc!" Cat shouted from across the campsite, her sword cutting through the last of the lynxes. "Run!" Her eyes widened as she realized Maddoc's position, but there was nothing she could do.

Sindri felt as though his limbs were slowed, and even his quickness wasn't enough to reach Maddoc before the creature could attack again.

The beast pounced.

Staring in horror, Sindri watched as Maddoc braced himself for its tearing jaws, the hunger of the creature's anger and pain. He seemed to ready himself for death, his eyes never leaving Davyn's face.

But death never came.

Just as the creature's paws were about to strike Maddoc, Elidor's knife sailed through the air. It sunk through the back of the lizard-creature's skull, past the scaled flesh, and cut deep into the brain. The creature's forward momentum carried it past Maddoc, its form suddenly limp and slack. It landed with a thud a few feet away, the hilt of the knife imbedded against the rear of its head.

"Oh, thank Paladine!" Sindri crowed, running to the wizard's side. "Are you hurt? Is it bad?" Maddoc's eyes never left Davyn even as Sindri inspected the long gash in his arm.

Catriona circled the camp several times, her eyes scanning the foliage above for more beasts.

"Are they gone?" Sindri asked.

She nodded. "I think that was the last of them." She lowered her blade, and strolled over to Maddoc's side. "This wound isn't as bad as it looks. It could have been much more serious." Cat's experienced hands rolled back the black velvet sleeve, pressing a cloth against the wound to staunch its bleeding. You're very lucky." She showed Sindri how to dress the wound, washing it with water and wrapping it in long strips of fabric from her backpack.

Elidor walked to Davyn, keeping his voice low so that the others could not hear them. "You could have attacked the beast before it ever got to the wizard."

"You could have thrown your knife sooner," Davyn replied quietly.

Elidor murmured, "There are other ways through the wood. You knew this route had varanus lynxes along it, didn't you? It isn't shorter, and it isn't easier. You chose it for a reason."

Davyn hung his head. "He might still have had power over his magic." His voice was hard, a resolute cast to his features. He lifted his head and looked Elidor in the eyes. "I had to know."

Elidor turned away.

Catriona stood up, leaving Sindri to bind Maddoc's bleeding arm, her expression concerned and wary. "You had to know," she repeated. Turning to meet Davyn's eyes, Catriona whispered, "No matter what it costs us—or Nearra."

Davyn recoiled as though struck. "That's not fair," Davyn began, but his tone was uncertain. He tried again. "We're fighting to save Nearra. I can't take the chance that he's only in this to get control of her again—to hurt her. We have to do anything and everything we must in order to make sure that we win, and that she's safe. If we fail, Asvoria will destroy her. I don't care about this legend of Asvoria or about her lost kingdom. I care about Nearra. I had to know. If Maddoc was faking it, he could betray us—and Asvoria would win. Then Nearra . . ." he gulped, looking away toward the wounded wizard before continuing. "We'd never see her again."

"We have to save Nearra," Catriona said. "But to do that, we'll have to compromise. We don't have the knowledge, or the power, to do this ourselves. No matter what we have to do, or who we have to work with, we have to help her. Nobody else is going to come for her. If we don't save her, nobody will.

"But you were willing to throw it away because you aren't willing to take a risk. I hope that you found your peace of mind, Davyn." The warrior sheathed her sword and walked away, her face grim. "Because you almost paid for it with Nearra's soul."

4   Dreams of Glory

The creature flowed like a river, its flesh altering with each step. The green leaf pattern rippled across its skin, changing it for a moment to a creature covered in ivy. As the creature approached the town, its skin changed again, replicating the color of gray stone and pale mortar. Only the bundle in its arms remained the same, the brown paper unchanging between its strangely iridescent hands.

The shattered town had been destroyed in Asvoria's time by the traitorous forces as they made their final strike against the armies of the sorceress. Now it stood forgotten in the middle of the northern forests of Solamnia, hardly more than a pile of stones. Some few buildings still stood among the ruins. Its name was as lost as the roads which led to it—and that was precisely why Asvoria had chosen it as a temporary shelter while she grew accustomed to her new form and to the changes in the world around her. So many things were different . . . and yet, so much was still the same.

"Ophion," Asvoria called out. "I am in here. In the garden."

The creature halted, its face moving and restructuring to give it a mouth and a throat.

"My Lady Asvoria," it replied, humble adoration in its voice. The sound was male, more for simplicity than from any actual sense of gender. It glanced through the fallen stones of an ancient wall, pushing aside the ivy that hid the open doorway beyond.

The area beyond had once been a lovely home, its rooms still marked by low, crumbling stone runners of foundation. With the passing of ages, it had become little more than a garden of lush greenery, ivy climbing the one stable wall, the other walls softened with old moss.

In one corner of the hidden garden, beneath a willow tree that grew from the cracks between the stones, a small pool of water bubbled up in a cleft of stone, swelling from deep beneath the earth. Beside the natural well knelt a delicate young woman.

Morning sunlight dappled her honey-blonde hair, streaking it with glittering highlights. She held her hands to her face, staring at the reflection in the little pool. She dropped her fingers from her cheekbones to her jaw, passing down her neck and over her collarbone.

"She is not unpleasant, all in all, though she does not surpass what I once was. Still." She preened like a little girl, pouting. "I miss my hair."

Ophion cocked its head and said nothing, watching as the woman rose to her feet and ran her hands over the simple, home-spun dress. It was similar to any that might be found in a peasant home in Solamnia.

Ophion knelt, lifting the package to her. She accepted it, tearing away the paper and allowing it to fall away into the weeds.

Inside lay a dress of green and gold damask, sewn in an ancient style with long sleeves and a flowing skirt.

Ophion looked away as the linen peasant's garb fell to Asvoria's feet. There was a rustle, and the soft sound of fabric against skin.

"You may rise." Her voice did not sound like a simple peasant girl, nor did it hold the quiet gentleness Ophion remembered from their first meeting. That had been Nearra, the original owner of the form. This was Asvoria's voice, stern and commanding, seductive and cruel—reborn within Nearra's flesh and returned to forge her kingdom anew.

The shapeshifter raised its eyes to see Asvoria straightening her sleeves. The gown fit her magnificently, its simple cut accentuating her regal form. "It will do," Asvoria murmured, her fingers catching against the smooth fabric. "Considering our current situation, more than acceptable."

Staring down at her reflection in the pool of water once more, Asvoria smiled. "Report, my most loyal servant." Her eyes never left the ripples below her, drinking in each movement, each breath. She controlled this form—at last.

The shapeshifter bowed its head, speaking in a voice that seemed to hold a disturbing lack of accent, nuance, or tone. "Nearra's friends have captured Maddoc. They have interrogated him. They head north from Cairngorn Keep, into the mountains." Ophion's face registered no emotions, the features only vaguely human.

"Do you believe they know of Navarre?" Asvoria's attention snapped to her servant.

"I do."

"Can they reach the tomb?"

"Yes, I believe it is possible. If you order me, I will go immediately."

Asvoria clenched her fists, anger sparking into barely controlled rage. "I will have my sword once more, Ophion. These cretins have already stolen my Daystar—the keystone of my power! I will not let them have the treasures of my tomb. Defilers. Heretics." Her body tensed, radiating with magical power. "The Daystar will be mine again. But I cannot spare the bone-griffin. It is collecting my armies, drawing out those of its kind, and others willing to stand beside me as I reclaim my rightful throne. Nevertheless, this is not the kind of task it is best suited for. This will take subtlety, Ophion—and that is clearly your domain."

She turned then, and Ophion was struck by the incongruity of it all. Ophion had known Nearra, the mortal whose shell now housed Asvoria's spirit, but the face no longer entirely resembled the gentle girl. The eyes were the same shape, the cheeks, the lips—but the rage that crossed her features was unlike anything that Nearra had been capable of understanding. Her movements were no longer hesitant or shy, but smooth and regal, every inch decreeing the training and poise of a born ruler. "They must not retrieve the Aegis."

She winced, as though some thing beyond her control shivered in her thoughts. Ophion began to stand. Asvoria snarled, placing her hand to her forehead. Ophion could almost see her eyes fading from blue back to violet as she forced Nearra back down into the darkness of their shared spirit, back to silence and emptiness.

When Asvoria continued, there was no sign of the inner conflict remaining in her eyes. "We will have to ensure that they are not able to continue with their little quest. And we shall have to reach the tomb before them—and steal the prize right from their grasping fingers." She knelt again on the stone, reaching down into the water beneath her and running her fingers through the clear, shadowed depths.

"It's Maddoc's influence, no doubt, that gives them such tenacity. That wizard is the only one among them with the courage and resilience to have any hope of defeating me. You said that he found someone who investigated the tomb some time ago, but could not enter the tomb himself? What do you know, Ophion?"

Ophion nodded, its limbs elongating as it knelt in the moss

nearby. "A failed attempt, milady. Maddoc found a ranger who had entered your palace at Navarre. The ranger's companions died, but he placed a spell around the entrance to the tomb proper. He could not pass through the gates alone, but he would not allow the treasure there to be stolen by others in his absence. Maddoc discovered this, gained the incantation to break the protective spell, and then destroyed the survivor."

Asvoria's face contorted. "How clever of him," she said wryly. "And the spell still holds?"

"Yes, my lady. It does. But your own defenses also still remain. They should keep Maddoc and the others at bay—for a while."

Asvoria laughed, a bitter sound in the primeval forest. "But not forever, Ophion?" She sighed, the boredom of a queen forced to play games with her lessers. "No. But enough, perhaps, to slow them so that we can find a way past Maddoc's troubling forethought. Then the Aegis will be by my side again, and I will take the Daystar from their fallen corpses."

Excitement sparkled in her wide eyes, and water dripped from her extended fingers back into the secluded well. "Tell me of Navarre."

"The years have taken their toll, my lady. There are only a few entrances now, most of them hidden by cave-ins and rockslides. Few of them are large enough for humans to pass through." Ophion's flesh shifted in color to match the stones, darkening to an even deeper gray as it spoke of Navarre. "There is only one entrance that invaders can safely use. Maddoc and his companions are three days from it, milady."

"Only one entrance that they know, Ophion . . . but I know another." Asvoria preened, smiling smugly. "Hidden among the traitors and cowards that betrayed me. We will use them, as well, my pet. One bloodline stands among the traitors, guarding the entrances and protecting the secrets of my tomb.

"But first, we must be certain that our forces are prepared before Nearra's friends arrive. I must arrange for Maddoc and the others to be as weakened as possible when they reach the tomb. By the time they reach the tomb, you will find the group to be easy prey." She reached again into the pool, and this time the water there began to swirl without the movement of her hand. The water swelled, breaking over the edge of the pool and trickling down the rocks.

She turned once more to her shapeshifter, reaching to touch its pallid face with long, slender fingers. "You must intercept this group, and obtain the incantation Maddoc carries or the Daystar. With either, I can get through the enchantments and enter my tomb. It is critical that you bring me one or the other, or the Aegis will be forever barred to me."

"But what of you? You will not join me on this journey?"

"I must travel more slowly than you, for my new body is not used to the rigors of magic that I now command. In a short time, I will have my power solidified, and the resistance within this flesh will be destroyed utterly. But, until then, you must do my bidding, and I will join you when I am strong again.

"But do not worry, Ophion. You will not be alone. I have a few servants at Navarre that still await my return. My Last Priest has heard me rise, he has listened to my whisper on the distant wind—and he will be prepared to aid you when you arrive in Navarre. And there are . . . others . . ."

Asvoria whispered to the water, murmuring ancient words of power. It shimmered, twisting first through the spectrum of the rainbow and then deepening to indigo, shadowy and thick like tar. Figures began to appear within the water, shifting and moving against the shadows, and bright green-blue eyes opened pair by pair.

Asvoria all but purred in pleasure, her lips curving into a satisfied smile. "Arise, my darlings," she breathed. The eyes multiplied, and the shadows slithered out from every crack and crevice. "There is work for you to do."

5 Tongues of Stone

Catriona's horse stepped carefully down the steep mountain path, keeping its head low. Below them, a charming valley spread out in rich greens, the blue of the river clinging to the mountain stone. The one blemish on the pastoral view was a terrible rockslide that had long ago fallen down the mountainside near the river. The rocks were a deep scar along the mountain. It stood out plainly, the color notably different from the green, lush valley that surrounded it.

Davyn gestured toward the scar. "The map says that this is where the manor house of Navarre once stood."

Maddoc nodded. "Legend says that the land was caved in by Asvoria's last servants, who swore to remain faithful to her even beyond death."

A shudder went down Catriona's spine. Her steed stopped for a moment, and its ears flicked forward and back. But it soon resumed picking its way down the path without guidance from its rider.

Davyn twisted in his saddle, squinting ahead and pointing at another site near the collapsed area and looking down at his map. "I see a cleft in the rock. Over in that area. It's hidden by brush, 53 probably piled up by that group Godwin mentioned—left there to keep out predators and treasure-hunters."

Elidor shielded his eyes, peering at the rock below.

"Where?" Sindri strained to see from the rear of Elidor's saddle.

"I'll show you when we get closer." Davyn said impatiently.

"When will that be?" Sindri asked.

Catriona smiled from her place farther back in line, glad that she was not the target of Sindri's curiosity today. Sindri chattered on about the beauty of the forest, the curious stone, the blue sky, and literally anything and everything that caught his attention.

Catriona tuned him out, listening to each solid clip-clop of Melia's hooves against the road. She remembered Nearra's laughter, her quiet courage.

I failed.

"Catriona, are you all right?" Maddoc's voice was soft, almost too soft to hear, and she was certain none of the others caught it over Sindri's constant banter. Maddoc rode at her heel, his hands loosely guiding the reins.

Catriona had convinced the others to let him ride without the rope binding his wrists. She told them the attack of the lynxes had proven he was powerless. And, somehow, despite herself, she felt pity for the old man. Maddoc had been stripped of his magic, his life, his fortune. Everything. He had less, even, than she when she had been excised from the Knights of Solamnia.

Ahead of them, Davyn and Elidor conferred, pointing at the forest opening ahead and checking the ground for signs of recent passage. Sindri bounced on the back of Elidor's horse, offering cheerful suggestions.

"It's nothing." She rearranged her expression, and faced forward in her saddle.

The black-robed wizard shook his head. "I know deception, Catriona, and it doesn't suit you." They rode in silence for a moment, and Maddoc continued. "You have every reason to be frightened. Navarre—"

"It isn't Navarre, all right?" Catriona snapped. Taking a moment, she closed her eyes and then continued more gently. "Maddoc, thank you for your concern. But, no, I'm not frightened."

"Catriona," Maddoc began again. "I realize that I'm no comfort to you, but I also realize that my life may hang on the balance of your sword. If we enter that place, and you are unready, then we all may die."

"And you're relying on me?" Catriona lashed out. "Maybe you deserve to die." Maddoc's face was impassive, untouched by her quick rage. "As you wish."

"No . . . no, Maddoc. I'm sorry." Catriona sat back in her saddle, pushing the long red hair out of her face. "I didn't mean that. Not exactly."

"Well, realistically, this is my doing, though I never intended it all to turn out this way." In the bright sunlight, Maddoc's face was craggy, pitted with lines. "Whatever else I may be, I am a scholar, Catriona. Asvoria was an experiment—an attempt to recapture lost knowledge. You may disagree with my methods, but the information we could have gained from her spirit—once successfully housed and controlled—could have been invaluable to the modern world."

"And Nearra paid the price." Catriona said.

Maddoc raised his head, staring up at the brilliant blue sky. "Yes. I know you disagree with that."

"Nearra was an innocent. And we—I—promised to protect her." Catriona turned to Maddoc, her anger still alive.

"And you feel that you have failed."

Catriona cursed herself for saying anything, for allowing the black wizard any access to her pain.

Maddoc continued, "But you haven't. Failed, that is."

Catriona couldn't help herself. "How?"

"Do you truly think any black wizard would be without an ulterior plan?"

She didn't think she wanted to know what Maddoc had planned, but she couldn't stop the words from being spoken. "What have you done?" A faint revulsion touched her tone, and her hand touched the hilt of her sword almost without her notice.

"Nothing as drastic as you may think." Suddenly, Maddoc changed the subject. "You were once squired to the Knights of Solamnia, were you not?"

Catriona started. But before she could say anything else, Maddoc continued, "Then you know the strength of an oath."

"Yes." Catriona was curt, her ire renewed.

"Then you'll understand that I made an oath, myself. And I intend to keep it."

She was taken aback. "What oath, wizard? And why would a man who chose the black robes care about his word of honor?"

"Some wizards choose the black robes for power. I chose them because they would lead me to knowledge. And knowledge, unlike power, respects honor as well as strength." Maddoc's steed swayed beneath him as they entered the forest at the low end of the road. Through the forest, the scar on the mountainside was less visible, but they could still see brief flashes of gray stone against earth and greenery, and the river's cheery burble drowned out the soft sound of hooves against loam.

"You lied to Davyn," Catriona said.

"I never gave him my word. There's a difference between trust and honor, Catriona."

"Nearra trusted me." Her voice was flat, and the hurt still felt fresh. First she had failed her aunt, then her oath, and now her friend—an innocent who had trusted her with everything.

"And you have not failed her," Maddoc said. "Not yet."

Catriona glanced at him sharply. "What do you mean?"

"I may not have magic, but I still have that which I sought most in my life: knowledge. I know Asvoria better than any man alive, and most of those who lived in her own time. If anyone knows how to restore your friend, it is I."

"You?" she snorted. "Why would you do that? You're the one who freed Asvoria in the first place."

"And lived to regret it." Maddoc shook his head, the leafy canopy of the valley floor casting strange shadows over his black velvet robes. "No, this was never my plan, Catriona. But I cannot restore what I have done." He lifted his hand and brushed a fallen leaf from his sleeve. "Not alone. And neither can you. I have the knowledge, and you—and your companions, of course—have the skill."

"A few days ago, you wanted nothing to do with Navarre. And now"—Catriona's eyes narrowed—"now you want to help us?"

"I've realized that it's the right choice."

"Why aren't you talking to Davyn about this?" she asked.

Maddoc's laugh was short and bitter. "For all I have done to raise him since he was a child, he now abhors me. Love turns to hate so very easily. You know that. You saw it in the eyes of your fellow squires, so long ago, did you not?"

Internally, she winced, though she kept her face impassive. Maddoc was correct—the eyes of the other squires, once her friends and companions, had been filled with disdain when she left the order. They had hated her for her weakness. For her fall from grace. It could have been any one of them. But it had been her.

She looked up and caught Davyn's eye as he glanced back to check on her, and in his gaze she saw the same disdain. Cat felt her face reddening, but she stared back defiantly until he looked away.

DRAGON SWORD

57

"What are you getting at, Maddoc?" Catriona's voice was hard-edged.

"Davyn is blinded by his hatred. Sindri, for all of his eagerness, is useless. Elidor does not have the strength of character I need to undo what I have done. I will not allow Asvoria to steal from me and not be punished for it. And you, you wish to rectify your failure to your friend, to Nearra. Together, we can achieve both goals."

"At what price, wizard?" Catriona kept her eyes on the ground, watching as her steed's light brown ears flickered forward and back again. The scar ahead seemed closer through the trees, looming from the bottom of the valley to its high cliff side, the rocks far larger than a person. "What do you want?"

"Your oath."

Catriona laughed aloud at the irony of it. "My oath?"

"Yes," Maddoc replied seriously. "We are both fallen from grace, Catriona. And we both have failures behind us that we do not wish to repeat. If anyone in this motley group can understand what I am trying to achieve—Asvoria's destruction—and why I must fight to achieve it, no matter what is denied to me, then it is you. We are very much alike."

She opened her mouth to deny it out of hand, but paused. Catriona couldn't entirely dismiss Maddoc's comparison, however much she wanted to.

After a moment, he spoke softly, "There is something I did not tell the others, Catriona—about the Aegis. A limitation that troubled me when I first read about the sword, though I assumed that I would eventually find a way around it."

She raised an eyebrow, unsure whether to trust him. "And that is?"

"That the sword's power is vastly increased when in the hands of a"—he grimaced —"woman. It can be held and used by a man, yes, but it is twice as powerful if a woman wields the blade."

Catriona stared at him. "Asvoria."

"Not necessarily. With the Aegis you could have the power to match her."

"And it would slowly corrupt me. You mentioned the Aegis was like a drug. You want me to wield it so that I'll become chained to it." Her eyes narrowed.

"Only if you kept the blade."

"And you wouldn't allow that to happen. Really, Maddoc, you overestimate yourself."

He did not reply. The dappled shade flickered across his hands and face.

They rode for a few moments in silence, her hand tapping rhythmically against the hilt of her sword. "Even if I were to trust that you spoke the truth, Maddoc," she said at last, "How could I trust that you would keep your word to me?"

He reached out then, his hand resting upon hers over the hilt of her weapon. "Because I, too, have nothing left to lose."

She met his eyes as they rode onward. "Then perhaps you do understand my position." She did not remove his hand.

"Cat," Maddoc's voice became impassioned. "I do not claim to be a good man. I am what I am. But we need each other. I'm not asking you to be a knight. I am asking you which is more important—your friend, or your anger. If anger toward me is all that keeps you from lending me your oath, then you are not the woman that I thought you might become."

"You have no right to judge me." But Catriona's tone was not as fierce as it had been before.

"Give me your oath that you will serve me, Catriona, and I can show you how to free Nearra. Asvoria will fall. I swear it." She heard an intensity in Maddoc's voice that had been missing since the loss of his magic. For a moment, it called to the shame she buried deep in her own soul. Offering an alternative . . .

Quickly, Catriona pushed Maddoc's hand away, and spurred her steed forward down the path toward the others. As she came out of the forest into the bright sunlight, Melia shortened her strides, coming to a halt by the side of a shallow river. Ages ago, a rockslide had tumbled into the river, shifting the river's course and forming a shallow lake.

Catriona raised her hand to shield her eyes from the sudden sunlight, staring up at the side of the valley. Rocks as large as houses rested against the side of the soft brown cliff, the earth around them packed tight by season upon season of rain and snow.

A waterfall at the edge of the lake may once have fallen straight from the precipice above. But now it tilted crazily, pounding at odd angles down the hill and over the jutting ledges of dark granite.

Up ahead, Elidor and Davyn had already dismounted, and Sindri's eager voice echoed from the high rocks. As Maddoc's steed trotted into the clearing, Catriona swung down from Melia's saddle, leading her horse toward her friends.

Elidor swung his hand up toward the waterfall's apex, the one spot where the water still fell straight down in its ancient path.

"Davyn," he called. "Is this where the entrance is?"

Davyn nodded slowly as he consulted the map once more. "This claims the adventurers marked the entrance with a flat boulder. The entrance lies beneath it." Davyn looked up, taking in every part of the landslide. "There." He pointed to a large, flat stone that lay across the scar of rock. "That's it. We'll have to find a way to move the rock." He glanced back as Maddoc dismounted his horse. "Without magic."

"Oh, boy! A real tomb!" Sindri smiled, his long hair flopping back and forth as he hopped in the sunlight. "I can't wait. I wonder what's in there! Maybe Asvoria's spell books. Wow, what I could do with that kind of thing!"

Catriona said nothing, placing her hand on Sindri's shoulder. She watched as Davyn and Elidor reached the stone marker. It was far too heavy for them to lift or move alone, so they tied several ropes around it, tossing the ends down to Cat.

She tied the ropes to Melia's saddle, conscious of Maddoc's eyes watching her every move. Urging the steed forward, Catriona pulled the rope with all her strength as Elidor and Davyn pushed from above.

Slowly—slowly, the stone moved aside.

Catriona gazed up at Davyn's face as he stared down into the unknown darkness, wondering what, if anything, he could see. Was there a passage? Treasure? Steepled stairs? Could he hear voices, or see movement? Was he thinking of Nearra as he stared into the depths?

"There's a cleft in the stone," Davyn called. "It leads down into darkness. Elidor, are you willing to go down there first?"

As Catriona watched him, too far away to hear the rest of the words they exchanged, she felt very much alone. At last, she looked away.

She met Maddoc's eyes once more, and understood him.

6   INTO THE EARTH

Elidor slid down the rope, the thick hemp twisting against his palms. The sunlight above dimmed and faded away. The hole beneath the rock was deep, more than four times the height of a man. When his feet at last touched ground, Elidor dropped the rope, and drew out his knives.

Though the light high above was faint, Elidor could see the outline of the circular chamber around him. On the ground, etched into the stone and sealed with once-colorful paint, was the letter A, surrounded by a dragon that curled protectively against the letter's form.

The walls were carved from solid granite. Statues stood around the perimeter of the circular room, their arms upraised to support what had once been a glorious mosaic ceiling. Elidor's eyes scanned the statue's faces, taking in the elegant, peaceful countenances and the graceful robes. He moved through the chamber silently, his blades flickering in the dim light.

A passage led from the wide chamber into the mountain's depths, and Elidor knelt at its entrance to study the patterns of dust. Putting one knife back in its sheath, he slid a finger along the edge of the corridor, inspecting the depth of the dust—and old footprints that lay against the stone. Faint echoes of wind drifted up from the passage, speaking of distant hollows in the belly of the mountain. He heard a distant trickle of water where the river had broken through the stone somewhere far below. There were no other sounds. No sign of life. It wasn't conclusive—but it would do.

He paused for a moment, feeling the cold gray stone beneath his fingers. It brought back old memories—memories Elidor preferred to stay buried. Her hair, cool like the stone, but purer . . . white . . .

Elidor jerked his hand back as if bitten, before more memories could surface in his mind.

Satisfied that nothing in the chamber would harm them, Elidor returned to the rope and tugged twice. Davyn's face appeared above, and with a wave, the others began to follow into the lower chamber. One by one they slid down the rope, their heavy boots landing with none of the grace of their elf companion.

Catriona knelt, drawing out her flint and steel to light a small lantern. As she blew the flame into life, Elidor winced. "You really have to use that?"

"Some of us aren't born with the eyes of the elves." Davyn chuckled faintly.

Catriona swung the door of the lantern closed so that it emitted only a faint glow. "There. I'll keep it dim so that you can see. And if there's trouble, I can swing it open, and Davyn and I can come to your rescue." Catriona grinned. It was meant to be lighthearted, but the sharp shadows of the lantern cast a menacing grimace over her face.

Sindri didn't bother with the light, scampering eagerly to the statues against the walls. He climbed up onto their bases and tugged at their stone arms. "My mother used to tell me stories about statues that came to life and told riddles." His voice echoed eerily through the long empty passages that Elidor had not yet explored. "Do you think these will move, Maddoc?"

"I doubt it." The wizard rubbed his palms together, soothing where the rope had abraded his skin. "But there are said to be worse things in the caverns." Maddoc shrugged. "Legends. Stories. Still, it is best to be on our guard."

Raising one arm as he looked at the copy of Godwin's map, Davyn pointed down the passageway. "There's a passage through here, and down the corridor to the left, after the branch."

"How far does the map go?"

Maddoc walked around the chamber, running his hand against the wall while Davyn looked down at the map. The wizard's footsteps echoed like faint pounding in Elidor's sensitive ears, blocking out the whisper of wind in the lower chambers.

"To the tomb itself," Davyn replied, "but not inside. The tomb looks like it is a separate building, surrounded by a large cavernous courtyard."

"That would be accurate, according to the legends I have studied," Maddoc added. "The palace is built into the walls of the mountains; the tomb was built within an underground courtyard. Many of these passages will likely lead to the edges of that interior cavern. We need to find the one that enters the cavern on the ground floor. The walls of the cavern will be far more difficult to climb down than this simple rope. Very dangerous, and potentially impossible to scale down to the ground. Unless, of course, you can fly?" When the others did not answer, Maddoc nodded. "I thought not."

"I'll be able to fly once I master the right spells. I can lift heavy things, you know. I just need to practice a lot more, and I'll be able to lift horses and maybe buildings!" Sindri's bright voice was out of place in the gloom, his purple cloak flaring out as he leaped from a statue's base to the ground.

While they spoke, Elidor moved a short distance down the passage, finding the branch that Davyn mentioned. One route led to the left, the dust scattered and brushed by footsteps several years old. The other, the right-hand path, was untouched. Elidor ran his hand over the floor, brushing aside the dust to see the carved granite beneath.

"Anything of note?"

Elidor looked up at Davyn, wiping his hand on his breeches. "Yes. This place is dangerous."

"Protected, you mean?" The ranger quirked an eyebrow.

"I've already made note of three traps." Elidor pointed down the hallway. "There, a tripwire. Over there, a hole in the wall that contains poisoned darts. And farther down, I see the marks on the floor where the roof of a pit trap is covered by false stone. Dust doesn't lie on false stone in the same patterns as it does on granite."

Impressed, Davyn straightened and peered down the right-hand corridor. "Another dead end?"

"No, the passage continues."

"Can you get us through it?"

"As long as there's no dracolich this time." Elidor's smile was thin. "It's a done deal."

Bit by bit, they maneuvered through what was once a small manor-house carved within the mountain. Sindri clapped his hands at every new discovery, climbing over furniture that lay in petrified rags, creeping down long hallways filled with rotted antiques. "It's a palace!"

"More like a catacombs," Elidor said grimly, as they creeped past a dusty skeleton, splayed out across the center of a corridor.

Moving through the manor-house took time. Doors bearing the same dragon entwined about the letter A swung open on ancient hinges that protested every movement. At each new turn, Elidor would tell the others to stay on safe ground while he checked the path ahead for traps.

At the end of one magnificent hallway, Elidor left his friends once again to vanish into the darkness. Soon Elidor heard Sindri's voice echoing down the hallway.

"He's been gone so long." Sindri's concern made Elidor smile, but he had no energy to yell back at him. Finding these traps took all of his concentration.

Maddoc's voice countered Sindri's words, a low rumble of sober unconcern. "He might have fallen prey to one of the traps here. Or one of the creatures." Elidor rolled his eyes to hear it, checking the ground with the edge of his dagger before proceeding another ten feet. The tiles of the floor were mosaic—perfect for leverage traps, or sliding panels.

Davyn retorted, "Elidor's better than that. He's fine. I know it."

"You have such faith in your companions," Maddoc countered. "You should know better, boy."

Elidor would have been pleased to hear Davyn's confidence, had it not so obviously been spurred more by Davyn's hatred of Maddoc. The elf sighed, slipping his dagger back into its sheath and standing in the gloom.

As the argument went on, Elidor slipped back along the passage toward his friends, watching the figures, lit by the brilliance of their lantern. They were so easy to see, easy to mark with an arrow. They would never even see him coming.

Davyn stood only a few feet from Maddoc, shaking his brown hair in front of his eyes like a bull preparing to charge. "I know Elidor. He'll be back. There's no trap in this mountain that he can't get through."

Maddoc smiled, obviously enjoying the debate. "I'd make a wager with you, Son, but I'm afraid I haven't anything to bet."

"Don't call me Son. *Never* call me that again." Davyn took a step forward, his hand twitching back toward his sword. "You're not a wizard any longer, Maddoc. If I want to cut your head off right here, nothing's going to stop me."

"Nothing," Maddoc said quietly, his voice like the hiss of an asp, "Except that by doing so you would lose Nearra's life."

Quickly, Catriona broke in, pushing between them. "I'm concerned about Elidor, too. He's been gone much longer than usual. This is a dangerous place." Cat turned and looked at Davyn. "Asvoria's place. None of us, not even Elidor, should ever face her—or her servants—alone."

"I'm going to go find him." Sindri leaped up, obviously trying to break the uncomfortable tension. "Elidor may need my magic!"

Disturbed, Elidor slipped out of the hallway shadows. "Trouble ahead," was all he said before sinking down into a cross-legged seat on the rough floor. "Only one way through. I think it might be a front hall. If I'm right, we might be able to access the tomb courtyard through the other side."

"But?" Cat tapped her fingers along the hilt of her sword.

"But." Elidor continued, "The trap is complex, and it can't be disarmed. If we don't negotiate it correctly, the ceiling—and half the mountain—will fall on our heads."

"That sounds really interesting!" Sindri perked up. "How do we make that happen?"

"The point isn't to make it happen," Davyn cut him off. "The point is to *not* make it happen."

"Oh." Sindri drooped. "That's not interesting at all."

"So how do we avoid the collapse?" Catriona asked. Elidor took his time answering, unrolling a set of tools from his backpack and going over them one by one. He counted them carefully, checking the steel tips and small mirrors.

"I can't do it alone." He rolled his tools back up. His gray leggings were covered with marks along the knees where he had knelt, and it was obvious that he'd placed his cheek along the floor to spot tripwires. "There are several markers throughout the hall that have to be turned off in a specific order. The trap is armed by using two keys. I've seen this kind of trap before. There's a keyhole at either end of the hall. They're both turned at the same time, disarming the ceiling's collapse. I haven't made it across the room yet—the floor's completely trapped—but I should be able to find the other keyhole fairly easily, now that I know how the one on this side was hidden."

"So you need someone on both ends," Catriona mused. "But none of us know how to pick a lock."

"You won't have to." He looked up, holding a lock pick to the light. "I'll pick it, but I won't trigger it. After I've got it set up, I'll arrange it so all you have to do is turn the lock pick to the side. I'll turn mine at the same time and the trap will be disarmed."

Davyn frowned. "That means you'll have to make it across without us, while the trap's still working."

Elidor nodded. "I can do it." He gathered up his tools again. "I'm going to have to climb across the room. Sideways. The others can stay beside the first lock, and turn it on the count of three. That way they unlock together. And only then will it be safe to walk on the floor." Elidor looked up, raising a finger. "This part's important. If we touch the floor at all before we turn the locks, then the ceiling comes down."

"And you'll be in the middle of it." Davyn said gravely.

With quiet seriousness broken only by an expectant smile, Elidor asked, "Are you up for it?"

"You always get that smile when we're about to do something extremely dangerous." Davyn adjusted his backpack on his shoulders. "Yes, I'm ready for it."

Elidor led them down a carved corridor whose walls had once been painted with bright pigments over the solid stone. Now they were faded, the brilliant and glossy paints chipped and worn by age, sections peeled away so that the barren rock below showed through.

"This isn't much like a catacombs." Sindri tugged more of the mural from the wall, watching the paint flake as he trotted along behind the others. "It's more like a . . . oh." His voice trailed off as they reached the main hall, and Sindri stared at the chamber before them.

The roof was high and arched, buttressed on both sides by rows of pillars. The pillars were slim and graceful, made of white marble, and they formed a small aisle on each side of the room. The walls were painted, much as the previous hallway had been, but here the colors still retained a portion of their once-delicate color. The walls had once been smooth, but time and the shifting of the rock face of the mountain caused long cracks and crevices through the stone. On the far side of the room, there was another long hallway, and Elidor thought he caught a faint glint of metal where he believed the second keyhole to be.

Sindri stuck his head into the room, pushing past Davyn and Maddoc but stopped by Catriona's strong arm. "Not too close," she reminded him.

"Oh, right. Right." Still, Sindri craned his neck around her, trying to see into the distant darkness. The room was so big that Catriona's small lantern barely illuminated the far wall.

Elidor ran his hand over the wall carefully, feeling the granite for natural finger holds. "There are plenty of cracks in these walls. I should be able to make it across easily."

He knelt at the edge of the archway that led into the main hall, drawing out his tools and laying them on the floor. "Cat, bring that lantern closer, would you?" She obliged, and he pointed out a small circle of pounded silver that had once been painted to match the bright colors of the wall. Elidor sat cross-legged by the lock, gently slipping his lockpick into the metal keyhole. As he maneuvered the long metal tools against the tumblers, Davyn and Maddoc shared a concerned glance.

Catriona watched Elidor's nimble fingers twist the thin lockpicks, rolling them expertly. Sindri sat on a fallen suit of rusted armor, chatting merrily with Maddoc—or, more accurately, at Maddoc—about his mother's prophecies. "She used to talk about kings living beneath the ground, golden chariots with flaming wheels, and knights of shadow and . . . oh, well, shadow and something. I wonder if she meant this place."

"Asvoria was a queen, not a king," Catriona said.

But suddenly, Sindri wasn't listening. He cocked his head, staring into the large room ahead. "Did you hear that?" No one answered, so Sindri slid down from his perch and stepped closer to the opening into the large hall. Catriona moved to stop him again, sighing at his stubbornness. He brushed her away, stopping at the edge of the hall and peering into the room.

"Turn off your lantern." Sindri dropped his voice to a whisper.

"I can't." Cat raised an eyebrow. "Elidor needs the light to work."

"But there's something in there." Balancing on the balls of his feet, Sindri tried to squint into the darkness, but the lantern light ruined his night vision. "Davyn, Maddoc—don't you see anything?"

"I see shadows," Maddoc explained, trying to discern what had made the kender so interested. "Nothing more."

Davyn knelt beside Sindri, listening with a ranger's trained senses. "I don't hear footsteps."

"No, it wasn't footsteps. It was . . ." Sindri scratched his head in exasperation.

The lock clicked. "Got it." Elidor scrambled up, carefully leaving one of his lockpicks still in the silver keyhole at the bottom of the wall. "Sindri, come here."

Sindri sighed, turning away from the main hall to kneel beside Elidor. Elidor showed the kender how to turn the lock pick, his hands sure and certain.

"I do know how to use one of these, Elidor." Sindri chuckled.

"Well, I suppose that comes with your heritage." Elidor smiled gently. "Just slide it firmly to the right. That's all you have to do. When I yell 'Now,' you push that tool, and I'll do the same on the other side of the hall." Elidor gestured beyond the slim white pillars.

"Ready?" Elidor asked with a smile. His companions nodded, and he added, "You won't forget how to work the lock, Sindri?"

Sindri beamed with pride. "Don't worry, Elidor. We'll be here for you."

"Elidor," Catriona said, her eyes worried. "What if the lock is enchanted?"

He smiled. "Don't worry, Cat. There are ways to unlock even magical traps that wizards don't want you to know. They didn't want me to know them, either—but I do." Maddoc glared at Elidor, but said nothing.

Elidor noticed how Catriona's eyes glanced away, studying the impassive Maddoc. Later he would have to find out what was bothering her. But not now.

Elidor reached out and gripped the edges of a large crack in the wall of the main chamber. He forced his foot into the crack, and slowly shifted his weight.

Creeping out farther into the room along the crack, Elidor felt for any irregularity in the wall. When he found a handhold, he pulled himself forward.

Minutes passed slowly, each cautious step along the creased

and broken wall a lifetime. Elidor balanced on ledges no wider than fingers, occasionally using the pillars at his back as support to get from one secure lodging to another.

"I tell you, something's moving out there," Sindri whispered.

"I don't see anything except shadows, Sindri." Cat squinted past the ranger's stalwart figure, her small lantern casting its flickering light over the massive chamber. "If anything were on that floor, we'd know it." She glanced upward at the ceiling, watching it cautiously for any signs of widening cracks or trembling stone.

"Not if it isn't touching the floor!" Sindri suddenly sprang forward, stopping with his toes just a hair short of the chamber's tiled entryway. "Watch out!"

As Sindri yelled, three of the shadows moved against the path of the lantern, skittering toward the light—not away from it. The shadows grew and elongated, their forms stretching into tentacled arms and sharpened claws. They surrounded Elidor, their bodies somehow even darker than the blackness of the cavern.

Elidor shivered, a sudden cold racing down his spine as he spun his head to look behind him. Ice formed in a crackling spider web across the wall where the shadows touched, slick and white and deadly. A terrible cold breeze whipped through the room, snuffing out the lantern's flame.

In the darkness, Sindri screamed, "Elidor!"

7 BROKEN STONE

Cat worked frantically to re-light her lantern as Sindri chanted, his panicked voice echoing through the large chamber. She heard the hiss of unfamiliar voices, and Elidor's pained cry. As the flame shimmered into life once more, Cat lifted the lantern. Beside her, Davyn had already drawn his bow. Sindri stood at the edge of the chamber, smoke drifting around his fingers and sparking faintly in time with his shouts.

Elidor . . .

The elf hung by one hand as shadowed claws slashed through the back of his leather armor. Another shadow dug its fingers into his arm, and ice frosted out from its touch, turning Elidor's skin blue and cold.

Two quick pulls of Davyn's bow, and two sharp twangs. A helpless feeling swelled in Cat's stomach as the arrows sank into the shadow—then slowly, like autumn leaves, tumbled to the ground.

Elidor pulled a glittering dagger from his belt, struggling to fight with one hand while two of the shadows continued their attempts to pry him from the wall.

The third came toward Davyn, Catriona, Sindri and Maddoc, all of whom were standing in the doorway. It stretched to nearly the size of an ogre, opening its mouth to reveal jagged teeth of ice.

The shock of its first touch burned like frosted flame. Screaming as it gripped his outstretched hands, Sindri jumped back. Agony coursed through his body.

Cat's sword leaped into her hand and flashed through the shadow. But when she withdrew her blade it was covered with a thick crust of ice.

"I don't think we're hurting them," Davyn said. He bit his lip, and launched another arrow at the shadows around Elidor.

"Maybe not, but it's slowing them down." Cat pointed toward the shredded area her sword had made in the shadow before her. "We've got to give Elidor a chance to get to the other side of this room. He's almost there."

Elidor swung from the wall, kicking out, and his feet connected with one of the specters. The creature enveloped his boots, but fell back from the force of the impact, and Elidor was able to swing forward and plant his feet in another crack. Defiantly, he stuffed his hand into a crevice nearby, shifting his weight forward a few more inches.

"Sindri!" Cat spared a second to search for the kender before she plunged her frigid blade into the shadow before her. The little wizard sat on the ground, holding his hands before his face and trying desperately to force feeling into his blue fingers. "Get up! When Elidor gets across the room, you have to turn the key!"

Sindri moaned, "I can't move my fingers!"

But Cat had no time to assist the kender, for the shade renewed its attack. It pushed forward into the hallway, its fingers slashing at the floor and spreading ice in a wide wave before it. As it reached Davyn, the ranger skidded and cursed, staring down at the ice as it cracked beneath his boots.

The shades near Elidor reached for his arms, trying to physically wrest the elf from his perch. His skin was blue with cold, and his fingers cracked as they clenched against the wall. Still he tugged himself forward again another few inches.

"Get one of them away from him," Cat yelled to Davyn. Her sword cut through the shadow in front of him. The shade howled, pain finally beginning to touch its ethereal core. "I can fight two at once."

"I've got an idea." Davyn pulled his next arrow out of his quiver, plunging the end of the wooden shaft into the lantern. When the arrow caught fire, Davyn drew it back upon his bow and released it toward of Elidor's attackers. The flame soared through the cavern, its light bright against the darkness, and then plunged into one of the shades.

The shadow screamed. Fire laced through its being, turning part of its shroud to ash. The creature trembled as the flaming arrow fell though its body to the floor. Ash flaked away from its form in charred clumps.

Davyn grinned, and drew another arrow from the lantern's flame as the injured shade dived toward him. Wind swelled behind it, shaking the lantern's fire back from a flame to a dim coal. Davyn released his second arrow, but the fire died before it reached the shade, crushed out by the shadow's approach.

Kneeling beside Sindri, Maddoc took the kender's hands within his own. He ignored the biting cold and stared into Sindri's eyes. "You may not rest, wizard," he said, too softly to be heard by the others. "Your sorcery is needed."

"I . . . I can't . . . I . . ." Sindri tried to flex his fingers. "My hands, Maddoc!"

"I know." Maddoc showed no sympathy, pressing down on the kender's hands until Sindri's fingers clenched into fists. The kender suppressed a cry of pain, his eyes widening. "But there is no time for weakness, Sindri." The old wizard pulled the kender to his feet. "Without you, your friends will fail."

Sindri leaned against the wizard's hands, trying to wiggle his aching fingers. "But . . . I don't know any spells against shadows. What do I do?"

"Stand here, Sindri." Maddoc knelt beside him, pushing the kender's purple cloak to the side. "Hold out your arm, this way." Gripping Sindri's elbow, Maddoc helped the kender shift his stance so that his arms were stiff, as though holding a ball before his chest. "Keep your fingers out."

"It hurts . . ."

"Sssh." His face serious, Maddoc placed both hands on Sindri's shoulders and turned him toward the specters. "Now . . . repeat after me . . ."

One of the ghostly creatures dragged its clawed hands through the air, carving ragged, frost-rimmed holes in Catriona's breast-plate. Cat growled, slashing again with her sword. The second specter howled at Davyn and lunged even as the ranger dodged backward down the hallway, the lantern in his hand.

"Fire, Cat!" Davyn felt the shadow behind him drawing nearer. He tore off the lantern's cover and tried to rekindle the flame. "We have to drive them off with fire."

Cat stepped forward to fend off the shade chasing Davyn with a stroke of her frost-covered sword. The handle was sticking to her fist and frost flaked away from her arm. "Hurry it up, Davyn. This is not as easy as it looks!" she called to him, darting in and out between the flowing creatures. Painfully, she shifted the blade to her other hand, clenching her right fist over and over to try and resurrect the feeling in her fingers. When the shadows coalesced around her once more, Cat struggled to block every grasping hand and shuddering claw, falling back toward Davyn.

Out of the corner of her eye, Catriona could see Elidor clinging to the wall, shoving his feet into the crevices step-by-step. The sharp claws of the shadow attacking him—thank Paladine, only one now!—had scored through his leather armor. It scrabbled at him, trying to tear him from his hold. She could see his fingers shivering in the cold. Catriona's heart sank in her chest. There was nothing she could do to help him, and the spectre wouldn't give up its attack.

Elidor would have to jump.

"Elidor!" Davyn swung the lantern wildly, driving the shadows back from Cat as she fell to her knees. Both of her hands were covered in ice. Her sword tumbled to the floor.

"Elidor, no!" Davyn yelled, seeing Elidor tense upon the rock. The thief was too far—the distance too great for any man to leap it and succeed.

Yet leap he did.

Elidor waited until the shadow's claws raked against him again, and then threw himself from the wall.

The shade roared bitterly, shadow-claws tearing against Elidor even as he passed beyond it. Elidor sank into darkness, an abyss beyond reckoning, and for a long, frozen moment, they couldn't see him.

And then Elidor fell to the floor just beyond the threshold. His body shivered uncontrollably against the hard floor of the hallway past the great chamber. Coughing, he crawled to his knees. Catriona couldn't help but stare in awe—there was no way the elf should have been able to make that jump.

And yet, he did.

"They're going after him on the other side!" Davyn yelled to Cat. She drew her paired dragon claws from her belt, her blue hands barely clenching the hilts. Davyn heated his sword in the lantern's renewed flame. With the swipe of his blade, he turned one shadow's arm to ash. The specks fluttered down on Catriona.

"He's going to make it!" This time, it was Cat whose faith in their friend was unshakable. Elidor crawled toward the hidden lock, as a shadow slashed at his arms.

"Cat, hold the lantern!" Davyn reached for his bow again, deftly swinging it from his back and ripping an arrow into place. She held up the lantern, and he lit his arrow before she returned her force against their enemies.

Arrow after arrow flew from Davyn's bow, piercing Elidor's opponent. Elidor drew out his lockpicks, lying on his belly as he worked the lock.

"I'm not sure I can keep going," Davyn said. "I can't . . ." But he never got a chance to complete his thought.

Just then, Sindri's spell took hold. Guided by the kneeling Maddoc, his voice swelled to a fevered pitch. A fireball burst forth from his fingers, with such force that it shook the stone hall. It raced through the two shadows before them, burning them to nothingness. The third shade, farther away, recoiled from the flame though it was injured only slightly.

"Now, Sindri!" Elidor's shout resonated through the chamber as the fireball died. He twisted his lock pick in the far keyhole. "NOW!"

Sindri dived for the keyhole, grasping at the pick Elidor had left behind. He turned the makeshift key, his eyes still watering from his fire-spell. But his hand, first frozen by shadow, then scorched by fire, faltered.

The key did not click.

The lock did not open.

"Elidor!" Davyn screamed, diving into the room toward his friend.

And a thousand tons of stone began to fall.

8 THE COST OF KNOWLEDGE

"Davyn!" Cat flung aside debris, digging into the mound of stone with both hands in a panicked frenzy. Maddoc tore at the rocks. Carrying the lantern, Sindri ran from spot to spot within the limited portion of the grand chamber. He searched anywhere he could reach, anywhere that had not completely fallen in, tugging aside loose rubble for any sign of Davyn.

"Here!" the kender yelled, jerking the edge of a green cloak from a rocky pile. "Cat! Maddoc!"

The others raced to join him, crawling over the fallen stone that Sindri had navigated so easily.

"It's him, Maddoc," Cat said as she forced herself into a small hole in the rubble, pushing past the kender. She pulled a stone from the pile, handed it through to Maddoc, and reached for the next.

"Oh, Davyn, no, Davyn . . ." Cat's eyes filled with tears. She pulled at the rocks, heedless of her own safety.

Maddoc caught her hand as she passed a rock through to him. "Cat, be cautious. He may already be dead, and you are taking too many chances. The ceiling is not sturdy. These holes in the rubble may collapse. We cannot afford to lose you as well."

Catriona gulped, and she nodded slowly. Tears rolled down her dusty cheeks. "You're right." She squeezed the old wizard's hand, and turned back to the rock pile. She moved more slowly, one rock at a time, keeping her eye on the tenuous balance of stone above her. Eventually, she cleared the upper parts of Davyn's body. His face looked shockingly white, his eyes closed. She tenderly brushed the earth from his cheeks.

A cough shook Davyn's body.

"He's alive!" Cat shouted. "Maddoc, help me get him out." Together, they shifted more rubble. Dust filtered down from the creaking ceiling of debris. Catriona's muscles tensed as she rolled a massive boulder to the side, allowing Maddoc and Sindri to draw Davyn out.

Maddoc gently carried Davyn to the hallway. He kneeled beside the unconscious boy, and watched his chest move with each labored breath.

"He's going to be fine," Maddoc murmured. "He's a tough young man. I taught him well."

Catriona muttered, "You taught him to deceive."

"I taught him to survive," Maddoc said. "He's my son. I did what I had to do, and I don't care if you condemn me for it."

The words echoed those she had spoken once, many years ago before the council of Knights of Solamnia. Cat reddened at the memory, but Maddoc didn't notice, for he was too obsessed with checking for Davyn's pulse.

Davyn's eyes began to flutter, and he inhaled deeply. Maddoc sighed with relief. He stared down at Davyn and seemed to catalogue every movement, every sign of life.

Content at last, the old wizard pushed away. He stood and took several steps down the hallway. "It's only a slight concussion. Davyn should be fine once he wakes up." He glanced back at Davyn once more before schooling his features to their usual solemnity. It was a rare moment, and Catriona's heart ached for him. She turned to say something, but at that moment, Davyn burst out coughing and sat up on his elbows.

"Davyn!" Catriona turned to take his shoulders in her hands and help him to a seat. "Are you all right? Does anything feel broken?"

"I don't think so." Davyn rubbed his head with a wince. "I took quite a knock . . . Catriona . . . Wait, where's Elidor? Elidor!" He rolled to the side, staring out into the collapsed chamber. His face fell. Stones now sealed the room, preventing any chance of reaching their friend on the other side.

"I'm sure he's fine, Davyn," Catriona said. "Only the ceiling of the chamber collapsed. Elidor was in the hallway on the other side. I bet he's over there being annoyed that we're stuck here." She feigned a smile that didn't reach her eyes.

"You almost made it over there, Davyn!" Sindri all but crawled over Davyn's legs and pointed at the huge mass of rubble. "First you zipped through there, and then you dodged past that first big one that fell, and then zoom, through the dust over there—then I lost you, but I could still hear you yelling for Elidor. That's how I knew where to look, you know." The kender's eyes shone as he punched Davyn lightly on the shoulder. "I bet you almost made it halfway there!"

"We have to dig through. Elidor may need us." Davyn scrambled to his feet.

"Ooh, that's a good idea." Sindri rushed to the edge of the chasm and began jerking at loose stones. The ceiling rumbled dangerously. "Well, maybe not."

"No, Sindri." Cat gripped the kender's cloak and pulled him back.

"The falling earth will have destabilized a good deal of the mountain." Maddoc said. "We cannot remain here."

"We'll never get to him this way." Davyn clenched his fist. He paused as he considered their options. "We'll have to find another way around." Spinning, he grabbed Maddoc's shoulder and slammed the old wizard into the wall. "Use your magic. Clear the corridor—teleport us across the room. I don't care. Take me to Elidor. *Now.*"

"It can't be done. At least, not by me." Despite the sharp jar of stone against his back, Maddoc kept his composure. "I've already told you. I have no magic, Davyn. I cannot help you." For a moment, there was a stark tension between the two, and Catriona feared the boy would strike the old wizard—or worse.

Davyn shook him again, and then shoved the old wizard aside. Maddoc fell to the ground, catching himself on his palms.

"Curse you, Maddoc." Davyn's face was still red with rage. "We should never have come here—never have listened to your wild stories about a magic sword. If Elidor is dead—then it's your fault. And I'll see you burn for it."

"It isn't Maddoc's fault," Sindri piped up. "It's mine. I didn't get the key to turn like Elidor showed me. My hands . . ." He held up his singed palms. "I did the best I could, Davyn." Davyn hardly glanced at Sindri, his anger focused entirely on Maddoc.

Cat stepped to Maddoc's side. "Davyn, stop it."

"We might still be able to get around this room. There were some hallways we passed back there that we didn't go down." Sindri stared stubbornly at the collapsed room. "That is, if you're sure you wouldn't rather dig? No?" He looked back at the other three and shrugged. "Okay, then, I guess we'll go back."

"Elidor has to wait." Catriona said seriously, taking Davyn's arm. "I don't like it any more than you do. But he'd be the first one to remind us what we're all down here for. We have to get to that tomb before Asvoria does."

Davyn stared out at the rubble once more, his fists clenching. "Elidor . . ."

"He'd tell us to go, Davyn. Nearra is important to him, too."

Grimly, Davyn agreed. "We'll come back for him."

"He had basic equipment on him, Davyn. A few days' food, water. Weapons. He may even find us first. He can certainly get around in these tunnels better than we can." Catriona took the lantern from Sindri and held it up to illuminate the hallway behind them. "He'll never forgive us if we stand here and pity him, and Asvoria gets to the tomb before us."

Bitterly, Davyn glanced at Catriona. "And if he's dead, there's no use wasting our time trying to find him. Is that right?"

"That's not fair—" Cat began, but Davyn stopped her.

"I'm sorry." He looked away. "I know you're right, Cat. It's the only thing we can do—but I don't have to like it." Davyn checked his sword, and sighed over his battered bow. "We'll just have to tie up Maddoc's hands again and get moving."

"Davyn, I don't think that's a good idea." Cat gestured toward the gray-haired wizard. "This wasn't his fault."

"You want to know a good idea?" Davyn snarled at Maddoc, turning to face the old wizard directly. "Tell me the incantation that will open the tomb, Maddoc. You want us to trust you? Then you have to trust us." Davyn shoved the old wizard's shoulder, pressing him back against the wall.

"No," Maddoc replied calmly. "I'll keep my bargain. When we get to the tomb, I'll tell Sindri how to undo the spell. Until then, it's a moot point."

"Not to me," Davyn said. "You're keeping things from us, old man, and I don't like it."

"Davyn!" Catriona gripped his arm. "Stop it. He can't do anything to hurt us. He didn't make the ceiling collapse—far from it, he helped Sindri cast a spell, an actual spell, and it may have saved our lives." She ignored Sindri's soft protest. "We're going to need all the help we can get."

"By Paladine, Cat. You don't actually *trust* him, do you?" Davyn said.

"No—well, a little. Enough to not treat him like a prisoner." She drew a dagger from her belt and handed it, scabbard and all, to Maddoc. "Keep this on you. Stay beside Sindri. Davyn and I will take up point and rear."

"When did you take charge?" Some humor crept into Davyn's voice, softening his words. "All right, Cat, I won't argue. Let's get a move on. If those shadows were servants of Asvoria, then it means she knows we're here—and she's planning for us."

Cat nodded in agreement, lifting the lantern and moving past Maddoc to peer down the hallway. She walked back the way they came with another glance over her shoulder toward the pile of rubble. After a moment, Maddoc followed, his hands folded in his long black velvet sleeves. Sindri and Davyn paused at the edge of the stone, looking back into the fallen chamber.

"There's nothing we can do," Sindri repeated, and Davyn nodded.

"I know." Before Cat's lantern faded down the hallway, Davyn turned and followed.

A few minutes later, Sindri went after him. No one noticed the thick weight that seemed to materialize in his pocket. Elidor had left the tool behind, after all. He would want Sindri to keep it and give it back to him later.

Cat's fingers moved over the heavy oak door. She traced the intricate dragon-and-*A* inscription, trying to find any knob, handle, or mechanism that would open the door. Davyn leaned against the wall behind her, holding the lantern. His eyes darted into the darkness. It had taken them six hours to get this far, following every corridor that led even vaguely in the direction beyond the collapsed hall.

"Anything?" Davyn shifted warily. "I'm telling you, you should have let me stay back at that Y-passage, check out the other side. If you're going to take all day here, I might as well go back and investigate it . . . meet you on the other side."

"What, by yourself?" Catriona rolled her eyes.

"I've been through worse. I could find Elidor, and with his help, I'd move twice as fast through these tunnels. We'd meet you at the tomb. If Maddoc gave me the incantation, I might even be able to get it open . . ."

"No, Davyn," Maddoc said coldly. "You aren't going to dispose of me that easily."

A half-hearted grin crossed Davyn's face. "It was worth a try, old man."

"I keep telling you," Sindri said, "there's no way you'll find anything without me. Now let me look at this door again." Sindri pushed at the door, trying to wedge past Cat. "Catriona, you've got to get out of the way."

Catriona stepped aside, running her fingers through her hair. "You've already looked, Sindri. I still think the only thing left to do is throw our shoulders against it and knock it in."

"That doesn't make any sense. Anyway, I think I had an idea about how it opens. My mother told me about secret locks on doors that are put right in the middle, you know? Anyway, there has to be a latch, because otherwise how would they invite guests inside? You'd think that they didn't want people to go in!"

Catriona sighed, leaning against the wall with Davyn. As Sindri went over the door again, Cat prodded Maddoc with her toe. The wizard looked up from his seat on the floor, his meditation disturbed. "Can't you teach him a door-opening spell?"

Maddoc sighed. "I could, but it would take days. I didn't specialize in such spells."

"What's wrong, Maddoc? Too illegal?"

The wizard tried not to rise to Davyn's taunting. "Spells of transmutation, particularly those that affect inanimate objects—are difficult. It would take days to teach Sindri the intricacies, the nuances. The fingering alone would take—"

"Found it." The lock clicked under Sindri's fingers. He grinned, and slipped Elidor's tool back into his pocket. "Oh, wow."

The door was heavy, thicker than Catriona thought, yet it swung without a sound, eerily silent on hidden hinges. Beyond, the darkness was broken by cheery firelight. Stacks of books taller than a person littered the room, and overstuffed couches faced the warm hearth. Two tables stood among the tall bookcases, with leather chairs that seemed only recently empty, as if their owners had stepped away for a cup of tea but would soon return.

Sindri took a step inside, his bare feet sinking into the plush carpet. "Hello?" he called into the library.

"What is it?" Davyn asked, pushing away from the wall to follow Sindri. "Hey, watch it, there might be traps."

"If there are, what are we going to do about them? Get Elidor to disarm them?" Sindri climbed over the couch, rubbing his hands before the fire. "Look at this! Hey, Maddoc! There's no wood in this fire! Wow, look at all the pictures on the wall—I wonder if they're like the ones in the Gallery of Despair! Are they enchanted? Do you think we'll vanish into them like before?" The kender climbed up on the furniture to poke at one of the landscapes hanging from the wall of the room. "Aw . . . I don't think these are magical at all."

Catriona and Maddoc entered slowly.

"Asvoria's library," Maddoc breathed, fingers brushing the leather bindings.

"Really?" Sindri popped up again. "It seems a little small. There can't be more than a hundred, hundred-fifty books here. Wouldn't a queen have had more than that?"

Maddoc smiled, removing one of the heavy tomes and flipping through its pages. "I'm sure she did—in her other palaces. Navarre was a small palace—a retreat for the nobility. It wasn't built to hold her vast treasures, only her favorite ones."

Walking cautiously across the carpet, Davyn studied the room. "There's another door here." He moved past the bookshelves, striding to the far end of the room. He pushed at a door half-hidden behind a tapestry of wolves hunting a doe. "Sealed. Like the first one. Sindri, can you take a look at this?"

But the kender had already joined Maddoc at the table, climbing on top of one of the leather chairs and poking at the book the wizard had selected from the shelves. "Is it a spell book?"

"A theoretical discussion, actually, one of Fistandantilus's lost essays. Astounding. I could spend years studying this."

"We don't have that much time," Davyn reminded him. "Now get over here, Sindri."

While Sindri studied the second door, Catriona walked among the bookshelves. Books of all descriptions covered the shelves, their bindings cracked with age but still sturdy. Between the books stood small objects of art, puzzles, and enameled boxes, their lids covered in jewels, golden tracings, or cloisonné pictures. She lifted a platinum bird from its stand, gasping slightly as it began to sing. Catriona quickly replaced it and the song died, the silvery wings ceasing to beat as soon as she took her hand away. "Magic."

"Oh, wonderful!" Sindri turned to see, but Davyn grabbed the Sindri's cloak by the hood and pulled him back. "Davyn!"

"Door."

Sindri sighed, and began to run his hands over the lintel and edges of the door. "It doesn't open like the other one," Sindri murmured. His finger slid against a grim face carved into the door.

Suddenly, there was a loud crack. Shocks of lightning trailed up and down the door. Sindri screamed, spinning from the door as though he had been slapped by a giant. He slammed into the overstuffed couch, flipped backward onto the cushions, and slid down to the floor.

Catriona leaped to his side. "Sindri!"

Maddoc looked up from his book, a frown creasing his brow.

"Sindri, are you okay?" Catriona brushed Sindri's dark hair out of his face to reveal his wide grin.

"Magic," Sindri said, awed. "The door's got magic on it." He coughed, and his eyes watered from the blow. "Maddoc, the door's magic! It's locked with magic."

"So I see," Maddoc said, turning back to the book nonchalantly.

Davyn looked from Sindri to the door. "So what does that mean?"

"It means that it's trapped. I can't open it. I don't know. Maybe Elidor could." Sindri sat up straight, climbing past Catriona onto the couch. "Can we do it again?"

"You can do it as many times as you want," Davyn sighed, running a hand through his dark brown hair. "But if it isn't going to get us through the door, then don't waste our time." Davyn kicked one of the fallen couch pillows across the room.

"I bet there's a key here, somewhere. They can't have made a door without a key." Sindri's eager tone made Catriona smile despite the situation.

Catriona looked around at the room. "If there's a key, maybe it's in one of those." She walked to the bookshelves and took down two small boxes, opening them and fingering through their contents. "But would a magic key look like a normal key?"

"It could look like anything," Maddoc replied, half-listening to the conversation. "Magical locks do not require such mundane materials as tumblers and gadgets."

Together, Davyn, Catriona, and Sindri began going through the contents of the room. Davyn and Catriona carried armloads of bric-a-brac from the shelves to a single pile by the door. Sindri went through them one by one, identifying them as magical, non-magical, and quite-possibly-magical. All the while, Maddoc ignored them, drawing more books from the shelves.

"Are you going to help at all?" Davyn snarled, carrying another armload past the table.

"I am helping," Maddoc said, his eyes never lifting from the book. Davyn muttered under his breath, tumbling the next load onto Sindri's lap.

"Davyn! Sindri!" Cat called from the last row of bookshelves. "Over here!" Catriona pushed aside a stack of books from the lowest shelf and held out a large glass sphere.

"Cat!" Sindri breathed. "That's not a key. That's a palontir!"

"A what?" Catriona set the sphere and its golden stand on the floor between them. The sphere was approximately ten inches in diameter, its glossy sides shimmering with incandescent rainbows over the clear emptiness of the glass ball. Inside, a faint twinkling of stars shimmered, illuminating Catriona and Sindri's faces with flickering light.

Davyn paused by the fire, staring over at them. "It's a what?"

Maddoc looked up from his book, staring fiercely at Sindri. "A crystal ball?" He stood, pushing away the tome before him. "Be cautious, Sindri. Palontir are dangerous."

"Crystal ball—hey! I bet we could see all sorts of other places in this! Davyn!" Sindri yelled. "I'm going to look for Elidor!"

Davyn rushed toward him, blood draining from his face. "Sindri, be careful. Maddoc knows what he's talking about. I've heard stories of those things trapping people's minds, stealing their souls. Don't try to use it until we know how treacherous it is." Davyn stared Maddoc in the eye. "If it will show us Elidor, then we'd better learn how to use it."

"You don't know what you're asking, my son. Palontir are rare for a reason." Maddoc closed the massive book he had been studying. He looked at Sindri. "Far too dangerous for a novice."

Even as the black-robed wizard stood, Sindri reached out to grasp the large crystal. He lifted it in both hands, staring at the orb's glowing, pulsing interior. "It's so light!" he called out. "Like a feather." Sindri tossed the ball into the air between his hands. The firelight glinted across its smooth surface.

"Sindri—no!" Davyn tried to catch the glowing orb. Catriona reached for the ball at the same time. Sindri protested, reaching up to grip the ball, but too many hands were in the way. The ball shifted in its flight, slipped between them, and crashed onto the floor.

"Oh," Sindri gulped. Thin glass slivers covered the wooden floor. A thick mist arose from the orb's fragments. The mist hovered for a moment, and then coalesced, thickening into a shimmery ball. It pulsed with light, shifting first to the left and then to the right. Fire flew in small bursts inside the mist, collecting into bright eyes that blinked in sudden awareness. The eyes stared first at Sindri, then Catriona, and finally focused on Maddoc with recognition . . . and hate.

"I don't think that was a crystal ball," Catriona said. "That mist is *alive*."

9   THROUGH THE DARKNESS TO THE LIGHT

D aylight filtered through the collapsed rock, illuminating the tunnel with a faint glow. Elidor pushed aside more debris, coughing. He pressed one hand through the crack, and pulled. A rock fell down, tumbling along the thin passageway past the elf.

He pressed onward, pulled aside more dirt and stones, until the crevice was wide enough to crawl through. As the first rays of morning warmed his face, he gave thanks to Paladine, Mishakal, and any other god he'd ever heard of. The path behind him into the mountain had been dark and cramped, and the slight incline of the cave-in had provided the only escape. The grand chamber was gone, filled with a thick wall of debris. The corridor beyond had also collapsed, and only this faint sunlight had guided him up, through the shifting rubble toward the sky far above.

One hand, then the next, and then his torso, inch by inch, Elidor climbed into the sunlight. He pulled his feet out of the ground and lay on a narrow rocky trail, relishing the feeling of cool air and warm sunlight. A few minutes later, he opened his eyes and took stock of the surroundings, looking down on the box canyon and the small village below.

Elidor scowled, recognizing the territory. "Of all places, I had to come up next to the village of Tarrent."

A dusty shadow, newly unearthed from the same crevice, said, "What's wrong with this village?"

"More than I could explain, Davyn," Elidor replied, watching as his friend shook dust and earth from his clothing. "You'll see."

The village was built in a circular pattern, the huts spread evenly around small gardens and carefully maintained roads. A larger building in the center, made of solid logs and packed earth, served as a hearthstead, a central location to govern the town. No road led into or out of the box canyon; the only means of access was to climb the long stone face of the surrounding mountains. The village was isolated, protected from the outside world and inhabited by those who did not choose to invite that outer world into their lives.

Even from their position on the mountainside, Davyn and Elidor could see a buzz in the town. The roadways were packed with people, and a train of three black horses led a wagon covered with dark blankets through the village roads. Elidor sharpened his vision, his eyes picking up details that others would easily miss. "It's a funeral." His eyes took on a hunted look, and his voice fell. "The Baron has died."

"The Baron?" Davyn stepped forward to stand beside Elidor. "How do you know that?"

"I recognize the banners on that wagon. I've been here before." Elidor's voice was flat, as though disguising some ancient pain.

Davyn started. "How can that be? I thought you said . . ."

"I said I knew this area." Shading his eyes, Elidor continued, "I found this canyon by accident, many years ago, while I was scaling the mountains in this area. There are tales of gold hidden in these mountains; I never knew those legends stemmed from ancient myths of Navarre."

"So, you know these people?"

"Yes." Elidor nodded. "But that doesn't mean they'll be happy to see me."

"Why?"

"That's far enough." Another voice broke in before Elidor could reply. "You'll do me the favor of dropping your weapons, of course." A guardsman stepped out of the brush with a bow raised, trained on Davyn and Elidor, watching for any sign of aggression. "We've had one death in the last day, gentlemen. I'd rather not add to the number . . ." His voice died as he caught sight of the elf's face. "Elidor? Is that you?"

Regretfully, the elf nodded, removing his long knives from his belt and dropping them to the ground before him. He gestured for the surprised Davyn to do the same, and Davyn complied.

"You won't be welcome back in Tarrent, Elidor. Particularly under these circumstances." The guardsman lowered his bow, and Davyn caught sight of strange, half-ogre features beneath the man's rawhide helmet. Obtuse brown eyes watched with sympathy beneath black wiry brows, and the man's voice held an accent that didn't sound like any place else in the world. It sounded ancient, undiluted by the passage of time.

"What happened, Gerhalt?" Elidor asked.

The guard sighed. "The Baron's been murdered."

"Murdered?" Elidor seemed shaken.

"Last night. His body was found in the hearthstead this morning, the killer's knife still lodged in his chest." Gerhalt's voice turned quiet. "You fight with knives, do you not, Elidor?"

Elidor didn't bother to respond to the question. "Tarrent is a small town. The people here have known one another from birth, their parents and parent's parents have always lived here. How could something like this happen? Was there a revolt?"

"No. No revolt. The winter was peaceful, and our stores are still good. There has been no unrest."

"Then what happened?"

Gerhalt shrugged. "I do not know, Elidor. It is a mystery to us all. But you are here, and that is too large a coincidence for anyone to ignore. The Baroness will want to see you."

"I'm sure she will."

The guard collected Elidor's and Davyn's weapons, slinging them over his back with the rest of his gear. "Let's go," Gerhalt said. "We'll need to be getting you into town now, so the Baroness can decide what to do with you."

Davyn and Elidor went with him, down a narrow winding trail to the village below. The small huts, formed of logs and mortared by grassy mud, looked as if they'd grown out of the canyon floor. The buildings were weathered by wind and rain. A small creek twisted through the center of the village, glistening in the morning sunlight, and a bridge led over the water to the hearthstead. A thousand people lived here; no more. Any larger population would have overcrowded the small, enclosed canyon.

As Davyn and Elidor passed beyond the first few huts, weeping peasants began to take notice of their approach. At first, they were stared at as strangers. The village children gaped at the first new faces they may well have ever seen. Then, sparks of recognition dawned in the faces of their parents. Whispers greeted them, and stares behind hastily raised hands.

"Elidor," one woman whispered. Her elf heritage was apparent in her slanted ears, but her squarish, chocolate-brown eyes were clearly a gift from some other parentage. She turned, lifting her skirts and running toward the hearthstead full-tilt, fear putting flight into her steps.

Davyn fidgeted, his hand seeking the sword that no longer

hung by his side. "What is this place?"

"It is a village in the heart of the Vingaard Mountains, lost to civilization long ago. And that is the way they wish it to be." Elidor's voice held regret.

"And you lived here?"

The elf nodded. "Long ago, when I was still a very young man, I ran away. Away from my mother's people, the Silvanesti. They hated the stain on my blood. My father was never good enough for them. I was even less. I was nothing." Old anger surfaced in Elidor's voice. "You can't imagine what it is like to be a half-breed, Davyn. I was . . . grateful for all that they gave me here: a home free of prejudice. By Mishakal, the blood of these people is ten times more sullied than my own. They never cared. I found this place by accident—but I made it my home on purpose. For a while." Elidor turned his face away from the accusing eyes that followed him from the crowd.

"It sounds like a paradise," Davyn said.

"Thief!" One man pointed at Elidor. He hissed, his tongue almost lizardlike in his mouth, "Liar. Betrayer! How dare you come back here!"

Elidor did not answer, meeting the man's eyes with a solemn, regretful stare. He turned back to Davyn. "There is no such thing as paradise."

A sobbing peasant woman fell to her knees as they reached the inner courtyards of the town. She gripped her young son and turned her face away. Elidor walked through it all, keeping his head down.

All of the individuals in the village had strange features, as though many different strains of people interbred though successive generations. Davyn could see dwarf features, elf features, and human features, as well as others that he could not place, scattered about like pepper in a rich soup. Elidor must have felt very much at home here once, Davyn thought as he glanced at the angry crowd. But something clearly had gone very, very wrong.

"He did it!" an old man cried. "He returned to kill Baron Darghellen! Give him pain! Give him death!"

"Now, Ryadin." Gerhalt stepped between Elidor and the old man. "Settle down. We're taking them to the Baroness, and she'll be the one to judge them. Not you, and not this rabble." Gerhalt tapped the man's arm with a short club. Gerhalt gently parted the crowd, turning to gesture Davyn and Elidor toward the bridge that led to the hearthstead.

"Gerhalt, you can't just take them to her." A short dwarvish woman wrung the apron of her skirt into a thick twist of fabric. "What if they attack the Baroness? What if that was their plan all along?"

"Go on home, Ellia. Nobody's going to be attacking the Baroness on my watch." The guard—who by now, Davyn could tell, made up approximately one-tenth of the entire guard force of the village—motioned for the people to move.

The bridge arched over the wide creek. It took three steps to cross over. The crowd gathered on the far side of the bridge, but did not follow them through to the other side.

Elidor did not look back. But Davyn turned around several times, watching the crowd gather, as if they were held back by some invisible force.

"They won't come across." Gerhalt wiped sweat from his brow, replacing his hat over his dark, curly hair. "By now, she's been told that you're here—and she'll be waiting." He stepped past two more guards, to the heavy wooden doors of the hearthstead.

The doors were painted red, covered in intricate tracings of dragons and fire, the colors vibrant and well-tended. It took two men to push a door open, and it gave a gentle squeal of well-used hinges. Gerhalt squinted inside, checking to see that nothing was blocking the entrance. Then, he extended his arm to Davyn and Elidor, all but saluting them into the building.

Warily, Elidor moved forward, entering the dimly lit hearthstead with Davyn on his heels. Inside the building, the room was wide and flat, the ceiling only a head taller than the tallest man. A dais covered in furs and woven green fabric took up one side of the chamber, and upon it rested a single chair—not an ornate throne, but a soft, covered armchair.

Light filtered down from windows in the thatched roof, propped open with long oak limbs that reached to the floor below. Empty lanterns hung along pillars, and two tall fireplaces, cold like the blackened mouths of the dead, gaped openly at Elidor and Davyn as they passed.

On the far end of the room, at the lip of the dais, a woman wrapped in furs stood beside the chair. She did not look up at them as they came closer. Absently, her fingers caressed the arm of the chair, brushing over the carved figure of a woman holding up the sun. White-blonde hair reached to the small of her back, looped about by three small braids to keep it confined into a thick coil. Her features were neither elf, nor human, nor anything else that could be easily defined.

She looked up at last, her soft pink lips tightened into a firm line. Her eyes and Elidor's met, and fury colored her porcelain white skin. She regarded him with a ruler's impassivity.

"Elidor the Fallen." Her tone was quiet, but it reached through the empty hall like a ringing bell. "My beloved."

"Vael," Elidor greeted her coolly.

She stepped away from the dais, and Davyn and Elidor could see a thick stain of red on the furs spread at the throne's foot. "I should have known when I saw the dagger in my father's back, that you had returned, Elidor. But this time you won't be vanishing from Tarrent while the moons are absent from the sky.

In fact, you won't be leaving at all.

"You and your companion are hereby charged with the death of Baron Darghellen of the village of Tarrent. You will surrender yourself to my mercy . . . ."

The doors of the hearthstead slammed closed behind them with a thunderous bang.

" . . . And you will be judged."

10   Freedom and Truth

Light rippled across the walls of the library, illuminating the bookshelves like a tiny star.

"The mist is alive," Catriona repeated.

Her voice seemed to echo within the ball of light, rippling the strange, luminescent matter as though it were water. The globe of light floated closer to the ceiling, and its two sparkling eyes slowly shifted to take in Catriona.

"Aaaaa . . . live," the globe echoed.

"It can talk!" Sindri jumped up. "Hello, ball of light! My name is Sindri!" Sindri bowed with a flourish. "This is Catriona, and this is Davyn, and this is Maddoc—"

As the ball turned to regard Maddoc, its colors suddenly shifted to a fiery red. Sindri gave a start of surprise. "Oh, I don't think it likes Maddoc. Hey, hey, ball? Look over here again." Sindri waved his arms above his head, trying to get the creature's attention.

"Sindri, we don't know if that's safe," Davyn said hesitantly.

"Sindri," the orb murmured, then the eyes blinked. "You are a kender."

"Hey! That's right!" Sindri jumped up and down. "I am a kender. And Catriona's a human, and . . . uh . . . what are you?" **101**

"I am a guardian. My name is unpronounceable in your language. Roughly," the orb said in a strange monotone, "it translates to . . ." A shimmering ripple of colored light danced across the surface of the orb. "But in lieu of . . . your ability to reproduce my name . . . you may call me . . . Seraphel."

"Seraphel." Catriona repeated numbly.

The ball turned so that its glowing eyes faced her. "I exist to protect good against evil." The ball shifted to a minty green. "Asvoria was my enemy. For an undetermined number of . . . years, I have been held captive here. Even though I felt her death, I could not be released until someone else engineered my freedom."

"Captured by Asvoria?" Davyn scowled. "You must not have been a particularly powerful enemy."

The orb rippled in the air. "I am a creature of good . . . and I am a guardian. But I am not omniscient, nor am I all-powerful. I am, however, protected against the powers of evil. Therefore . . . her only option was to incarcerate me."

"Until we freed you." Sindri climbed up onto the couch, staring up at the glittering orb with wide eyes. "Isn't that wonderful?" Davyn and Maddoc didn't seem to agree. For once they were unified in their uncertainty about the hovering creature.

Catriona moved to a leather chair by the table and sunk into it without ever taking her eyes from the floating orb.

"Now what are you going to do, Seraphel?" Sindri smiled, eager to hear the creature's response. "Do you have any family?"

"All creatures of good are my kin," the orb replied. "But I am eager to leave this place, it is true." The orb spun again, its shining eyes taking in each one of them in turn. "I will leave, but not until I know you are safe. That is my gift to you, for my freedom. Sindri, Catriona—you are creatures of one with my own heart. Your nobility shows within you . . . but your companions . . ." The eyes sparked red as they regarded Davyn.

"In your past, you have served evil." Seraphel's rippling colors changed and altered as it stared down at Davyn. "But you have not yet found the end of your path. I will not judge you . . . not today. Choose wisely . . ." The orb paused for a moment, as though about to say more, but then fell silent.

It then turned to Maddoc. "You, on the other hand . . . redemption is not something you choose. You have turned your back on every opportunity, on every hope. Your robes are as black as your heart, wizard. I have seen your type before, littering the bloody fields of ambition." The orb pulsed, and red became its dominant color, spreading through the incandescent shimmer of the glowing creature. "I see no reason to allow you to live."

"Wait a minute." Catriona started up from her seat. "You can't just kill Maddoc." Her face seemed pale among the library stacks, the crackle of the fire glinting like a soft candle against Seraphel's brilliant light. "We're on a quest." She stepped forward with purpose. "And we need his help."

Seraphel's sparkling eyes turned their full regard to the red-haired warrior. "He is evil. He has made his choice. He will suffer the consequences." The angelic voice held no anger, no cruelty, only a sense of implacable certainty. "Has this wizard not done evil to you? Are his works not in opposition to the very nature of your being?" Catriona flushed, lowering her eyes.

Maddoc scowled, folding his hands into his black robes. "I despise creatures like you. Oh, yes, guardian, I have met your type before. You are narrow-minded, weak-willed, unable to see that the world cannot exist with only light. Each day must have its night. Would you drive all evil from the land? All knowledge? All sacrifice?" Despite the obvious power of the shimmering being, Maddoc lifted his head and refused to show fear. "The gods themselves have chosen that this world will live half in light and half in darkness. Do you dare to place yourself above the very creators of Krynn?"

The glowing creature pulsed. "Your arguments are meaningless. You are a black wizard, a servant of Nuitari. You will be destroyed."

Sindri climbed onto the back of the couch, gesturing wildly. "Not everything that is evil is bad!" He shook his head. "We need Maddoc."

"We do." Catriona agreed, refusing to meet Davyn's eyes as the ranger colored visibly.

"I can't believe this," Davyn suddenly interrupted. "The guardian is right. Look at us. We're trapped in a ruined palace, trying to beat Asvoria to her greatest treasure, and arguing to save Maddoc's life." He spat out the words with contempt. "*Maddoc*, Catriona. The man brought Asvoria back in the first place. It's his fault we're here, his fault that we're racing against time to save Nearra—if she can be saved." Davyn stared at the others as though they were experiencing a shared hallucination.

"Davyn—" Cat began, but he continued, raising his voice to drown out her protests.

"Listen," said Davyn. "I know you think you can redeem him. I'm not stupid. But Maddoc isn't something you can win or lose." He paused, looked sideways at Maddoc, and went on. "As long as he gives us the incantation first, you won't fail anyone by letting him go . . ."

"Fail anyone?" said Catriona softly.

Davyn continued, "I know what you've been through. You can't replace that by saving Maddoc. You can't pretend like it never happened, and you shouldn't think that you can." Davyn's balled fist struck the table. "I'm sorry, Cat. But I can't watch you be manipulated by him—like I was."

Catriona stared at her friend in shock. "Davyn, this isn't the time or the place." She rose, placing her hands on Davyn's shoulders. "I know how you feel about Maddoc, and I'm not letting him manipulate me. But we can't abandon him. We need him to unlock Asvoria's tomb and find Nearra. If he can undo what he's done to Nearra, how can we turn our backs on that?"

Throughout it all, Maddoc stood silently, watching the two discuss his fate as though he still held the world in his hands. He kept his eyes on the guardian, resolutely looking up at the glowing creature as though daring it to defy the very laws of the gods. Catriona looked back and met Maddoc's eyes. "We can't afford to lose another member of this party. Maddoc is an ally—no matter what happened in his history."

"Your purpose is to gain access to Asvoria's tomb?" the orb asked, its surface shimmering through robin's egg blue to deep indigo.

"The door's locked." Sindri ran to the sealed door and pounded on it lightly. "It's trapped with magic. We can't get through it. There's probably a key in this room that will unlock the magic trap, but if we do that, it might blow up. I'm more of a spell caster, not really the kind of kender you might think . . ." He gasped, and his words died away as the ball of light flushed pink, then orange, then green—and the door swung open.

"A gift." Seraphel's shining eyes seemed almost to smile. "Your freedom, in exchange for my own, good kender. Take the woman, and the ranger, and go. May you best Asvoria, where I could not."

Sindri jumped up, his purple cloak swirling. "Thank you, ball of light!"

Seraphel shifted, sparks drifting down from its hovering presence to die out against the cold stone floor. "Leave me with the wizard. His fate will be relatively swift." The light advanced on Maddoc, and for a moment, Sindri forgot all about the unexplored hallway beyond the open door.

"Hey! No!"

Across the room, Catriona released her hold on Davyn's shoulders and turned to face Seraphel. "Asvoria put you in that prison. She's more powerful than we are. We need all the allies we can get." She kept one hand on Davyn's shoulder and pointed to Maddoc with the other, "I can't let you murder him, no matter how noble your intentions."

"You have no choice. There will be no further discussion." Seraphel's light flashed across the spectrum of red. "Will you not beg for your life, wizard?"

Maddoc withdrew his hands from his sleeves, his face alive with anger. "Never."

Seraphel flashed, and Maddoc's face contorted with pain. The black-robed wizard's mouth opened into a silent O of agony, and he fell to his knees, body shaking with pain.

Catriona and Davyn stared, stunned by the power unleashed upon their once-enemy Maddoc.

"No!" Sindri screamed, leaping over the couch to Maddoc's side. Maddoc clawed at the table, knocking the books to the floor with a crash. He choked, his lungs emptying of air as the guardian pulsed with scarlet light.

"Do not grieve, kender," Seraphel said, hovering over Maddoc. "This is a victory."

Sindri tried to grab Maddoc's robes, to pull him away from the guardian. "I won't let you!"

Catriona's weapon leaped into her hands. She jumped over the fallen books to stand between the guardian and the fallen wizard, holding her heavy sword in both hands like an executioner over a chopping-block. "Seraphel, stop! Davyn, help me!" Davyn froze, faltering. "Davyn!"

Davyn slowly drew his sword. "Catriona's right. I hate it, but she is. I can't let you kill him, Seraphel. No matter how much I wish I could. As long as Maddoc holds some key to my friend's return. I have to protect him." A pained scowl flashed across his face as he joined Catriona.

Sindri reached inside his cloak, digging into his pocket with fumbling fingers. "Hold on, Maddoc, just . . . don't die." The wizard, of course, could not reply. Sindri began to pull out a sheaf of thick canvas.

"Back away." Red and angry, Seraphel burned against the ceiling and Maddoc gasped. Davyn lifted his guard, advancing with Catriona. Though their swords would likely not harm Seraphel, the act of their defiance seemed to have confused the guardian. "If you choose his side," it said threateningly, the red glow spreading to encompass the entire room, "then you will share his fate."

Agony ripped through Catriona's limbs. It felt as though her muscles were being torn from bone. Davyn howled, and his sword fell to the stone floor. He reached for the table, falling over the edge as his face reddened with pain. Catriona balled up upon her knees, still trying to strike at the guardian with her sword. By now, Maddoc was nearly unconscious, his eyes gazing emptily at the guardian, defiant until the end.

Sindri's fingers spasmed as he unrolled the canvas. He held it high above his head.

And suddenly, the pain vanished.

"Sindri . . ." Catriona wheezed, gripping her sword and staring at him. "What have you done?"

"Don't look at it." Sindri's eyes were squeezed shut, but he unscrewed one to look at her. "Go out the door. I'll put it on the table."

"What . . ." choked Maddoc, gesturing toward the canvas. Above them, the ball of light hung in the air, its sparkling light now a sorrowful yellow-green. Seraphel's eyes flickered back and forth over the painting in Sindri's hands.

Sindri looked abashed. "I'll just put this here on the table, and when Seraphel's finished, uh, looking at it . . . well, we'll already be long gone."

Cat took in the fraying edges of the canvas where it appeared to have been cut by a knife, the faded smatterings of paint along the edges. "Sindri!" Catriona gasped. "That's a painting from the Gallery of Despair! How could you!"

Maddoc spluttered, "You cut down one of my paintings?"

Sindri grimaced. "Of course not. I conjured it! I was thinking it would be useful and suddenly here it was, in my pocket."

Catriona exchanged a wry grin with Maddoc. But she didn't say anything. They left the library quietly, Catriona's arm about Maddoc's shoulder to support his still-weak steps. Sindri danced merrily from the room, slipping small treasures from the pile by the fireplace into his pocket before he followed Cat into the hallway.

As Davyn passed through the doorway, he turned back to stare at the guardian for a long moment. The floating creature hovered over the painting, sparkling eyes completely focused on the colors on the canvas. "Choose wisely," the guardian murmured to itself.

Davyn whispered, "I will . . ."

11   A Portal Opened

Elidor stood at the window of the hearth-stead, watching the funeral pyre outside. Thick smoke rose against the blue sky. Weeping women knelt at the edge of the bier, leaning together like willows in a rainstorm, their sobs echoing through the village. The Baroness stood at the back of the crowd, her head bowed, masking her silent grief. The funeral was over, and the pyre was little more than a bonfire filled with ash and regret.

Davyn shifted uncomfortably, folding his arms against his chest. "When will we know?" Davyn said, leaning close to Elidor so that Gerhalt would not hear their discussion.

"Her judgment?" Elidor shrugged, his face unreadable. "The village of Tarrent is not like other places on Krynn. They believe in trial by testing. It is likely that Vael will choose some sort of physical test to see if we are responsible for her father's death. If we fail, we will be proved guilty by their law. And if we are guilty," Elidor hung his head, his blonde hair falling in front of his eyes, "then we will be executed."

Davyn turned, staring at the furs on the ground of the large building. The hearthstead was cold. A brisk wind drifted through **109** the open skylights that allowed sunlight to enter the gloomy chamber. Gerhalt stood in front of the closed doors, his eyes trained on the two prisoners.

Sighing, Davyn ran his hand across his chin. "And if we pass the test?"

"Then we will be released." Elidor shook his head. "But we need more than that."

"You've got to be kidding me." Davyn took Elidor's sleeve, pulling him away from the window. "You don't think that escaping from this place with our lives is enough? The others are still trapped somewhere in the mountain. Asvoria is coming—if she isn't there already." His voice dropped to a desperate whisper. "And we have no way back into the mountain to find them. We're going to have to get out of this canyon, reconnoiter, and go back through the original entrance. We might end up days behind them, or more." Davyn sized up Gerhalt before whispering, "We might be able to make a run for it. That guard doesn't look like he could stop us both. And even if he called for help, there are probably only about twenty trained guards in this whole village. We've faced worse odds before."

Elidor shook his head. "Impossible. These people are hunters. If we flee, they'll find us. Believe me."

Davyn sighed. "What happened here, Elidor? Why do these people hate you so?"

Elidor walked back to the window. "It's more important right now to understand that I know this village. I know its customs. I know its people. And, most of all, I know its secrets."

"Secrets?" Quickly, Davyn lowered his voice as the guard raised his eyebrow and muttered. "What secrets?" Davyn whispered, glancing back to his friend.

"There is a portal hidden somewhere in the village. I never knew where it led, only that the Baron guarded it with his very life. But now I think I know. The portal leads back into the mountain—to Asvoria's tomb."

"How can you be so certain?"

"Long ago, Baron Darghellen told me that the people here were the descendants of servants and guardsmen of an ancient queen. That they had escaped being buried alive . . . but he wouldn't tell me how. He told me that the portal would one day be opened, and when it was, the key to the Obsidian Heart would be found."

"The Obsidian Heart? What's that?"

Elidor shrugged. "I don't know. The Baron was very secretive. All I know was that until the portal was opened, the key to the Obsidian Heart would be a secret. Only after it was opened would the key be revealed—or some such. I'm not sure why he chose to tell me about it. Typically, only the Baron was intended to know such secrets. Then again, I thought he was telling tales—only stories. Now that I have seen Navarre . . . I believe he was telling me the truth, as he knew it. His people fled Navarre, long ago."

"Paladine." Recognition flashed across Davyn's face. "These people once belonged to Asvoria. They were her slaves."

Elidor nodded. Before he could continue, the doors swung open. White hair flowing behind her like a cape of snow, Vael strode purposefully into the hearthstead, with two more guards at her heels. Her eyes shone with tears but her expression revealed no sorrow. At the side of the throne, she stopped, and a vague uncertainty crossed her porcelain features. Instead of sitting in her father's place, she turned and stood at its arm, pulling her long blue cloak about her body as though it were the regal robe of a king. The three guards encircled Elidor and Davyn, leading them to the area before the throne.

"You stand accused of the murder of my father," Vael plunged in without preamble. "As are the ways of my father, and his father before him, you have two choices. Accept the judgment, or prove your worth before your peers within the village."

"We do not accept," Elidor countered. "Vael, listen to me. I am sorry for your father's death, but we are not the ones you seek."

Vael's face did not change. "Then you will undergo a trial of my choosing."

"Vael." Elidor's quiet voice seemed to rein her anger, and the Baroness watched as he folded his legs and sat upon the floor before her. "Darghellen was a father to me when I had none. I would never harm him."

"You hurt him more than you know when you left without saying goodbye, Elidor. Why should I believe anything you say now?"

"Vael, not like this." Elidor paused to look at the black-vested guards that surrounded them. "We were close once, and I, too, grieve."

"No, Elidor. It will be explained here. Now. You say you cared for my father?" Her voice cracked like a whip. "Then honor his memory and his death."

"We did not murder Baron Darghellen."

"Then how are you here?"

Elidor paused, his head lowering like an animal's as he considered his answer. Instead of forcing the elf to admit his failure in the underground palace, Davyn stepped in. "Your Excellency." He bowed slightly, uncomfortable with formality. "My name is Davyn, friend of Elidor. I traveled with him here, but we were not planning to come to this village. We were headed to Navarre."

At the mention of the name, Gerhalt stepped backward, making a sign in the air against evil. The two other guards reached for their swords, but Vael lifted her hand and they fell still. "That word is a curse in this place. It reminds us of ancient legends of slavery and pain. Do not say it again, lest the old ways come to haunt us once more."

"I'm sorry. I didn't know." Genuine regret tinged Davyn's words, and his courtesy seemed to soften the Baroness's anger. She gestured, and the guards put their weapons away—but their eyes followed Davyn with renewed suspicion.

Vael glanced again at Elidor, then continued, "You are an outsider, Davyn. You should know that we are not an unreasonable people. We are peaceful, although when we are wronged, we can be vengeful. The village of Tarrent does not take outsiders into our midst with ease. And, I expect, they will be even more reserved after this. My father was a strong man. He guided us through many dangers, and kept this place prosperous. He opened his heart to those who have no other home, and that heart was broken—stabbed by a friendly blade." Vael turned to the throne, her fingers brushing its carved arm.

"What happened to him, Vael?" Elidor asked.

"Late last night, after his usual evening of work, my father left our home to come to the hearthstead. He told me that someone had asked to meet with him in private—not unusual, as the Baron often listened to his people's problems and offered quiet counsel. Our home stands against the hearthstead, with a door that passes directly into this building." She gestured to a small door at the back of the room. "It was never difficult for him to come here and meet with anyone who requested his assistance. We are a small village, Davyn." She turned to him again. "And we are very close.

"Beneath our village is a portal that has been sealed longer than memory. Tales say that it was our means of exodus from slavery. We keep it sealed, but there are legends that say a powerful queen sleeps in death far below us. Her spirit seeks to find us, to destroy us for abandoning her and refusing to remain and be buried alive at her side." As Vael spoke, Elidor nodded, this part of the legend familiar to him. "We do not remember the name of that ancient queen, only the stories of her tyranny. This canyon is our haven from her power; our safety and our home. In all that time, no one has ever opened the portal beneath the village." Vael sighed. "Only the Baron and his family know how to open it. Only I . . . and my father."

"Elidor told me that when the portal was opened the key would be revealed," Davyn said cautiously. "What kind of key? What will it open?"

Vael shrugged. "I do not know. My father was the one who knew the details of all those legends. He was going to teach me, teach me everything, but last night . . ." Vael's bright eyes shimmered with tears, and she took a deep breath "I awoke late last night to the sound of the portal opening. I ran here to discover what had happened. It was pitch black inside and I had to light a torch. That's when I saw that the entrance to the portal chamber was indeed open. That's also when I saw my father." Vael's voice broke, and she paused to recover her emotions before continuing.

"My father—at the base of his throne. I was too late. The life had already left him. He lay, cold and alone, with a dagger in his breast. The wounds on his body were made at close range. He knew his killer." Vael paused, turning away to look out the window at the funeral pyre, and Elidor felt the weight of the guards' eyes upon his empty dagger sheaths.

Vael breathed a long shuddering breath. "I started yelling for the guard. I knew that Gerhalt and his men were right behind me—it was only a matter of seconds." Vael shook her head, remembering with great pain.

"As I knelt beside my father's fallen body," Vael continued, "I heard the portal closing and footsteps behind me, running through the hearthstead. Even with the torch, it was dark, so dark. I couldn't see his face. I rose to chase him, but lost him in the morning fog. All I can tell you is that the form was male. Slender. Swift of foot." Her gaze lingered on Elidor's lithe, flexible form as though comparing it to her memory.

She turned, and gestured to one of the guardsman, who approached with a cloth-wrapped bundle. Vael took it from him, and opened the wrappings just enough to show an ivory handle. "This is the knife that murdered my father." She folded the brown cloth over it once more, and then handed it to Elidor. "Whoever did this left the knife behind when he fled back into the village."

"So whoever did this must have killed the Baron after he opened the portal. But why would someone open the portal, but not go through it?" Elidor asked.

Vael shrugged. "Perhaps he was releasing someone from the tunnels below." Her pale eyes lingered on Davyn, taking in his leather armor and mud-covered boots.

"Then you would have seen two forms in the hearthstead." Elidor shook his head, his hair falling into his eyes as he fingered the clothbound bundle. "Perhaps the portal was opened to send someone else through . . ."

"Whatever reason, those who did this also murdered my father. You claim that it was not you, and I . . ." Vael grew quiet, gazing down at Elidor with unreadable eyes. At last, she finished, "I am willing to give you the chance to prove that." Vael stepped down, placing her hand on Gerhalt's arm as the guard assisted her from the dais. "Your trial, Elidor and Davyn, is to find the person who did this. If you succeed, then my father's spirit will be avenged, and you may go free. You have one day." Vael turned to the stalwart guardsman. "Stay with them, Gerhalt, and see that they live up to this task."

"I will, my lady." He saluted her, his fist rising to his shoulder.

"Vael, we have friends still trapped in the caverns." Elidor stood up before her. Vael barely came up to his shoulder. "We will find who killed Baron Darghellen. But we also wish to go through the portal, and seek our friends below. They need us, Vael. The death of your father is only the first of many, unless we return to them in time."

"These friends," Vael said softly. "Did you say goodbye to them before you left them in the darkness, Elidor?"

Elidor grew quiet, and for a moment it seemed he would reach out to touch her cheek. Before he could, she looked away. Straightening, his hands falling to his sides, Elidor watched silently as Vael turned and began to walk away. She kept her head high, each step bearing her across the empty hearthstead—away from him.

12   Long Forgotten Lies

Davyn and Elidor walked through the town's bazaar, trying to ignore the villagers' hard-edged stares. Gerhalt walked a half-pace behind them, his hand on the hilt of his thick club. Elidor wasn't sure if the show of aggressiveness from the guard was to keep them in line—or to keep the citizens of Tarrent at bay.

"Gerhalt," Davyn asked, "Who has access to the hearthstead at night?"

"The only people who enter the hearthstead are the Baron, his daughter, the seneschal, the guards, and citizens who have an issue to take for judgment. At night, the hearthstead is closed."

"Did you notice anything unusual last night?" Davyn asked.

The guard shrugged. "Most people here go to sleep early. Even the local gaming house closes a bit after dark. Anyone walking through the street would be noticed by my guards.

"I questioned my men as soon as I heard what had happened. Last night was quiet as usual. The only people walking through the town that night were huntsmen returning from checking their traps, a few kids out after curfew, and Roland, the Baron's seneschal, returning from a meeting with the Baron at the hearthstead."

Davyn frowned. "No one saw the Baron after the meeting?"

"The Baron's house is next to the hearthstead," Gerhalt replied. "There's a doorway that connects the two buildings. No one would have seen him travel back and forth—it was as simple as opening the door. The guards didn't notice anything out of the ordinary until they heard Vael calling for them."

"What about the dagger?" Davyn turned to Elidor. "Maybe that's a clue."

"I've never seen a dagger like this before." Elidor unfolded the cloth to show Davyn the weapon beneath. "It's nothing like the ones I carry. And it seems out of place here. I mean, how many people in the village have daggers with ivory hilts and gold filigree?" Indeed, the dagger that Vael had found was ornate, its workmanship ancient and elaborate. It appeared to be more of a ritual dagger than a true weapon, the blade in perfect condition despite its obvious age. The ivory on the handle was yellowed with age, a perfect counterpoint to the intricate gold lacing that criss-crossed the pommel. The dagger's blade was inscribed with the symbol of a dragon wearing a crown, wrapped about the letter A.

Davyn peered at the blade. "Asvoria."

"It's identical to her symbol, the one we saw in Navarre." Elidor looked thoughtful. "Vael said she heard the portal open and close. Someone must have gone through it. Someone else besides the man she saw running through the hearthstead."

"It might have been Asvoria." Davyn wondered aloud.

"But wouldn't Asvoria have the magical power just to open the portal without assistance? Why would she need the Baron? No." Elidor shook his head. "I seriously doubt Asvoria came herself. But there was definitely someone else involved in this. Maybe it was someone who worked for her, trying to meet her when she reached her tomb. Or someone to open it for her, before she arrived."

Gerhalt scowled. "This village is founded on the myth of the ancient queen that enslaved our ancestors. If this—Asvoria?—exists, then she would find no allies here."

Elidor did not answer, folding the knife back into its wrappings and tucking it beneath his belt. He watched the flow of people around the bazaar, seeing them ebb around him as though his very presence was contagious. Once they had been friendly, greeting him by name and smiling to see him each morning. Those memories seemed a hundred years old.

"Gerhalt, is anyone missing?"

"Missing?" The guard raised an eyebrow.

"Yes." Elidor turned to face him, running a hand through his sandy blond hair. "Is anyone missing? Have your guards heard about anyone that hasn't been seen since last night?"

"No. Most people came out for the funeral. We're a tight-knit town. If anyone had been kidnapped or anything, we'd know."

"That's my point. Someone went through the portal—but no one is missing. No one outside the town would know where the portal had been hidden, what the security was in the hearth-stead, or how to get the Baron alone. So we're dealing with at least one person who lives here. And since the person who went through the portal hasn't been missed, he wasn't from the village. But the other one was. The man who ran past Vael was definitely someone from the village." Elidor frowned.

"It had to be someone who could move around at night without being noticed." Davyn said. "Someone who could leave the hearthstead, while the Baroness was calling for the guard, and still not arouse attention."

Elidor stopped in the street, ignoring the people who pushed past them rudely. "Gerhalt, you said that there were huntsmen out that night. Can we talk to some of them?"

"Certainly. There are several. Most of them live on the outskirts of town. Where do you want to start?"

"I don't know, Elidor," Davyn said. "Maybe we should speak to the seneschal. He'd be the one most able to get the Baron alone, and Gerhalt said he was seen out last night as well. We'd be better off speaking with him first, rather than traveling around trying to find a score of huntsmen one by one, all on a vague hunch."

After a moment, Elidor nodded. Still, he seemed uncomfortable, his blue eyes shadowed. "All right, Davyn. You're right. Gerhalt?"

The guard pointed north. "He lives this way. Come on. But I'll warn you, I'm not sure he's going to take kindly to questions." He patted Elidor's shoulder. "Especially from you."

The three walked to the edge of the village. At last Gerhalt stopped in front of a large house, built of stone and wood. A white fence around the yard enclosed a small vegetable garden, where a fourteen-year-old boy knelt, tilling the soil with strong hands. He pulled up a particularly difficult weed, glancing up as Gerhalt tapped politely on the gate. Brushing his brown hair out of his eyes, the boy let his gaze flicker past the guardsman and rest on his two companions. He stared at them, worried.

"Ayudar, we need to see your grandfather," the guard said soberly.

"Yes, sir." He wiped his hands on his pants and rose, his bare feet sinking into the earth. He stepped onto the porch, entered the house, and closed the door.

After a moment, Ayudar opened the door again and held it ajar. "My grandfather is happy to speak with you now, gentlemen."

Gerhalt led the others into the house, brushing past Ayudar quietly. The structure was small, but in this small village it seemed almost palatial. They entered a study, decorated simply but with a certain forethought, the furniture well-made and carefully arranged. An elderly man with a kind face sat behind a small desk near the front window. He placed a quill back into its holder as he looked up at his visitors.

"Roland." Gerhalt bowed slightly, and both Elidor and Davyn did the same. "These are the individuals accused of the Baron's death. They're charged with proving their innocence by finding out what happened last night."

Roland's dark face was sober, his brown eyes stern but not unkind. He was a slender man, his human face marked by a strange grayish cast to the skin. His features were even, but coarse, tinged with non-human blood.

As Gerhalt spoke, Ayudar entered, carrying a pitcher of goat's milk and some biscuits. He placed them on the table shyly, and Roland nodded his head. "Thank you, Ayudar. You can go back to your chores now." The boy nodded, and then left, closing the doors to the study.

"Elidor." Roland smiled. "I never thought to see you again. Please, have a seat."

"That sentiment's been expressed a lot," Davyn murmured, as he and Elidor took a seat on the couch. Gerhalt stood uncomfortably by the doors.

"Roland," Elidor said. "As I remember, you were the one who spoke to the Baron on my behalf when I asked for the hand of his daughter."

"So I did." Roland's smile faded. He poured himself a cup of goat's milk and took a sip. "A pity that the Baron didn't take my counsel. You would have made a fine counterpart for his child."

"But a poor Baron." Elidor couldn't conceal his anger. "You told him that, as well."

"Was I to hide my true thoughts from my liege?" Roland shook his head. "My first duty was to him. You knew that. You are a thief, Elidor. Not a leader of men."

"And because of that, he gave me a choice. Marry Vael and remove her from the succession or break our engagement, so that she could follow him as leader of Tarrent." Elidor's voice began to rise. "That was no choice at all. Vael was his only child. If she didn't take the throne, then it would break his heart. And she loved him. She trained all her life to be the Baroness, to make him proud." Elidor clenched his fists, looking away. "I couldn't do that to either of them."

"And now you've returned." Roland set the cup back in its saucer. "Why?"

"Not for the reason you think, I'm sure."

Davyn quickly stepped in, "You already know that the Baron was murdered. There are few clues. You were out late last night, and you met with the Baron. Why?" Davyn crossed his arms, waiting for an answer.

"The Baron and I were concerned. Hunting in the area hasn't been good lately, and if it doesn't pick up before the first crop harvest, Tarrent will have serious difficulties through the next season. We were discussing rationing grain over the next few weeks to get us through the shortage."

"And about what time did you leave the hearthstead?"

Roland shrugged. "Late. The Baron was most interested in exploring every possibility."

Interrupting, Elidor asked, "Vael told us that the Baron had a meeting late last night. Is that the same one?"

"I would assume so."

"Did the Baron leave when you did?"

"No, I believe he remained in the hearthstead. He wanted to go over the reports one more time." Sipping his milk nonchalantly, the seneschal continued, "I returned directly home, dropped off my reports here at my desk, and went to bed. I didn't know about what happened until I heard the commotion."

"Did you see anyone else on the street near the hearthstead?"

"A few huntsmen. Josiah, Mavis, and Corsian, I think. I wasn't paying much attention. It was late, and I was in a hurry to get home."

Davyn nodded. "We should speak to them as well, Elidor." When the elf didn't answer, Davyn rose from his seat.

"One more question, Roland," Elidor asked. "Was Ayudar awake when you came home?"

Roland shook his head. "No. He was asleep in his room, with the door closed."

"So your grandson didn't hear you come home? He can't verify your story?"

"I'm afraid not." Roland grew sober. "Now, if you don't mind, I have a great deal of work to do. Good afternoon, gentlemen."

Gerhalt bowed slightly at Roland's clear dismissal. "Thank you, sir." He turned to Elidor and Davyn. "Let's go, then."

As the door closed behind them, Davyn took Elidor's arm. "This is getting personal for you, Elidor. I don't like it. We have to find this killer, and fast. There isn't time to get tangled up in your past. Not now. Catriona, Sindri—they're counting on us." He shook Elidor's arm. "Can you do this?"

Elidor jerked his arm away with more force than he intended. "I can. It is only that this place holds memories that I cannot deny. It's hard to ignore them. If I had stayed, perhaps the Baron would be alive right now."

"Why didn't you stay, Elidor?" Davyn asked as they walked. Gerhalt politely fell a bit behind, sensing the conversation was private. "I mean, even if Baron Darghellen said that you couldn't marry Vael, why not stay with her in Tarrent?"

"And explain to her that she had to choose between me and her duty?" Elidor demanded. He paused, rubbing his eyes. "I couldn't put her in that situation. She had a future here. One she was trained for since the day she was born. I wasn't going to put that in jeopardy."

As they walked through the village toward the hunter's cabins, Elidor recounted the incident. "It wasn't as though the Baron was cruel when he told me. He was apologetic. He offered to talk to Vael for me, but I told him no. We talked through the night about my options, about what the future held. I promised him that I would try to make something of myself." Elidor's mouth twisted wryly. "But the moment I left Tarrent, my life went back to what it had been before—thievery. I thought I had changed, here in this canyon. But I hadn't. I was only hiding from myself."

"Elidor," said Davyn, looking concerned, "Stop."

"Look out for number one, Davyn. That's what I do." The elf shook his head, narrowing his eyes. "For a while, I forgot to do that. I did what was best for *her*. And now look at me. She hates me. She sees me for what I am, nothing but a half-breed thief. You can't go back, Davyn. You can never go back."

They reached the hunter's cabins by midafternoon, climbing the side of the canyon to find a small cluster of homes that were hidden within the thick forests. Gerhalt pointed as they approached. "That cottage belongs to Josiah. Mavis lives a bit down that way, and the curl of black smoke just beyond those poplar trees is Corsian drying meat, I'll wager."

At the first hut, Elidor and Davyn met a plump woman and her husband, Josiah. They were kind, though a bit concerned to see a guard and two strangers at their door. After only a brief period of questioning, Josiah's travel was catalogued, his movements checked, and his location established.

The second man was much easier to discount. A sprained ankle, twisted early in the evening at the pub, prevented him from being the man Vael saw running away from the hearthstead. A few moments of conversation about his swollen ankle, propped upon a pillow, was all the evidence that the pair needed.

The three walked down the lane to Corsian's home as the midafternoon sun beat down upon them. Green grass swayed to either side of the little trail, nearly obscuring the view of the village. A small thatched hut stood at the end of the lane, smoke puffing out of its chimney.

As they approached the house, though, they quickly realized that the smoke was not coming from the chimney. It was rising from the hut itself.

The home was on fire.

"Water!" Elidor sprinted toward the hut. "Get water!"

From within, there came the terrible sound of screams.

Surprised, Davyn watched, frozen for a moment, as Gerhalt ran to the nearby water trough and began filling two buckets.

"Boy!" The guard's shout jerked him out of his reverie. "Carry these!" Davyn gripped the bucket-handles, dragged them to the side of the hut and dumped them upon the flames.

Fire roared from the thatched roof, engulfing the home in a scorching blaze. It leaped out the window and crept down the sides of the home, trickling like water from roof to ground. As Davyn and Gerhalt watched, Elidor kicked the door, rattling it once, twice, then knocking it in.

"Elidor, what are you doing?" Davyn yelled as Elidor tore off his cloak and tossed it away. "You'll be caught in the fire!" But still Elidor rushed into the building, ignoring the fire all around him.

Inside the hut, flames roared across the birch rafters, swelling through the rear rooms of the house like a living thing. Elidor shielded his eyes from the glare, as he searched the small hut. From one of the two side rooms, he heard a pounding, and a scream. Rushing in, he noted a burning mat on the floor, covering what seemed to be a storm-door.

Quickly, Elidor kicked aside the mat, revealing a door beneath. It was square, wooden, with a metal ring on top that could be pulled to provide access. Wrapping his belt around the center of his hand, Elidor grasped the ring and pulled. He shouted with pain as the heated metal seared his flesh even through the leather, but the door came free.

Beneath it, in a small wooden room, a man lay on the ground. His hands and feet were tied to a wooden beam behind him, and he stared up at Elidor in terror, seeing the flames behind the elf. Any moment, the house would collapse upon them both, filling the lower chamber with fire and heavy wooden beams.

"Help me!" the man shouted.

No ladder led down into the room, nor any other means of descent. Elidor took a quick glance above his shoulder at the creaking, fire-laden beams above him, and, with no other possible choice, leaped down. A knife flashed into his hands as he set about cutting the woodsman free, noting the heavy bruises on the man's face. "Corsian," Elidor said, "Can you walk?"

The man nodded, wincing. "I think so. But I'm very weak. Two days . . . without food, and only a little water."

Elidor glanced around at the empty barrels that were housed in the cellar. "Help me push this beneath the opening." Together, they scooted the barrel to one side, and Elidor helped Corsian climb on top. He pushed the man onto his shoulders, standing upon the barrel and holding him while Corsian climbed into the house above. "Hurry!" Corsian reached down, lying on the floor of the room above. As the rafters began to crumble, Elidor grasped his wrist and leaped up.

With Corsian's arm around his shoulders, Elidor stumbled out the front door and they both collapsed a short distance from the hut. As they did, the roof at last crashed to the ground with a thunderous, ashen crunch.

"Elidor!" Davyn said, as he and Gerhalt rushed to Elidor's side. The elf smiled up at them, his face blackened a bit by the ash. "Are you all right?"

"A bit singed," the elf groaned, "but fine. Corsian?"

The woodsman beside him was not as lucky, though he was breathing and smiling slightly. His face was purpled from the bruises of many blows, one eye swollen nearly shut from his injuries.

"I owe you," he gasped. "I've been down there for . . . two days." He coughed, breathing in deep gasps of clean air. "Then . . . just this morning . . . the fire."

"You were down there for two days?" Gerhalt's voice was incredulous.

"Yeah. Two days." Corsian nodded wearily, the fire casting strange shadows across his injured face. "I was asleep, just got home from checking all of my traps. I woke up because someone else was in the room. It was a man, a tall man, with strange features and eyes . . . bright blue eyes . . . He hit me over the head with my own cudgel, tied me up. I caught a glimpse of him when he was leaving, after he'd put me down there. The funny thing was—he looked just like me. Exactly like me. I know you'll think I'm crazy . . ."

"You're not crazy," Elidor said grimly.

"Ophion. Asvoria's shapeshifter," Davyn said, his hand balling into a fist. "If Ophion was here, that means the shapeshifter's almost certainly been masquerading as Corsian for two days. The creature's been all over the village. It could have talked to anyone. Even if we assume Ophion's the one that went through the portal, the person helping it could be almost anywhere."

"Wait," Gerhalt said thoughtfully. "If this—Ophion?—went through the portal last night, then whoever was helping him must have set this hut on fire to cover their tracks. Ophion wouldn't have been here to do it."

"Corsian, do you know who set fire to your house?" Gerhalt asked the woodsman.

"No. I heard people in my house both last night and the night before. Talking—it sounded like male voices, but I couldn't make out more than a few of the words. Something about someone named Asvoria. That was it, the 'Last Priest of Asvoria.' Something about a bloodline, some kind of duty . . . strange things. I couldn't understand what they meant."

Elidor said, "A bloodline . . . the Last Priest of Asvoria. Maybe one of the people who escaped the tomb with the other servants was still loyal to her. Perhaps even waiting for her to return."

"Passing along the duty from one generation to the next, is that it?" Davyn scoffed. "That's dedication."

"It's very possible." Gerhalt considered the idea, his weathered hand making a fist against the ground. "The legends of the ancient queen that haunt our village do speak of a traitor within the ranks of the original escapees from the dark place beneath the mountain. But it was only a legend—a story to frighten the children into their beds late at night."

"Perhaps it is more than a story, Gerhalt." Elidor stood. "And whoever burned this hut—and tried to kill Corsian—had to be someone who knew we were going to come out here." Elidor agreed. "And someone who had something to gain by covering it up."

"The only person who knew we were coming up here to question the huntsmen is Roland." Davyn's worry reddened his cheeks.

"But why would Roland kill the Baron—his oldest friend?" Gerhalt asked.

"Roland." Elidor's eyes narrowed. "It all makes sense. Roland has always had his eye on the throne. Don't you see? Seven years ago, he tried to convince the Baron to let his daughter marry me, and to remove Vael from succession to the Baronial throne. If Vael hadn't been able to succeed the Baron, the throne would have fallen to Roland."

"But Vael did succeed her father," Gerhalt said. "She's the new Baroness of Tarrent."

"She is, for now." Davyn's train of thought paralleled the elf's own. "We were Roland's lucky break. He didn't know we were going to show up, but now that he does, he has the perfect scapegoat for as many murders as he thinks he can get away with. This killer has already blamed her father's death on you." He looked at Elidor. "What's one more?"

"Paladine," Elidor breathed, his face turning pale. "He's going to assassinate Vael and blame me. We've got to get back to the village."

13   Protections

The darkness parted like velvet curtains, swirling back before her upraised hand. The belly of the mountain was hollow, holding a courtyard the size of a palace grounds. Once, the palace had been built into the side of the mountain, half standing under the sun and half carved into the mountainside. The outer glory, the gardens that had spilled down the mountainside by the river, had been nothing compared to this underground patio with its phosphorescent wonders.

Asvoria closed her eyes, remembering those days when her magic had brought forth life from the very stone. It was once a paradise, where water trickled along carefully maintained fountains. Strange vines had curled around delicate iron frameworks. Flowers had lined the stonework paths. On the far side of the cavern, a statue made of pure onyx had depicted Asvoria holding aloft the Aegis, the Daystar clasped to her stone breast. The palace proper was carved from the very mountainside, and bronze doors opened between the garden and the rear of her magnificent home.

But no more. Now, the grand cavern was faded and decrepit. The garden, once bright with flowers, was a tangled jungle of rocks, made light by softly glowing fungi that spread across the distant stones. The iron trellises were rusted and fallen. The bronze doors were green with age, and the waterfall was a fetid pool.

Only the statue still remained as it was, standing black and glistening on its pedestal. Behind it, a mausoleum had been erected, its sides as black as the statue, exactly as she had instructed.

Asvoria frowned. With a sweep of her hand, a thousand sparks fell upon the barren rock, and flowers of glowing light rose from the cracks in the once-dark earth. The walls erupted in fountains of twisting vines, green and silver that arched from the walls, curling about iron frameworks.

"Much better." Her blonde hair shifted across her shoulders, and violet eyes the color of dark twilights gazed out at the building. "So lovely," she whispered. She bent down to touch the bones of a skeleton at guard. He stood where he had died, still wearing the rotted armor of a guardsman. On his breastplate was the insignia of a dragon surrounding an ornate letter A.

Asvoria sighed. "One of my last faithful." She gazed about. "There were so few of you. There should have been more. A hundred servants, fifty guardsmen, and seven of my finest wizards were to be interred with my body. But where are they?" Her fingers brushed the skull's cheekbones as though touching a beloved friend. "Did they abandon me, at the end? How very sad. I hope they were punished. If not," she smiled sunnily, "I shall have to remember to find their descendants and do it myself." Standing, Asvoria stretched, nearly purring with amusement. "Ah, the possibilities this new body allows me."

My body. My future. Not yours.

"Be quiet, you impudent girl." Asvoria laughed at the voice within her soul. Since her imprisonment, Nearra had been a constant plague. "You weren't doing anything with it except wasting your life pining after some woodland barbarian. You should be pleased that you were chosen—chosen to give me new strength, so that I can bring this world back to order once more."

Asvoria laughed cruelly, lifting her damask skirt and stepping over the body of her fallen guardsman. "But I cannot do it without certain tools. My Aegis, buried with my body in my tomb, here at Navarre. Ophion seems to have slowed down your little friends well enough. If it is a very lucky day, perhaps he's even killed one or two of them. Wouldn't that be lovely?" Nearra's only reply was a cold and bitter silence, trapped within the depths of the shell that they shared.

Asvoria threaded her way down the shattered garden paths, the broken stone crushing beneath her feet. Lavender and soft green fungi cast an eerie glow upon the high walls of the cavernous garden.

"My tomb . . ." Asvoria reached out her hands as she approached the statue next to the mauseolum.

Suddenly, there was a sharp crack, and a sheen like silvery metal erupted from thin air. Asvoria fell backward onto the path. Her head snapped up, and rage illuminated her eyes. Not even bothering to rise from the ground, she held out her hands, and fire erupted from her fingers.

The spell-fire reached the base of her statue, and then turned away as though blocked by an arch of solid stone. Where it grazed the strange protection, magical blades began to spin in the air, revealing the power of the guardian spell. As the fire died, the whirling steel became invisible once more, hidden within the same spell that shielded the tomb from approach.

"Maddoc!" Asvoria cursed, springing to her feet and shaking the dust from her skirts angrily. "Ophion told me that the old cobbler had control of a protection on the tomb, but I did not think it was this strong." She reached forth with her magic, eliciting sparks as she brushed against the magical framework of the shielding spell. "If I had my Daystar, I could tear this apart with hardly an effort." The sparks flew faster, and Asvoria jerked her hands away, canceling her spell. "Fools!"

You can't get through it. Nearra noted with satisfaction.

Asvoria didn't care to answer, storming from side to side on the path as she considered her options. "I could break my way though with sheer power, but the magical explosion might collapse the cavern. Performing the disenchantment more gently would take months—even years—and I don't have that kind of time. I need my Daystar."

Maddoc will never let you have it. He wants to make you a prisoner; he won't accept anything less than all of your power for his own. There's no negotiating.

"Be quiet, girl!" Snarling, Asvoria picked up a rock and hurled it at the tomb. It collided with the magical barrier, sending sparks flaming down from the impact. "I'll just have to wait," she mused, tapping her chin with a long, elegant finger.

"Your little friends will be so busy looking for my sword that they won't see danger stalking them. They already turn their back from the evil within their midst, ignoring all in order to seek me out."

Asvoria smiled. "Yes, all I have to do is wait. Wait for them to seek and find a darker truth than they ever imagined . . ."

14 THE LAST PRIEST OF ASVORIA

Davyn, Elidor, and Gerhalt raced down the twisted mountain path. The sun had long ago fallen beneath the rim of the mountain, and they were guided only by moonlight.

They reached the first row of village huts, panting for breath. "Where's Vael?" Elidor asked Gerhalt, gripping the guardsman's sleeve.

"She could be anywhere," Davyn cut in. "But we know where Roland is." He pointed across the street at the white-fenced house. Candles in the window illuminated the home with a cheery glow. Through one window they could see a tall male figure moving about inside.

"He hasn't gone to find Vael yet. We're in time," Gerhalt said with a sigh of relief.

"Or else he's already done it, and they just haven't found her," Elidor countered sharply, heading for the house. "Either way, he's not going to get away with this. I'm not his tool to play with, and neither is the village of Tarrent." The elf leaped the fence easily, and his companions hurried to follow him through the small vegetable garden.

135

The door to the house was closed, but Elidor didn't bother to knock. He turned the handle and pushed the door open, Davyn and Gerhalt on his heels. "Roland!" Elidor yelled, his voice echoing through the cottage. "Roland!"

They found the old man in his study, rising from his chair with a sheaf of paper in his hand. He pulled a set of wire-rimmed glasses from his face, staring angrily at the intruders. "Elidor! Gerhalt! What are you doing? How dare you barge in here!"

"We know it's you, Roland," Elidor growled. Although neither he nor Davyn carried weapons, the serious intent in their eyes caused the seneschal to fall back a step.

"Know?" Roland scowled. "What is it that you believe you 'know,' Elidor? That I sabotaged your wedding with Vael? I told the Baron what I believed. If he chose to accept my advice for the best interests of the village, then that was his choice, and I agree with it—"

"I know what you did to me, Roland. This isn't about my wedding to Vael. This is about her father—and your ambition."

"I don't know what you mean." Roland's voice was angry. "And I'll thank you to get out of my home immediately. Gerhalt, remove them."

The guardsman, standing by the door in his black vest, stared somberly at the seneschal. "I'd advise you to listen to them, sir. They have some pretty compelling evidence."

"Evidence? What kind of evidence? Evidence of what, exactly?"

"Vael's father was killed by two individuals. One of them passed through the portal just after her father died, while the other remained in the village. The guards are patrolling the canyon thoroughly enough that they found us within minutes of the time Davyn and I climbed out of the collapsed tunnel. No one could have left the canyon without their notice, so that means the murderer is still in Tarrent.

"The only people on the streets of Tarrent at the time of the murder were you, the woodsmen, and some kids who were breaking curfew." With an emphatic gesture, Elidor pointed at Roland. "And you were the last one to see the Baron."

"Two of the woodsmen couldn't possibly have been the person that Vael heard running from her father's murder." Davyn leaned against the wall, his face dark in the candlelight. "The third, I'm afraid, had his cottage burned."

"Burned?" Roland seemed surprised, but Elidor pressed him.

"Don't worry, Roland. Corsian's still alive, and he's going to be fine. He told us a very interesting story about being kidnapped—and about the man who held him hostage while a shapeshifter used his identity." The elf stood eye-to-eye with the aged seneschal, refusing to back down. "The shapeshifter's gone now, hunting our friends in the passages below the village, but its companion is still here. Right here, in fact."

"You believe I conspired with a . . . a shapeshifter? To kill my oldest friend? Elidor, you've gone completely mad. Now, I simply must insist—"

Davyn growled, "You'll listen to him, Roland." The threat apparent in Davyn's voice made Gerhalt step forward and place a hand on Davyn's shoulder. Davyn leaned back against the wall again, but his fingers twitched in anger.

"You're the one with the most to gain, Roland." Elidor pressed on. "If Vael and her father are no longer on the throne, you inherit leadership of Tarrent. The same way you would have if Vael had married me, and her father had disinherited her. What I don't understand is why you work for Asvoria, Roland. Your people are going to be among the first ones she destroys when she gets her power back. Tarrent, this canyon—all of it, gone. Is that what you want?"

Roland protested, "Elidor! You can't possibly believe this! I've always done what was best, for Tarrent and for the Baron. I know no one named Asvoria. I've no idea what you're talking about. Listen to reason, Elidor."

"You don't know what I'm talking about, but I'll bet you do recognize this." Elidor withdrew the cloth-wrapped bundle from his belt and pressed it into Roland's hands. The wrapping fell away, leaving the ivory-hilted knife in Roland's hand.

"Where did you find this?" Roland blanched, his face turning as pale as the ivory in his hand.

"That's the knife that murdered Baron Darghellen." Gerhalt said flatly. As Roland staggered a step backward, Gerhalt caught his elbow and helped him to sit. "Breathe, Roland, you're turning green."

"That knife belongs to the last priest of Asvoria." Elidor tapped the stylized A on the blade. "We saw that symbol countless times down in Navarre. A, for Asvoria."

"No, no . . . you're wrong," Roland protested weakly.

"You've seen the knife before." Elidor could tell by the seneschal's pallor. "Haven't you?"

"A for Asvoria?" Roland stared at the knife, shaking his head. "No. A is for Allieth, my wife; Anya, my daughter; and for Ayudar, my grandson. Family . . . family tradition, on my wife's side. This knife has been passed down for generations."

"Passed down . . ." Elidor whispered, making a sudden realization. "It's not yours."

Roland looked up at them with horrified eyes. "This dagger belongs to Ayudar. My daughter gave it to him, just before she passed away. But he can't . . . he wouldn't have . . ."

"Passed down, you say, for generations. From mother, to daughter . . . to son." Davyn stared at Elidor. "The last priest of Asvoria."

"Where is Ayudar right now?" Elidor demanded.

"Why, he's in his room, asleep. The boy's been through so much, with the death of the Baron . . ." Roland's voice faded and died.

Gerhalt walked down the slight corridor to the boy's door, slowly drawing his club from its holster. He glanced back at the others, his suntanned face lined with worry, and then turned to the door.

Tap-tap-tap went his light club against the door. *Tap-tap-tap.* But there was no response.

"Ayudar?" Gerhalt called, lifting the door handle with one hand while tightening his grip on his weapon with the other. "Ayudar, are you in there?"

The guardsman swung the door open, and candlelight from the main entryway streamed into the boy's room. Aside from a bed, a small desk, and a lantern, the room was empty.

Ayudar was gone.

"No, it can't be. Ayudar's a good lad, a quiet lad. He takes after his grandmother . . ." Roland began, tears pricking his eyes.

"That's what we're afraid of, sir," Davyn said. "We've got to find Vael."

"She was in the hearthstead," Roland said. "Going over the list of things we will need in order to survive to the first harvest. She said she couldn't sleep. I was going to take her some milk later on this evening, just to make certain she was all right." Roland looked into the kitchen. "That's gone too. Ayudar must have taken the tray when he left—I'm such an old fool, I didn't hear him go. I must have been wrapped up in my papers, busy with my work . . ."

"We've got to get to the hearthstead." Elidor spun on his heel, but Roland caught his shoulder before he could pass by.

"Take this." Roland pushed the ivory-hilted dagger into Elidor's hand. "Protect Vael. But please, if you can—don't hurt my grandson. He's all I have left in this world." For a moment, Roland seemed very old and frail. Elidor nodded, placing the knife back in his belt.

"We'll try, Roland. That's all I can promise." Clasping the old man's arm, Elidor gave him a somber nod, and then released him. The three men hurried into the night toward the council building. Behind them, the seneschal sank into a chair by the fireplace, weeping with his head in his hands.

Rage fueled Elidor's steps, hurrying him through the village at top speed. He had a death-grip on the dagger, and his muscles tensed with anger at each step. The knife cut so deeply into his palm that a faint line of blood trickled down the hilt, but he did not notice.

"Elidor." Gerhalt stepped in front of the elf. "You've got to calm down."

"Calm?" Elidor snapped. "You've seen what Asvoria's done to this village. To its people. Ophion . . . Ophion's killed Baron Darghellen, and its accomplice might kill Vael."

"And you're going to kill Ayudar." Davyn caught up to them, breathing hard from the sudden sprint.

"That's right," Elidor said. "And he deserves his fate."

"Will you kill Nearra next?" Davyn asked quietly.

Elidor's face was frozen. "Asvoria won't hurt this village again. I swear it. This is the one place where different races truly live in peace. Nearra is one woman. I may regret that the decision had to be made, but when the time comes, I will make it. Just like you did, in the forest, with Maddoc. Better to watch a man die, than to risk betrayal."

"I don't believe that anymore, Elidor," said Davyn with an emphatic gesture. "I was wrong."

The concern on Gerhalt's face spoke volumes. "Elidor, I knew Ayudar's mother. I watched when he was born. I saw him raised, and I have seen each day of his life as he lived it.

If he's guilty of this crime, then I will see him punished. But murder?" He shook his head. "No, Elidor. I won't judge one crime with another."

"Sometimes the only way to protect yourself and the ones you love is to kill, Gerhalt. Davyn knows that, as a hunter, and so should you." There was no apology in Elidor's voice.

"You sound like Maddoc."

The condemnation from Davyn shocked Elidor, and he turned to face his friend. "That's enough." He sliced the air with the dagger. "We don't have time to argue. Ayudar is with Vael, and *he* isn't going to let blind conscience stop him." Elidor spun on his heel, leaving the others to follow.

From the bridge over the village, Elidor could see that the hearthstead was still lit. The large wooden doors were open, and a shaft of light stretched across the hard earth. He raced forward, legs pumping, with Davyn beside him and the burly Gerhalt close behind. Vael's name heavy in his mind, Elidor burst into the building. He feared to see the worst—blood on the furs of the dais, a body sprawled at the base of the throne.

But nothing moved in the grand hearthstead other than the fire, crackling and snapping in one of the tremendous fireplaces and casting a grim glow through the wide room. Unlike the cheery warmth of Roland's small cottage, the fire did little to warm the hearthstead.

"She's not here," Davyn said with relief.

"You're wrong." Elidor pointed. By the throne a small pitcher of milk lay tipped on a silver tray, its contents spilled and trickling slowly onto the furs. "She's here."

"Where?" Davyn spun slowly to try and take in the entire chamber.

"Vael said she heard the sound of the portal closing when she found her father's body. She also referred to the 'portal chamber.'"

Elidor scanned the room. "The passage to the portal's got to be here, somewhere.

"Ayudar knows we'll find out it was him. He's going to try to get through the portal and find Ophion. It's his only chance. Once the portal is open, he won't need her anymore. That's when . . ." Elidor's voice broke, his eyes tearing through the room with barely-contained rage.

The pillars that held the high wooden roof stood stoically around the chamber, and light from the fireplace illuminated fallen paperwork near the throne on the dais. Elidor traced the path Ayudar would have taken from the front door to the throne, kneeling to brush his fingers against the furs where the milk had spilled. "Davyn, do you see any tracks?" he murmured intently.

Davyn scanned the hard-packed earth floor of the building, shaking his head. "It's . . . too dark. I'd need more light, and even with light, the ground's fairly hard. It wouldn't hold a good print."

"Over here!" Gerhalt called from the fireplace. He knelt beside the fireplace, poking at ashes that had been strewn against the floor over the hearthstone. "These are from the fire. They shouldn't be out here, they should be inside the hearth. Something scattered them."

Davyn jogged to his side. "You're right. Something knocked them out of the fireplace."

"Not something. Someone." Elidor's nimble fingers were already working on the hearth, searching the fireplace stones for any sign of movement or hinge. Sweat beaded on his forehead from more than the fire's heat, and his eyes darted from stone to stone with a thief's calculating glance. Old lessons, honed during his childhood, fluttered through his mind. Check for discoloration. Check for dust. Find the pattern in the stones. Which one doesn't fit? Which one has been touched recently, or moved, or stands out even a hair?

He'd been in trouble before, felt his own life hanging by a thread—but this wasn't his own life. If he couldn't figure out how to get to the portal, Vael would die.

Elidor blinked into the hot flames of the fire in the hearth. He was too close to the flame, but it didn't matter. Better that his hands singed to the bone so long as he found her before . . .

"Elidor, hurry."

He didn't need Gerhalt's encouragement. Sliding his fingers beneath burning ash and hot coals, he felt something: a lever. Ignoring the pain, Elidor pressed it down, praying that it wasn't trapped. The side of the fireplace, three stones wide and four tall, just large enough for a man to crouch through, slid open, flicking more ash over the hearth.

"Found it," he breathed.

Davyn clapped his shoulder. "Good work, Elidor."

"I pray we aren't too late." Drawing Asvoria's dagger from his belt and testing its heft and weight, Elidor stepped through the opening and into the small tunnel beyond.

The opening was small and cramped, built into the stone and dirt of the earth and supported by thick wooden beams. Unlike the delicate stone structure of Navarre, this earthen passage had been packed by hard-working hands without the benefit of magic. The ground was brushed with dust and a faint smell of mold pervaded the air.

"We don't need a torch," Elidor said over his shoulder. "There's a light ahead—it must be Ayudar and Vael. Hurry."

He crouched, moving down the corridor on bent legs. The knife was in his right hand, and despite the fact that it held Asvoria's symbol, the sturdy steel reassured him. The passage was dark and small, poorly illuminated, but Elidor hurried forward, hardly bothering to silence his movements.

The slope was steep, and wet from the nearby creek that flowed around the hearthstead. "Watch your footing," he whispered. "The mud is treacherous."

"Elidor, I think—" Davyn's words were suddenly cut off by a cry of surprise. His feet slipped, and he fell forward, forcing Elidor to lurch forward too. Elidor flailed and then he tumbled, sliding down the passage. He dragged his hand against the wall in a desperate hope to slow their approach. But it was no use.

Still gripping the knife, Elidor reached the end of the passage. He rolled to his feet, twisting like a cat to regain his balance. In a flash, he was crouching again, the knife weaving in his hand as he took his bearings. The passage opened into a small chamber directly beneath the hearthstead. Davyn skidded down the muddy passage behind him, landing hard at Elidor's feet. In the tunnel, he could hear Gerhalt skidding to a halt, his arms braced against the stone and slimy earth.

But Elidor hardly noticed, staring straight ahead across the small cave in which he stood. From the light of a lantern placed near the center of the room, he could see a tall stone obelisk embedded in the wall, the symbol of Asvoria carved deeply onto its face. The stone was black, some kind of obsidian, very out of place against the muddy granite walls of the chamber. It had no handle, and no hinges, standing firmly against the side of the cave like a sentinel over some ancient grave. Still, Elidor hardly noticed it.

He did notice Vael, standing beside the black stone, her white hair a stark counterpoint and her face pale and frightened. The blade of a thick hunting knife glinted against her throat, and Elidor could see Ayudar's suntanned face, contorted with fear, over her shoulder.

"Elidor," Vael whispered, shuddering against Ayudar's knife. Her pale eyes met Elidor's, thousands of lost moments passing between them in an instant's time.

"Put your weapons down," Ayudar insisted, his voice high-pitched and panicked. Fear shone in his eyes, and the knife trembled in his hand. "Put them down *now*, or she dies."

15   THE TOMB OF A FALLEN QUEEN

That's really it?" Sindri gazed across the tangled garden, standing on his tiptoes so that he could see the black mausoleum. The light of Catriona's lantern barely reached that far, shining like a pale beacon through the massive chamber. It illuminated twisted skeletons of iron and stone that jutted up from the garden's wilderness. A soft mist of luminescence lit the walls, faintly illuminating the massive cave.

"Yes, Sindri." Maddoc sat down at the edge of the passageway, leaning back against bronze doors that had long ago fallen from their hinges. They lay now, tilted against the ground, creating a natural lean-to beneath their long, flat surfaces. "But we've been walking for nearly twelve hours. There are likely to be things in that jungle that we do not wish to face under our depleted strength. Catriona is quite right. We can rest here, and face the tomb when we are more prepared."

Noting Sindri's crestfallen face, Maddoc continued, "In any case, it gives us the opportunity to work on your spellcraft, Sindri. There are some spells that will be very useful once we have reached the tomb, and I want you to study them while we rest." 147

"Wonderful!" Sindri climbed back over a chunk of stone that had once adorned the distant ceiling.

"Stay away from him." Davyn grabbed Sindri's sleeve and jerked him away from the old wizard. "If it wasn't for him, we wouldn't be in this mess in the first place. And this"—he knocked a leather bag of spell components out of Sindri's hand—"isn't helping anyone."

"Hey!" Sindri yelped.

"This is a waste of time," Davyn said, tugging harder on Sindri's sleeve. "We need to go back. We can't stay here, tomb or no tomb. Elidor is in these passages somewhere. We can't abandon him. We have to go back and find him."

"Let Sindri go, Davyn." Catriona pulled Davyn's hand away from Sindri, and the kender quickly scrambled away. While Maddoc calmed Sindri, Catriona drew Davyn off a short distance. "Davyn, we need to talk."

He turned toward her with fire in his eyes. "Yes?"

You have to stop this, Davyn. I know that you expected to find Elidor down here. We went through miles of corridor, looking for him. We've been walking at least a day, if not more, and found no sign that he's even been in these passages. That cave-in was significant. At least two other areas of the palace collapsed."

"What are you trying to say?" Davyn sat down by the wall, rubbing his calves wearily. "That I have to accept that Elidor is dead?"

"Maybe." Cat ran her hands through her hair, shaking out the dried sweat from their long march.

"No. We missed a section, somewhere. Another passage—a door we didn't see, maybe behind a tapestry or something. Hidden in the wall. We can't just give up. We have to go back—we have to look again . . ." Exasperated, Davyn pounded a fist against the stone wall with hard, short thrusts.

"Some of those traps back there are pretty deadly. We avoided what we could, but I thought Sindri was dead at least twice. Elidor's got no light source, and very little food. I just don't want you to wait for him, Davyn. If he meets us here—then we'll celebrate. But otherwise . . ." Catriona shook her head. "There's nothing we can do."

Davyn sighed, shaking a small stone out of his boot. "I'm not giving up on him."

"I'm not asking you to. But I am asking you to remember why we're here in the first place."

Catriona watched as a scowl crossed his even features. Davyn was prone to flashes of anger, but he was also a true and loyal friend. He had turned his back on the man who had raised him in order to support what was right. Elidor was his closest friend—but at this point, he was also a liability. "We have to stop Asvoria and drive her soul out of Nearra—and that means we have to be ready to face her, even without Elidor. This time, she'll be more dangerous. She'll be used to her new body—Nearra's body—and she will use it to make us powerless. Davyn, listen."

Catriona was serious, the steel in her eyes tempered by her own past. "There comes a moment in each of our lives when we have to face our weaknesses, Davyn. I'm not any stronger than you are, but I know where mine are."

"And you're saying that I don't?" Davyn asked.

"You were willing to take off Maddoc's head rather than let him help us. You want to give up on our quest to go find Elidor, who may not even be alive."

"Elidor's not dead," Davyn replied stubbornly. "And Maddoc's going to betray us. It's his nature."

"You might as well say it's in my nature to fail," Catriona said. Her eyes shifted to Maddoc, and then dropped to the floor. When

149

she continued, her voice was a rough whisper. "My life, Sindri's, and all those people Asvoria's planning to rule, may hang on the balance of your sword. If we enter the tomb, and you're not ready, then we could fail, and more people than we know could die." The words weren't hers, but they were the right ones. An image of Maddoc on his horse, his eyes boring into hers, flitted through Catriona's mind.

What do you want, Maddoc? She had asked him while the sun beat down through the forest leaves.

Your oath . . .

"Catriona? Cat?"

She snapped back to awareness, suddenly realizing that Davyn was staring at her. "I'm sorry." She rubbed her eyes. "I'm just tired."

"We all are." Davyn smiled faintly. "You were right. We should rest. Tomorrow, we'll try to open the tomb. And I can't promise that I'll be everything you need me to be. But I can promise that I'll do all that I can. Is that enough?"

"Yes, Davyn, of course it is." Clasping his shoulder, Catriona tried to shake off the feeling of a dark cloud overhead, a sense of impending doom that had suddenly chilled her. "It's all I can ask."

I do not claim to be a good man. But we need each other. I am asking you which is more important—your friend, or your anger.

With Maddoc's words echoing in her memories, Catriona walked away from Davyn and left him to consider what she had said. Sindri and Maddoc looked up as Catriona approached them. They had begun a small fire beneath the shelter of the tilted bronze door, its light hidden by the door's shadow.

"Is everything all right, Catriona?" Maddoc raised an eyebrow, leaving Sindri to puzzle over a small bag of spell components. She shrugged, walking past him.

"I'll take first watch," she said, striding toward the glowing garden. Her eyes slowly adjusted to the darkness beyond the fireside, allowing her to pick her footing down a twisted, broken path. The softly glowing moss that grew on rocks here and there, and clumped high up upon the cavern walls. The purplish glow was not enough to cast shadows, hardly shedding enough light to guide her toward a boulder upon which she could sit. Sighing, Catriona pulled herself onto the shallow stone, staring out at the strange underground jungle; the broken pieces of an ancient past.

"This is a *real* manticore horn?" Sindri said. "Ooooh . . . spell . . . powder. Stuff. These are wonderful!"

Catriona could not make out Maddoc's reply, muffled as it was by the strange acoustics of the garden. Without the lantern's direct light, she had lost the impression of the tomb, but she knew it was still there. Cat closed her eyes and felt it, hulking at the edge of her mind like a sleeping giant. When it was awakened, what would they find within?

"Catriona?" Softly, Maddoc's voice came from just beyond her shoulder.

She sighed. "You should get some sleep."

"Sleep?" The old wizard harrumphed. "What, in the same campground as Davyn? Is Sindri going to protect me from my son's hatred?" Maddoc sighed, crouching to sit on the cold stone beside the warrior. "No, Catriona. I am far safer here, alone or with you, than I am by my son's side." The wizard's peppered hair seemed blacker among the shadows of the cavern.

"He says you are going to betray us," Catriona said at last.

"Davyn?" Maddoc sighed. "Yes, I knew he would. He has never understood that logic—like magic—is neither good nor evil in itself. It is a tool, like any other, to be used without the restraints of morality."

"You genuinely believe that, don't you?" she asked, the shadows on her face hiding any emotion.

"Have you thought about my offer?" Maddoc replied without answering. "Once we have rested, we will move toward the tomb—and the final traps there. I do not know what magic Asvoria used to protect the final resting place of her most cherished treasures, but they will be powerful. The Daystar will aid us, that is certain—but if Asvoria's servants are already there, or if she long ago placed guardians within the tomb—I do not know if it will be enough."

"We will work together and overcome them," she said fiercely, her eyes glinting in the flickering light. "That's what we do, Maddoc."

"Without Elidor? With Davyn constantly threatening to place a knife in my back? With a kender whose strongest magic is his imagination?" Maddoc gestured back at the camp dismissively. "Those are your tools, Catriona. Use them how you will."

Cat looked around, trying to settle herself despite Maddoc's words. She stared out at the shadowy tangle of vines that clambored up the broken trellises. The stone walls near the doorway were faded and gray, with bright flecks of paint here and there that may once have been patterns. Iron bars, rusted and broken, lay across the path. It would take several hours to reach the tomb, crossing the overgrowth and the treacherous pitfalls of the once-garden. "You didn't mention yourself, Maddoc," she realized at last, turning to stare at him.

"That is because I am not your tool. As I told you before, I cannot afford to take chances. If I have the opportunity to kill Asvoria—"

"Nearra," Catriona interrupted, but Maddoc paid her no mind.

"—then I will do so. Unless she can be controlled, she is a danger. I brought back Asvoria's soul to learn from it, not to be subject to it. And if that is betrayal, then so be it. But I tell you this now because I believe that you deserve to know."

"Why, Maddoc?" exasperated, Catriona turned to him. "Why are you telling me this? I could go back right now and tell Davyn. If I did, you would be put back in your bonds, your hands tied. We might even be forced to leave you behind, here, while we go to the tomb. Can we trust you beside us? I don't know, Maddoc!" She picked up a small rock and sent it sailing out into the darkness.

He turned to her, his voice gentle. "You have another choice, Catriona. With but a word from you, I can be transformed. Give me your oath, and I will use that conviction to fuel the Aegis. Without conviction, the sword is powerless . . . and we are doomed. This group is fragmenting, Catriona. Surely you see it, as well as I. I am offering you a fair return for your oath. In exchange for your honor, I will give you something to believe in. Something to fight for, and a fight that I believe you can win." When Catriona did not respond, he reached out to take her hand in his. She started in surprise, fingers trembling and jaw set determinedly. Maddoc continued, his voice a low, dark baritone, "I swear that if you do, Asvoria will fall, and we will save Nearra."

Catriona stared at him for a long moment, then pulled her hand from his, standing and walking into the darkness. She stood with her arms crossed protectively over her chest. She shuddered, once, as though her memories shook her from the inside. For a moment, she saw her aunt, a knight of Solamnia riding her black charger across green fields. She felt the bandit's knife against her skin, heard them offer an exchange for her life—and then she saw the eyes of her fellow squires as she was led to the trade in chains.

"I should have died fighting," she whispered.

"That is the past, Catriona." Maddoc stepped behind her, his body against her back and his hands gently touching her shoulders. "The past is gone, and we cannot live there."

"I've lived there for so long." She clenched her jaw, her hands balling into angry fists. "It's my life, wizard. That's who I am—the squire who failed."

"Is that all you are, Catriona? One moment, out of thousands? You chose to live in that moment, and you're still there." Maddoc's hands clenched her shoulders, nearly shaking her with the force of his argument.

His ferocity made her pull away again, reaching as though to draw her sword. "Leave me alone, Maddoc," she snapped. "Or I'll make Davyn a very happy man—by spilling your blood right here and now."

Maddoc raised his hands in submission. "As you wish, Catriona." She breathed deeply, lowering her hands from her weapon, and he continued. "After all, I am nothing more than a wizard stripped of his power. What am I to fear? You will not need me to return Nearra to herself, I'm certain. Go on, by yourselves, without me." Maddoc turned slightly, smiling quietly.

"No, Maddoc, I . . ." Cat shook her head, arguing with herself. She knew the wizard was baiting her, but she couldn't help responding. "You know that we need you."

"But not enough to trust me, is that it, Catriona? Not enough to give me the one thing I want—the one thing you need—to know that I will be your ally. Not enough to find your conviction. Why are you so afraid of redemption? Is it because you have lived so long with failure that you fear to find what you would become without it?"

"Why me, Maddoc?" She said forcefully. "To replace Davyn as your pawn?"

"No." Maddoc's face fell, and she could tell that she had hurt him. In a way, it felt good to poke a hole through the wizard's calm demeanor, to see that he could feel pain. "To redeem my failures. And perhaps yours, as well." His voice was quiet, and for the first time, Catriona sensed no amusement, no games.

"Never mind." Gathering his robes, Maddoc stepped back onto the path that would lead him back to the fire. "Perhaps we are all doomed to live in the past, after all." His voice was low, hollow. As she watched, he strode back to the campsite and was greeted by Sindri's eager questions.

Catriona stood in the darkness, staring back at the encampment. Maddoc and Sindri began discussing spellcraft in low tones, while Davyn curled up near one of the stone walls, his blanket not disguising the fact that he slept with his sword unsheathed and ready. The small flicker of the fire illuminated them in a soft golden light, showing every crack and crevice of the beaten bronze door under which the encampment had been made.

She leaned against the wall, feeling the cold stone against her arms. Catriona growled to herself, angered by the feeling of uselessness. What if Maddoc was right? Was she living in a single moment, refusing to move on?

I failed, she reminded herself. I deserve to be in pain.

The thought surprised her. It felt like something that had come from outside herself, a punishment leveled against a child by their parent. Is that what I am? She wondered. A child, afraid to face the real world without my "comfort"—my failure— that piece of me that defines me?

She shook her head again, angry. She wasn't defined by her failures.

A faint laugh back at the campsite caught her attention, and she saw that Maddoc, too, had bedded down. Only Sindri sat awake, drawing a small wooden flute from his pocket that she vaguely recognized as one a bard in Ravenscar had played upon. After a few sour notes, Sindri began to play a soft tune. The faint sound made her think of days when life had been simpler.

Sindri played, very quietly, and Cat had to strain her ears to hear the song. It soothed her, but her mind still replayed the conversation with Maddoc over and over again. Every tool they had against Asvoria was being taken from them, one by one. She was turning her back on Maddoc's offer.

It was too much for him to ask.

Why? she asked herself. Because he has no right to ask it, or because I am afraid to give it to him—to anyone? Even, she thought softly, to Davyn and Elidor.

My friends.

The hours passed slowly as Catriona thought through the problem, trying to understand herself beneath the starless sky of Navarre. Eventually, even the tireless kender curled up under his purple cloak, snoring softly. She envied Sindri his good nature. Nothing, no matter how dire the trouble around them, seemed to bother him.

Catriona sighed. It seemed as though she had been alone forever, with no one to turn to, and no future to look forward to. It was a comfortable path, she realized, one that didn't expect much of her. She couldn't fail, because she had never set a goal.

Well, she had a goal now. *Nearra*.

She walked slowly back to the encampment, staring down at the glowing ashes and faint flicker of the dying fire. Without thought, she walked to Maddoc's side, staring down at the sleeping wizard with quiet green eyes. For a moment, she considered waking him, accepting his offer. She imagined his smile as she told him that he was right, that she needed a future as much as he did. Biting her lip, she began to kneel, her arm reaching out toward the gentle rise and fall of Maddoc's chest.

"Cat?" Davyn's sleepy whisper startled her, and she spun to face him. "How long have I been asleep?"

Catriona rose and went to him, smiled with a calmness that she didn't feel. "A few hours. I was just checking . . ."

"And a good idea, too." Davyn shot the sleeping wizard a look and slid out from under his blanket. "I wouldn't be surprised if he tried to sneak off tonight, and warn her."

"Asvoria? Come on, Davyn. He's got as much to lose as we do. She'd destroy him before she'd even allow him to open his mouth."

"I guess that makes her smarter than we are."

"Stop it, Davyn."

But Davyn read something in her face that she couldn't hide. "He's getting to you, isn't he?" She turned away, but Davyn stood and turned her back, staring intently into her green eyes. "Don't listen to him, Cat. He's a liar, and he's evil."

"Davyn—"

"I'll take the rest of the watch," he cut in. "I think you need to get some sleep. You're not thinking clearly, Catriona, and we're all going to be relying on you tomorrow." Davyn's voice was kinder than before, almost as if he understood the struggle she felt. "Tomorrow, you'll look back on whatever he said to you, and you'll laugh at it. For now, just go to sleep."

"You're right, Davyn," she shot another glance at the wizard, but Maddoc remained asleep beneath the tilted bronze door. "You'll wake me in a few hours?" He nodded, and she clasped his wrist. "Thank you," she said quietly. He handed her his blanket, and she curled up against the wall across the passage from the others.

"Don't worry, Cat. I'll keep an eye out." She closed her weary eyes. A faint brush of wind swept briefly down the passage, ruffling Davyn's dark hair.

"Sleep well, Catriona," he whispered, turning his gaze to the wizard and his kender apprentice. He stood over them in the darkness, staring down at their sleeping forms with a strange half-smile. "I'll be watching you."

CHAPTER

16   BLOOD AND PROMISES

"Put your weapons down!" Ayudar screamed again, and pulled Vael's head back by her long white hair. "This is no joke, Elidor. I mean what I say. I'm not afraid to kill in the name of Asvoria." The youth's expression was panicked, and Elidor was more frightened that he would injure Vael out of fear than out of ruthlessness.

"I know that, Ayudar," Elidor said grimly. He slowly crouched to the floor with his hands out, Asvoria's ritual knife held loosely against his palm. "You've already proven it." Elidor's eyes flickered over the youth, his captive, and the obsidian portal. To his relief, Vael didn't seem to be hurt. The fire in her eyes was anger, not fear, and although there was a knife against her neck, she seemed tense and prepared for anything.

Elidor gestured to Gerhalt, and the guardsman regretfully lowered his club. "You killed the Baron. We know exactly what you're capable of."

"That . . . That wasn't my fault . . ." Ayudar stammered, looking from side to side to try and read the expressions on their faces. "But . . . but . . ." He tried to smile, and his knife hand relaxed for a moment against Vael's white skin. "He deserved to die."

"Who told you that?" Elidor asked cautiously.

Ayudar stepped back, drawing his knife up again beneath Vael's chin. "He betrayed her. He, and all of his ancestors. They walked out on her and turned their backs on their oaths. They had the chance for immortality in her service—an eternity in the afterlife at the side of the greatest queen who ever lived. And what did they choose?" The young man's voice rose as though repeating words that had been ingrained into him, his hand shaking dangerously. "They chose a life of exile. This canyon is death, death that forever keeps us from our purpose at her side. Well, I'm . . . I'm the one who has to change that. It's my destiny." He glanced around the small chamber, keeping the obsidian obelisk at his back and clenching the knife with white-knuckled fingers.

Elidor could see that the young man was frightened, clinging to the things he'd been taught for—how many years? Since his childhood, certainly. "It's your destiny. Just like your mother and your grandmother before you."

Elidor's words made the young man puff up with pride, lancing the emotions that Ayudar must have hidden all his life.

"That's right. All of us, for generations. My mother's family has always served the queen, always kept her memory alive. We've waited for her for generations, keeping her secrets and watching over the people of the canyon until the day when she could come and take her revenge. Now I'm the last one. The last priest, her only true disciple. And she's come for me. For me!" He jerked Vael toward him, his voice breaking as he ordered, "Now, drop your weapons, and step back toward the passage."

Even though he could see the fear in Ayudar's eyes, Elidor had no choice. He watched as Ayudar's strong arm pressed the knife against her, completely certain that the young man would slip, killing her in an instant if pushed too far. It was clear that

Ayudar didn't want to murder Vael, but he felt as though he had been forced in a corner—and like any animal, he could snap if pushed too hard.

"It's all right, Ayudar," Elidor said quietly. "You're in charge." The elf left the knife on the floor, stepping back to join Gerhalt and Davyn. The guardsman's club was on the ground at Gerhalt's feet, the older man's face dark with concern and barely-tempered rage. The lantern near Ayudar and Vael cast flickering shadows across the small cave, making it difficult for Elidor to tell when the knife was against Vael's skin, or inches away. He exchanged a dark look with Davyn, hoping that the ranger was watching for any opening.

"Where does the portal go, Ayudar?" Gerhalt said. "And how do you know it will open?" Good man, thought Elidor. Keep Ayudar talking. Make him comfortable. And then when he relaxes . . .

"I saw it open before. We . . . we made the old man do it. The Baron thought I'd kidnapped Vael. But it wasn't Vael. It was all the shapeshifter, with her face."

"Ophion." Davyn's brows met in a frown. "It tricked the Baron into believing you had Vael. A father's love for his daughter—and he'll do anything to keep her safe."

"So why did you kill him, Ayudar?" Elidor asked quietly. "He opened the portal, did what you wanted."

Ayudar's face contorted in shame and grief. "It wasn't my fault. The Baron tried to grab Vael away from me—tried to get her away from the knife. But it wasn't Vael, you see, it was the shapeshifter. Ophion changed form. The Baron grabbed me instead . . . we struggled."

"And the knife slipped," Davyn said, understanding. "Or Ophion pushed it."

Ayudar nodded, his eyes haunted. He straightened, trying to regain his composure. "But this time, I'll do it for real." Vael stood stiffly against him, the knife at her throat. "You might not take me seriously, Elidor, but you should. You should.

"I know you, Elidor. When you left this village, I was only a child—but children hear tales. And I know that the Baron thought of you as a son. And you left him. But you came back for Vael, didn't you? Didn't you?" His wide smile was nervous. "So I can use her to make you do what I want. And I'm serious. I'm . . . I'm serious about killing Vael. So you just listen to me.

"Vael's going to open the portal. Then she and I are going to go through. It's enchanted, you know. Only the rightful ruler of Tarrent can make it open. Which means that after she opens the portal and we go through, it will close. And there's no way you can follow us—unless you become the next Baron."

"And let you kill her on the other side?" Elidor asked, stepping closer. "No."

"Listen to him, Elidor," Vael said softly.

"No. I can't leave you," Elidor whispered. "I won't let him kill another person I love." Elidor felt as though he were being filled with boiling water. He fought with his anger, refusing to allow it to dull his instincts. "Ophion has already gone through the portal, Ayudar. Did you really think Ophion wanted you to come, too? You're a murderer and Ophion left you behind to suffer the consequences."

"No! Ophion wanted me to come. But first I had to take the Baron's body back to the hearthstead. Ophion told me no one should suspect we had breached the portal. I left the body on the dais, and I ran back down here. But . . . But, it took too long. By the time, I returned the portal had closed. And then I knew; I had to find a way back through it. Back to my queen!"

"Your queen?" Elidor spat. "Your queen cares nothing for you. She has what she wants—a quick path to her treasures. Do you think she'll be happy to see you, if you do make it to her side?"

Elidor shook his head. "She'll destroy you, or enslave you. You mean nothing to her."

"You're wrong!" Ayudar screamed. "The queen is a holy woman. She keeps her vows. Ophion promised—"

"Promised?" Elidor laughed. "Ophion's word is no more trustworthy than its features. A shapeshifter gives its word freely, and breaks it with equal speed."

"You lie." Ayudar shook Vael, the knife flailing at her throat, and Elidor felt his skin crawl. Ayudar glanced toward the portal, dragging Vael by her hair to the large obsidian slab. "We do this now, before you can talk me out of it."

Ayudar kept one hand in Vael's hair, the other held the knife loosely at her throat. She began to struggle, reaching up to grab his fist, but he jerked her against him with a sharp breath. "Please," he whispered, the desperation in his voice stabbing through to Elidor's heart. "I don't want to have to hurt you."

"Vael," Elidor murmured. "Do as he tells you." Behind him, his sharp senses noticed Gerhalt and Davyn moving slowly to either side, taking advantage of Ayudar's trouble with Vael to shift to more defensible positions.

"Open the portal," Ayudar said sternly. "Open it." He reached for her palm, pushing it forward to touch the dark obelisk. Vael's white hand struggled in his grasp, but Ayudar's grip on her wrist was too much for her. Her palm pressed against the portal stone.

Vael glanced back at Elidor, unspoken words in her eyes. He could do nothing but watch, every nerve urging him to leap to her defense. But the knife never wavered from her throat. "Say the word," Ayudar hissed, his breath coming in nervous gasps. "Open the portal!"

Forced to obey, Vael whispered, "*Thiraxus*."

Ayudar held Vael's hand against the stone as Asvoria's signet began to shine. The coils of the dragon seemed to move. Then, the obelisk rumbled and shifted, moving deeper back into the cave wall. A bitter red light slowly spread across the stone. First the edges of the obelisk were slightly tinted with light, and then the stone itself began to take on a red hue.

On the wall above the reddening obelisk, a small sign flared, burning brightly against the dark stone. It was a stylized bronze dragon, its head raised in a fierce roar. Davyn whispered to Elidor, "The key!" And suddenly Elidor understood. The key to the Obsidian Heart. It wasn't an item, but a sign. A sign that would guide them through the tomb's entrance—or unlock the door.

No one else seemed to notice the dragon. Their eyes were fixed on the obelisk as it shifted from opaque to transparent. Through the veil of red light Elidor thought he could see the entrance to a corridor.

"My queen!" Ayudar shouted. "I am coming!"

"Now!" Elidor shouted, diving for Asvoria's knife in a forward roll. He gripped it in one hand, using the other to propel himself forward. As he did, he heard Ayudar cry out. Elidor came up in a fighting stance, the ritual knife held level before him.

Vael's hair was a shifting tide, her body lashing out as she kicked Ayudar in the knee. Ayudar tried to grip her, but he fell backward. The knife slashed in a fumbling arc across Vael's shoulder, opening a terrible gash. She fell back onto the cold floor.

Elidor swung the ivory-handled knife, hoping to catch Ayudar's wounded leg with the blade, and force him to surrender. As much as he would like to kill the boy, Elidor knew that Ayudar wasn't evil. He remembered Roland's agonized face, and swore not to bring the old man any more pain than he was forced to.

But Ayudar had desperation on his side. The young man shifted out of the way. He leaped back on his uninjured leg and returned the attack with his thick hunting knife.

He cut open Elidor's pant leg at the knee, slicing a thin line of blood. Elidor snarled and struck out again, driving Ayudar back.

With a roar of anger, Gerhalt lifted his club and lumbered forward, trying to force Ayudar away from Vael, who still lay on the ground. The boy fell back against the portal, checking to see if he could slip through the stone. But the ritual had not completed, and the obelisk was still partially opaque. Ayudar scrabbled for a moment against the stone, trying to force it open with his will, then spun back to face them with a feral glint in his eyes.

"I didn't want to do this," he began, his words like a fanatic prayer, "But you made me, Elidor! You made me!" Ayudar's knife plunged down toward the fallen Baroness.

With a leap so swift it could not be tracked by the eye, Elidor jumped to Vael's side. He blocked the downswing of Ayudar's blade with his own, but he lost his grip and the ritual knife clattered to the ground. Ayudar smiled. "I guess you're getting old, eh, Elidor?"

Davyn grabbed Vael and swung the Baroness out of the way, placing himself between her and danger. "Elidor!" she shouted, fighting to get free of Davyn's grip despite the blood that stained the shoulder of her white gown.

Gerhalt charged Ayudar with a bellow, wielding his club in one hand. The boy dodged. But he was too slow. The guardsman slammed Ayudar into the wall beside the portal stone. Ayudar flailed, his arms swinging wildly, and he struck overhanded.

Elidor shouted, "Gerhalt!" but his cry came too late.

Ayudar screamed in anguish, as his knife sank into Gerhalt's back. The guardsman fell to his knees before Ayudar, the hunting knife sticking out between his shoulders.

His face sick with fear and anguish, Ayudar turned to hurl himself through the portal. "My queen!"

Everything seemed to move in slow-motion. Elidor charged forward, feeling every shock of stone beneath the soft soles of his boots. He saw Gerhalt slump to the ground, looking up at Ayudar with something between stunned amazement and fatherly concern. He heard Vael's scream, saw her slip through Davyn's guard, her white hair streaming out behind her, stained by blood and portal-light.

Elidor leaped over her to Ayudar, but the boy was too fast. He reached again for Vael. Elidor grabbed Ayudar's arm. He succeeded in forcing Ayudar away from Vael, but lost control as the boy danced back toward the portal stone—and through it.

Ayudar laughed wildly, holding up his bloodied hands in triumph. "Free!" Elidor fell to the ground at the base of the portal, his hands empty. The shock of his fall stunned him for a moment, and the elf looked up to see Ayudar standing over him, the blade of Asvoria's dagger in the young man's hand.

Between them, the transparent stone began to thicken, its pale red glow fading as the ritual began to end. Elidor tried to move toward it, but his wounded leg at last gave out. He tried to stand, cursing his weak flesh, but knew he would never get to the stone before it sealed once more.

"I'll kill you, too, Elidor!" Ayudar snarled. He raised the knife to slash downward at the elf. It was a motion born of fear and hatred, anger and desperation.

"Ayudar!" Vael called fiercely. She knelt beside Gerhalt's crumpled form, pulling out Ayudar's blade and raising it above her shoulder in a smooth movement. The boy turned, his eyes wide with glee. In his moment of triumph, Ayudar saw no danger. Vael's eyes were cold, bearing not only the rage of a woman who had lost her father, but the oath of a Baroness protecting her people and of a woman protecting the man that she loved.

She hurled the hunting dagger.

The knife spun in the air, catching a stray flash of golden-red light, and then bit deeply into Ayudar's chest. Ayudar staggered back, clutching his chest as though stunned to find the hilt of his own knife protruding from his breastbone. He glanced up at Vael, his eyes confused and strange. He stumbled, leaning against the wall of the corridor, his hand smearing a bloody trail on the stone.

"Free . . ." he whispered once more.

Then, with a soft sigh, he fell.

"Gerhalt," Vael whispered, bending over the guardsman's body. Breath still lingered there, brief and shallow, but as sturdy as the old guardsman himself. "We have to get him upstairs. If we staunch the wound, I think he may be all right." She pressed a makeshift bandage to his wound, wrapping it there with the long blue length of her own cloak. The obsidian stone stood above the fallen man like a marker, smooth black sides reflecting none of the lantern's soft light. The red glow that had bathed the chamber was gone, and the lantern seemed a dim star after the sun had set.

Davyn wrapped Elidor's wounded leg with a long bandage torn from his cloak. The elf seemed almost frozen, glancing from the black portal to Vael. "Are . . . are you wounded?" he finally ventured, trying to keep his voice still.

"Yes." Vael drew her tunic around her shoulder. "But I'll be fine."

"You're not fine. You've lost a great deal of blood." Davyn knelt beside her, pulling the cloak aside to take a look at her arm. "It isn't deep, but it is long. You'll need to clean this and put herbs on it." He tore another swath from his cloak and pressed it to the wound. Vael winced, and Davyn gave her a small smile. "You're very brave, my lady."

"Thank you," she said, but her gaze remained on Elidor.

Davyn exchanged a look with Elidor, then stood. "We should go—soon." He paused, then continued. "Our friends are in great danger. We can't stay. Still . . . I'll go get the guards to bring help for Gerhalt . . . Make certain he'll be all right. Before we go." Davyn cautiously adjusted the bandages around Gerhalt and whispered, "I'll be right back." With another glance at Elidor, he began to walk up the passage back toward the hearthstead.

"Davyn," Vael said, and he paused. "Tell the guards that I command them to return your weapons. Yours, and Elidor's as well. Give them this, and they will obey you." She handed him her signet ring. Davyn took it between his fingers and nodded silently.

"Vael," Elidor began as Davyn's footsteps retreated.

She shook her head, placing a hand on his lips. "No, Elidor, you kept your part of the bargain. You found the man who killed my father. I'll keep mine. The portal will be opened again, and you can go save your friends."

"It's not that easy." He took her hand in his, the pale skin like silk between his fingers.

"My father's spirit is at rest. He wouldn't oppose our union now, Elidor." Vael spoke softly, almost as though she were afraid of the words. The Baroness's face retained its stoic bravery, but her eyes asked the question she could not say.

"Vael . . ." Elidor began.

"I will not ask you, Elidor. Never think that I would beg for any man." She held her head high. Although her skin seemed made of ice, her hand was warm in his. "But I offer this—if you remain here, in Tarrent, then we will rule together. The village needs to rebuild, and if this queen is truly returning, then we will need our heroes."

Elidor took her shoulders and drew her into a gentle embrace. "Tarrent is in danger, Vael. But I can't save it by hiding here, or

REE SOESBEE

even by giving it leadership. Asvoria is in Navarre. She's down there with my friends. They're in trouble, and I can't abandon them. If we're successful, we'll save a friend who needs us very badly." He looked down into her eyes. "But that means I have to go after her."

"You have always run from the past, Elidor." Her voice was quiet, somber. Any accusation that might have found a place in her words was drawn out by the deep calm in her eyes. "You don't have to be an adventurer anymore. There is enough prosperity in Tarrent to give us a life of plenty."

"This isn't an issue of the past, Vael. Nor has it ever been an issue of money or of power." Elidor's face was pained. "My past . . . I am still only a thief, Vael. You deserve better. Until I can be something more, for you and for myself . . . I can't stay."

She reached to draw his face into her hands. "No, Elidor, You have never been 'only a thief' to me."

He sighed. "Tarrent is the only place I've ever felt at home. I will miss this village."

"You will miss only the village?" she asked softly.

Elidor looked down, meeting her eyes gently. "No. I will miss you, as well."

"Then why leave?" she whispered, and her voice made his heart ache.

"Because I have promises to keep."

"You have changed, Elidor," she said candidly, and he could not meet her eyes. "Once, you left me despite your promises. Now you return to your friends, to keep them. But I think," she paused, and her eyes measured his. "It has made you a better man. I wish my father could see you now. I think he would be . . . very proud of you."

"Vael," Elidor said. "I've never meant to hurt you. I've always—"

"No." She put her fingers over his lips. "You don't need to explain. Seven years ago, I didn't understand how you could leave so easily. How you could hurt me, when the love was so great between us. But now I see. Sometimes, love means that you can't hurt someone, Elidor. And sometimes, it means that you *must* . . ."

Slowly, Vael pulled away from him, crossing her arms as though a cold wind chilled her. "I can't promise to wait for you. Tarrent needs a leader, and a leader has responsibilities."

His arms fell to his sides. "I know."

"But I will . . . for as long as I can." It was more than he expected, and the words filled Elidor with a sudden bright spark of hope.

Lifting her head with a touch of imperious grace, Vael whispered, "So it is goodbye again, Elidor. No," she cut him off before he could respond, "Don't say it. I find that, in the end, I prefer not hearing your goodbyes." Davyn's footsteps could be heard in the corridor, and Vael reached to press her hand once more against the obelisk. "*Thiraxus.*"

Two guardsmen followed Davyn into the portal chamber. The shimmer returned, and the obsidian began to turn red.

As it became transparent, Vael instructed them to retrieve Ayudar's body from the other side. "He will be buried with a quiet ceremony. I do not think his grandfather . . . should suffer for the crimes of a lineage that is now dead and gone." The guardsmen did as she commanded, carrying the youth's body away in gentle hands.

Vael paused after they had gone, breathing softly as though something weighed upon her heart. She reached into the pocket of her long blue cloak and pulled out a small wooden flute. She ran her fingers along the intricate carvings, the elven workmanship apparent even to Davyn's untrained eye.

"Remember this, Elidor?" she said without looking up. "You gave it to me years ago. You said it would remind me that we were . . . that I would be part of your family. I have carried it with me since the day you left." She held the flute out toward him. "The time has come to return it to you."

Elidor took a step back. "No, Vael, you should keep it. To remember me."

Vael shook her head. "I no longer need your flute to reassure me. I have much more than that now." She smiled and tucked the flute under his belt, forcing him to take it.

"Good luck, Elidor." Vael turned away, sweeping across the small cave to the passage that led to the hearthstead. She paused as Davyn passed her, staring back at the elf. "Take care of him, Davyn," the Baroness commanded gently.

"My lady," Davyn said seriously. "I will."

She left them, then, in the glow of the scarlet stone as it turned transparent, her feet making no sound against the slick stone. Elidor stared after her as Davyn clapped his hand to the elf's shoulder. Davyn stepped up to the opening portal, lifting the lantern from the floor. Davyn handed a set of knives to Elidor, and the elf numbly placed them back in the sheaths at his waist where they belonged. "Do you think you'll see her again?" Davyn wondered aloud.

Elidor said nothing, and after a long pause the ranger shrugged, not expecting an answer. Stepping through the red glaze of the portal, Davyn called, "Are you coming, Elidor?"

Finally, the elf nodded, tearing his eyes away from the passage back to the hearthstead. Somewhere above them, they heard the stone fireplace slam closed, echoing hollowly through the earth. Elidor turned slowly, kneeling to pick up the ivory-hilted dagger from the floor where it had fallen. He held it for a moment, turning the knife in his hands and casting a fleeting look back at the corridor.

But the hearthstead above was silent, and the portal behind him was beginning to lose its scarlet glow. Elidor placed the knife in an empty dagger sheath. The glow of Davyn's lantern on the other side was beginning to move away, the scarlet light of the portal dangerously darkening. "I love you, Vael," he murmured, closing his eyes and listening to the silence.

After a moment, Elidor turned away, and did not look back again.

17 BETRAYAL

When Catriona awoke, she had the sensation that a good deal of time had passed. Though the shadows that surrounded her were no more dense than before, her muscles ached from hours of lying against the stone floor. How long had it been? Hours? Davyn was supposed to wake her up after only a short time, just enough to beat back the weariness.

She sat up, feeling her pounding head ease as the blood slowly began to return to her frozen limbs. She rubbed her neck and looked around. Nearby, Maddoc lay quietly on the ground, and Sindri huddled beneath his short cloak.

Davyn was gone.

Catriona pushed to her feet, shaking her head to clear it. "Maddoc, Sindri," she called quietly, checking her weapons. "Something's happened to Davyn." Maddoc sat up quickly, peering into the darkness. Sindri did not move at all.

"Sindri!" Maddoc shook the kender, then stopped with surprise. "He's not asleep."

"What?" Cat rushed to their side, kneeling and drawing back the kender's purple robe. A dark bruise had spread across Sindri's temple, but his breathing was even. "Oh, Sindri!"

Maddoc took the kender's head in his hands, checking for a pulse and any other signs that Sindri had been injured. "He's been knocked unconscious. I have some herbs that may help me wake him, if you give me a little time." The gray-haired wizard's fingers opened one of his belt pouches.

Catriona nodded. "I'll look for Davyn. If someone's broken into our camp, they may have hurt him, as well." She hurried to the fire, stoking the faint coals into a small blaze. From that, Catriona lit a wax taper and then headed into the corridors from which they had come. A brief search revealed no sign of the ranger, no mark of any fight or struggle. She returned, and searched just beyond the fallen brass doors, hunting for any tracks. She was no ranger, but she didn't see any obvious disturbance in the rocky earth, nor did she find any sign of Davyn.

She knelt by a patch of soil, studying it for markings. Although the earth was scuffed, she could not tell if it was an obscured boot print or simply an area marred by time. "Why is it the ranger that runs off?" she wondered sardonically. "He's the one who's supposed to do the tracking—not be tracked himself." She sighed, standing straight with her hands on her hips. "This is hopeless."

"Catriona!" Maddoc called from the encampment. "Quickly!"

She rushed back to the fire, her boots clapping against the stone. Maddoc cradled Sindri's head lightly as the kender's eyes blinked into awareness. Cautiously, the wizard helped him drink water from one of their flasks. "Careful, Sindri, careful," Maddoc said with a frown as the kender coughed up the liquid.

"Sindri, what happened?" Cat took Sindri's hand, gently shaking it to get his attention. "Where's Davyn?"

"Oh, I had the strangest dream." Sindri reached up, feeling his bruised temple gingerly. "You wouldn't believe it, Cat. It was like some kind of a different world. A world where Maddoc was teaching me spells and I was hovering over flying cities, and then Davyn came along riding on a phoenix. It was marvelous!"

"Sindri," Cat said, exasperated. "Don't you remember what happened? Who hit you?"

But the kender wasn't listening. "Oh, Cat, there was this other part of the dream. I was talking to the wizards at the Tower of High Sorcery, and they were giving me an award—and suddenly, someone was taking it from me. They were taking it right off me, Cat, digging through my pockets. Well, I tried to find out what they wanted, but they didn't ask.

"Oh!" he cried, sitting bolt upright. "I remember! It was Davyn in my dream. But he wasn't Davyn. And it wasn't my award he wanted. It was the Daystar. But that's such a silly dream. What would Davyn want with the Daystar? And anyway, it's right here . . ." The kender paused, his hands flashing through his pockets. "I thought I put it right here. Oh, dear. Did I set it down somewhere?" With a kender's usual lack of concern for his possessions, Sindri shrugged. "I'll have to go looking for it, I suppose."

"No, Sindri, you didn't leave it anywhere." Cat felt a cold fist closing over her heart.

The kender looked up at her innocently. "You can't actually mean that Davyn took it? Well, if he did, we'll have to ask him. I mean, it's one thing when someone doesn't want something, and they set it down, but it's entirely another to take it out of someone's pocket." He paused. "Well, no, maybe it isn't." The moral quandary seemed to stall Sindri for a moment, but then he shrugged, grinning. "If Davyn wanted it, why didn't he just ask?"

"I don't think it was Davyn, Sindri," Maddoc said.

"Ophion." Catriona said.

Maddoc nodded.

"How did it happen? Why didn't we realize it?" Cat was furious. "It *was* Davyn. It knew what Davyn knew—how to treat you, what to say to me. How did Ophion know those things?"

"Asvoria now has control over Nearra's body. She has been watching for a very long time, Catriona. She may not have been able to act while Nearra was in control, but do not fool yourself into believing that she was not listening. Anything Nearra knows—Asvoria knows. The question isn't how." He scowled. "It's when. And most importantly of all—where is Ophion now?"

"Ophion took the Daystar." Catriona gave Maddoc a despairing look. "There's only one thing it could want to do with that."

"Enter the tomb," Maddoc agreed.

Sindri bolted to his feet. "Oh, gosh! Davyn—I mean, Ophion—is going to use the Daystar to get into the tomb? But that's marvelous! We should hurry, I don't want to miss it." He trotted into the garden, leaping up onto a boulder and peering across the softly illuminated garden.

Cat's eyes were nearly red with anger, and Maddoc grabbed her before she could stand. "You've got to calm down, Catriona. If we go charging into this fight, Asvoria will destroy us. There are only three of us left, and we will face Asvoria and her shapeshifter. Our odds are not encouraging. If you rush off to seek vengeance, we won't just fail. We will die."

His words chilled her, but she pulled away. "Then we'd better catch Ophion before it gets to Asvoria."

"Cat, Maddoc!" Sindri whispered loudly from atop a small rock just within the garden. "I see a light. I think Ophion's close to the tomb. Come on!"

"He's not even angry, is he?" Cat murmured, kicking out the fire and handing her taper to Maddoc.

The wizard smiled, his gray eyes dark. "Why should he be?

Despite all of my attempts to make him a proper wizard, he is still a kender. The sense of propriety and ownership that we give items simply doesn't exist for him." He sounded strained. "And the idea of Ophion stealing the Daystar—well, he sees it as just another adventure."

Catriona reached out to stop Maddoc before he started down the path. "If Davyn was Ophion," she said uneasily, "why didn't he kill us in our sleep?"

"That, my dear," the wizard replied, "is the most disturbing question of all." He paused, and when he spoke again, his voice was soft. "There's something I need to tell you, Catriona. This tomb—it was built after Asvoria died. She was their immortal goddess-queen, you see. She would not build her own tomb, so certain was she that her reign would never end."

"So Asvoria has never been inside her own tomb?"

He shook his head. "No. And more—she does not know its secrets. Not as I do. I researched the tomb extensively, even though I could not find its location. The main chamber is filled with her treasures—yes—but her sword, the Aegis—it is not among the rest." Maddoc continued emphatically, "It is hidden in a separate chamber, to keep it safe in case the tomb was found and its treasures looted."

"Why didn't you tell us this before?"

"And trust that Davyn would allow me to live, once my usefulness had gone?" He lifted an eyebrow. "You must think I'm a fool. I had planned to play this card if Davyn convinced the rest of you to end my life. Until then, it was my secret."

Catriona thought about it for a moment, but could not argue. "Can you find the chamber?"

"I believe so. But if Asvoria, or her minions, have arrived at the tomb before we do, she will know that it is not among her treasures."

"And she'll guess, you will know where it is." Suddenly she understood. "We were protecting you."

"Yes." Dour, Maddoc denied nothing. "But I was also giving you what you wanted—Asvoria has come here to find me, and to use me to get inside her tomb. I didn't use you or your friends any more than you used me, Catriona. And we are both but steps away from our goal. Nearra is within your grasp, Catriona. She's here, and she's waiting for us."

She snorted. "Is there anything else you haven't told me, Maddoc, so long as you're being confessional?"

He chuckled. "Only one thing. And it is a great trust that I tell you this, Catriona. Understand me, I do not do it lightly." He breathed a long, remorseful sigh. "The Aegis—it has a certain sentience, as I described it before. Once a woman lifts it—if it allows her touch—then no one can take it from her. If you wield the Aegis, then you will have to voluntarily give it up when we are victorious."

"And you said you weren't going to let me keep it," Catriona mocked. "Your lies are showing, Maddoc."

Her voice was gentle, and his lips twisted into a slight smile. "Better that you know this now, when the chance of you carrying the sword is very real. Would you rather I hadn't told you?"

Catriona glanced toward the tomb, and a shiver ran down her spine. Davyn was supposed to be here—Nearra would listen to Davyn. He could call her out, bring her soul to the surface, and help her fight Asvoria's control. The sword felt heavy in Catriona's hand, and her armor constricted her chest, shortening her breath as the metal bound her. She was a fighter, a warrior, someone who solved problems with her blade—

"Catriona!" Seeing the doubt in her eyes, Maddoc took her shoulders in his hand and pulled her to him, staring down at her with dark foreboding. "Conviction. You must act with conviction. You cannot forget that."

"Davyn—Elidor—they're both gone now." She stared, composing her face and breathing in her courage. "I have to do this, don't I?"

"Yes," he said. "But you *can* do it."

"I know," she said, more for herself than for him. Her hand clenched and unclenched around the hilt of her sword, and she managed a small smile. "I know."

Maddoc's troubled look lightened. "We can do this if we work together. You and Sindri keep them busy in the tomb—try to draw out Nearra. Make her think. If she's busy fighting Nearra's spirit, then Asvoria won't have the energy to discover what I'm doing. We both know that you can likely defeat Ophion in a fair fight, and with Sindri's help, you should be able to hold your own. I'll seek the Aegis, and I'll find you."

"The incantation . . ." Cat began, but Maddoc quieted her.

"You no longer need it, Catriona. Ophion—and soon, Asvoria—has the Daystar. They can remove the enchantment now. It was always an alternative, although I feared the power of the medallion would alert her to our location. But she's found us in spite of everything. With the Daystar, she can put down the spell . . . And enter the tomb."

Catriona's eyes were probing. "Maddoc, what will you do once we have the Aegis?"

"That, my dear,"—he smiled—"is entirely up to you. You remember my promise, and my price."

Before Catriona could respond, a sudden shudder rocked the cavern. Catriona spun and saw a brilliant golden light surging forward from the tomb. Sindri was already too far away, but she leaped in front of the wizard, shielding his body from the blast. The shockwave of light roared past them, uprooting small bushes and hurling Catriona and the others to the ground. She felt the earth ripple with the power that was released, shuddering beneath her. White spots covered her eyes, half-blinding her in the sudden return of darkness. Sparks flew around the obsidian tomb in the distance, for a moment standing in a solid, luminous arch, and then disintegrating to the ground as the shield broke apart and vanished.

At her side, Maddoc gasped, coughing as dust swirled though the cavern in the wake of the blast. "She's used the Daystar, as I knew she would." he said bitterly. Quickly, he rolled to his knees, reaching for Catriona. "Are you all right?

"I'm fine," she said, still a little shaken. Catriona pushed herself up from the ground where she had fallen, shaking her head to clear it of the spots in her vision. Maddoc took her arm, helping her to stand as Sindri capered easily over a collapsed boulder.

"Wow, did you see that?" Sindri crowed. "Ophion must have used the Daystar to reverse your spell, Maddoc, but wow! Boom!" He tugged on the wizard's robes, eager to learn more. "Did you know it would do that if someone used the Daystar on it? Was that a backup plan?"

"Yes, Sindri." The wizard tried to make out the tomb, but the garden in between still had too many tangled branches in his way. The light they had been following was gone, swept away by the burst of radiance, but it was clear that Asvoria's shapeshifter had reached the tomb. Maddoc slowly released Cat's arm, staring intently past rubble and small rocks that tumbled warning from the ceiling above. "I had hoped not to need it, though, as it would draw them to us."

"Asvoria and her shapeshifter."

"Yes." Maddoc nodded, his face ashen. "But it's too late. Ophion will take the Daystar—and the Aegis—to Asvoria. She may even be with him—or approaching. You have to get to the tomb. *Now.* You're both faster than I am, and I have neither Catriona's strength nor Sindri's swiftness." His eyes were haunted. "Don't let them get away with our last chance to gain the knowledge of Asvoria—and to save the life of your friend."

"But Maddoc!" Sindri looked appalled. "I can't fight Asvoria without you! I mean, you've taught me a lot about spells—but I don't know if I have the words memorized—I might get the chicken foot mixed up with the lizard's tongue, and what about the powdered ocre? Maddoc, I need you!"

The wizard's face was drawn, and he put a hand on Sindri's shoulder. "Go. I'll meet you there. The seconds you save may mean the difference between salvation and failure."

Catriona didn't argue. She knew that Maddoc was right. With a salute, she turned toward the tomb. "Come on, Sindri. We'll see him again in a few minutes." Side by side, they sprinted, Catriona's long legs covering the distance far better. Despite her armor's weight, she drew ahead of Sindri, and he redoubled his efforts in order to keep up. The two of them raced forward, covering as much ground as they could. Three were stronger than two—but they would have to sacrifice that strength in order to gain time.

Catriona and Sindri burst out of the undergrowth into a rocky courtyard that may have once been earth, covered in ornate stone tiles. A statue stood above the clearing, as black as the tomb behind it. Catriona knew at once who it was. "Asvoria."

"She doesn't look at all like Nearra," Sindri said, squinting up at the stone visage. "Except maybe around the eyes."

Behind the statue, the tomb was carved of pure obsidian, with eerie, dragon shapes set at regular intervals against its lustrous stone. Time had not altered it. It glistened as though newly-built. The main doors had once been covered with vines that bloomed with pale white roses, but the vines were dead, only bitter thorns remained upon blackened vines.

The doors were open, and the stone was chipped and splintered as though by a single, terrible shock. A cold breeze shivered Catriona's skin. No luminescence penetrated the halls of the tomb itself, and no shimmering fungi grew near enough to cast its subtle glow. She could barely make out the reflection of light somewhere within the building, echoing in wall after wall of polished obsidian. Cat reached forward into the doorway, unsure, and then clenched her hand into a fist. The spell was gone.

"Stay near me, Sindri." She raised her sword and stepped forward through the doors of the ancient tomb—and into the darkness beyond.

18 A Little Misdirection

Elidor slipped along the narrow passageway, helping Davyn follow behind him. The corridor that led down from the portal was long and twisting, half-collapsed in several places—but they squeezed through and continued. At one point, they found a recent cave-in that marked the foyer where the cavern had collapsed. Grimly, they made their way around the rubble, eager to continue on where they had been blocked before.

Davyn paused, placing his hand on the stone and listening.

"Davyn—" Elidor stopped in the hallway, the lantern in his hand. "They won't be there. Even if they were still in the area, the sheer amount of stone filling that room . . ."

"I know." Davyn's hand fell. "Do you think they're all right?"

Elidor allowed a slight grin to creep across his delicate features. "I don't know. Why don't we go find out?"

Davyn chuckled at Elidor's confidence, and followed him into the darkness. Many hours later, with aching legs and palms red from gripping the rough stone, the two came out onto a shallow ledge. Elidor leaned out slightly, staring down into a massive cave that was only faintly lit by purplish luminescence.

Davyn reached down and broke off a small sprig of the moss, rolling it between his fingers until it turned a soft indigo. He began to brush the plant off his fingers against the stone, and then froze. "Elidor," he said, "Look."

"The tomb." Elidor gripped Davyn's arm and pointed. A large black building guarded by the tall statue of a woman stood near one side of the cavern, past piles of fractured stone and ancient ironwork. Strange, stunted plants desperately reached toward a stone sky, trying to live on the faint light of the moss that spotted the ceiling and chasm walls.

The tomb stood at the far edge of a great cavern, lit by the phosphorescence of stunted plants that lined the walls. Around it, the massive cavern arched, covered in shadows. They had exited a small, hidden entrance in the wall. On the opposite side of the cavern, a number of openings hung like lanterns on the cavern, surrounded by elegant stone balconies. The centerpiece of that wall was a pair of giant bronze doors, lying at strange angles due to the passage of time. The elf's keen eyes followed two glimmers of light as they moved below, through the cavern. Separated by at least thirty feet of distance, one seemed to be chasing the other toward the great tomb. The lights seemed like fireflies, skittering down broken paths. "Look!" Elidor pointed.

"One of those lights has got to be Cat and Sindri." Davyn knelt at the edge of the ledge, peering toward the floor of the cave intently. "The other is probably Ophion, chasing them. We're just in time. Can we get down?" His eyes took on a predatory shine.

The elf put out the lantern so that the light would not warn Asvoria's servants, latching it to his belt. They would not need it, as the moss would show them handholds and crevices far more readily without the lantern's harsh glare. Elidor nodded to Davyn, reaching out below the ledge to test the stone. "The cavern wall is irregular. We can climb down. It will take some time, but we are closer to the tomb than they are. We may make it before the second light."

"Which means we'll get to Cat before Ophion does." Davyn grinned. "Let's go."

The wall was rugged, and they had no rope, but luckily both were stalwart. Elidor lowered himself easily down the rough stone, smiling at Davyn as the boy dropped from one thin ledge to the next. Elidor's count was accurate; by the time they were once again on solid ground, the first light had reached the tomb—but the second was still distant, its flicker rising and falling in the thick brush of the once-beautiful garden.

A bright flash of yellow light burst from the tomb, rolling across the garden like an ocean wave. The ground lurched, and Davyn staggered, though Elidor rode the earth's shift on lightly balanced feet. For a moment, they could see a shield of magic, arched over the obsidian building—then it sputtered, twinkled, and fell apart like a thousand sparks disintegrating from arch to ground.

Blinking as the light receded, Davyn shielded his eyes and tried to make out the tomb. The black building still stood. "That must have been Maddoc taking down the shield spell." Davyn gave a startled gasp. "They're inside."

The two crossed the cavern, choosing their steps carefully around jagged iron trellises and broken stone. Finally, the obsidian tomb lay before them, its shining walls a stark reminder of the portal in the village of Tarrent. The dragons which coiled subtly along its sides seemed to shift in wary knowledge of their approach, coils twisting around the hidden letter A. The statue, which stood before the doors, glared down at them with stoic, angry eyes. Davyn stopped to snarl up at her.

"She doesn't look like much."

Elidor glanced up, then looked away. "Never judge a woman by her appearance, Davyn. She'll tear you to ribbons before you can even say her name. You've seen Cat when she's mad."

Davyn gave a faint chuckle, then turned toward the open doors. "Seems we're not the first ones inside."

Elidor's sharp eyes caught the glimmer of a flame within the garden behind them. "It looks like Ophion is gaining ground."

"Then we should hurry. But that's no reason to throw caution to the wind." The ranger knelt to inspect the tracks and damage done to the heavy obsidian door. "Broken by magic. The cobblestones here are too clean to bear clear tracks, but I'd say multiple people went in, one wearing harder boots, and one barefoot."

"Sindri?"

"Small, that's for certain, but it is not clear enough for me to be sure."

Elidor quirked an eyebrow. "Sounds like Catriona, Sindri—and either Maddoc has gotten his magic back, or Sindri's finally mastered a spell." Nodding, Elidor tried to see into the tomb. "Shall I light the lantern so that you can see?"

"And give ourselves away to whoever's chasing Cat and Sindri? No. I'll live." Davyn shook his head. "Here." He scraped some of the soft purplish moss from a nearby rock, cupping it in his gloved hand. "This will give us a little bit of light, but won't shine like a lantern will. Want some?"

Elidor declined. "I can see just fine, thank you." His blue eyes curved as he smiled.

Davyn drew his sword, holding it in his other hand and gesturing to Elidor to go in first. Elidor smiled, understanding. If there were any traps in the building, they would need his sharp senses to find them before they were set off. Together, they entered the tomb. The walls inside were pure obsidian, their black shadow drawing in the feeble light of Davyn's mossy bundle. Somehow, the luminescence made the tomb seem darker, as though the dim light was fighting a losing battle.

The tomb was much larger than it appeared from the outside. Directly across from the entrance, a coiling corridor led down, deeper into the tomb, and forked at every few turns. As they headed down the corridor, their footfalls echoed, reflecting back from every corner in the building. The black walls were mirrored, shining back images that flickered with the light that Davyn carried in his hand. At some points, the obsidian reflected his image as though he were in two places at once. Other times, the walls hid themselves completely in the darkness, giving the illusion that the passage continued. Davyn and Elidor maneuvered through the passages for several minutes, trying to find their way in the coiling maze.

Voices, a female and a male, echoed through the strange hallways. Although Davyn could not make them out, he caught their tone—concerned, quiet, seeking. "Sindri?" he called. "Cat?" The voices fell silent. "Anyone there?"

Catriona and Sindri walked through the darkness, trying to find the source of the faint illumination deep within the mausoleum. "How is Maddoc ever going to find us?" Sindri asked, his still-bruised face upturned.

"He'll find us," Cat replied confidently, keeping her sword ready for an unforeseen attack. "We've been walking through these corridors forever. He's probably somewhere in here with us at this point. He wasn't that far behind us. Some sort of head start we got, getting lost in the tomb."

"It wasn't our fault," the kender protested. "It's confusing in here. All the reflections, and the echoes, and the false rooms—it's like someone didn't want us to get in here. I mean . . ." His voice trailed off, and Sindri cocked his head to listen. "Sssh!"

A moment later, the echo reached Catriona's less sensitive ears.

" . . . Sindri . . . Cat?"

"That's not Maddoc," she said grimly.

"No!" Sindri brightened. "It's Davyn!"

Catriona's heart froze. "Are you sure, Sindri?"

"Yes! Oh," he caught sight of her forbidding look. "Davyn . . . is Ophion. That's right." Sindri listened again. "He knows we're here. He's calling for me now. What do we do?"

"If he's trying to lure us out, then he can't have found the Aegis yet. And if he hasn't found it, then he still needs us. If he thinks we're going to fall for his Davyn impersonation, then he's vulnerable." The warrior readied herself, leaning her back against one of the black obsidian walls, and smiled. "Call him to us, Sindri. We'll make sure he never gets back to Asvoria."

"Davyn?" Sindri put his hands around his mouth and yelled as loudly as he could. "We're here, Davyn. Over here!"

Grinning, Davyn called back, "Stay where you are, Sindri. I'm coming."

Elidor gripped Davyn's arm. "We might do better if we split up. Whoever was chasing them will be here soon."

Davyn nodded. "The passage forks again here." He pointed at the left hallway. "You take that one. We don't have much time."

Elidor clasped Davyn's wrist in a brotherly shake. "We'll find them." He stepped nimbly toward the corridor, releasing Davyn, and gave him a fierce grin before vanishing into the obsidian darkness.

For a moment, Davyn stood alone in the tomb, listening to the distant footfalls and wondering if other feet were padding along black passages. Holding aloft the bundle of luminescent moss, he turned to the passage on the right and entered, watching as two copies of himself against the walls repeated his every move.

Footsteps reverberated through the tomb, and Davyn could not tell which were his own and which belonged to the others. He felt along the wall beside him, hoping to feel where the passage opened, as he could not trust his eyes. The moss bundle he carried seemed to refract like a prism, sharing its light from every angle as it bounced from mirror to mirror. Once, in the reflection of an obsidian wall, he thought the saw Catriona's red-flame hair—but before he could reach for her, the light shifted, and she was gone.

"Here, Davyn!" The kender's voice seemed to taunt him.

He followed Sindri's voice, hoping it would lead him through the maze. Each echo led him another step, as his eyes desperately tried to pierce the gloom. Was the figure before him Elidor? Was it Cat? Was it his own reflection, darkened within mirrors of obsidian and stone?

At last, the ranger caught sight of Sindri in the darkness. The kender's purple cloak picked up the light of the moss bundle, making Sindri seem otherworldly against a background of dark stone walls. Davyn lowered his sword and hurried toward Sindri, reaching out toward the kender.

"Thank Paladine, you're all right." Davyn knelt next to his friend. "Where's Catriona, Sindri?"

"Right here." Catriona stepped from behind the hidden corner, her red hair a bright star in the darkness. The sword in her hand fell like an executioner's axe from on high.

Catriona's sword threw up sparks where it struck the obsidian floor, and gouged a deep path in the soft stone. Davyn barely had managed to throw himself out of the way of her downswing. She raised her sword. She wouldn't miss again.

"Catriona!" Davyn was stunned. "What are you doing?"

189

"Killing a shapeshifter," she replied tersely, her sword slicing through the air once more. Davyn parried, his sword over his head as he scrabbled to find his footing on the slick floor.

Catriona pressed her advantage, kicking Davyn's other hand out from under him as he tried to stand. He stumbled once more, but rolled across the floor, his weapon held tightly in his hands. Catriona charged, but Davyn reversed, passing under her guard and kicking at her ankles.

Catriona fell hard, landing on one knee with a roar. The movement forced her sword out of her hand, and it skittered across the smooth floor. By the time she spun around to face Davyn again, he was rising.

Her eyes flashing angrily, Catriona lunged from her position, driving her shoulder into Davyn's stomach, with all of her strength. His breath was knocked out of him, but he still had enough power to grip both fists around the hilt of his sword. He slammed Catriona between the shoulderblades with the pommel. He hit her once, twice, but she lifted him from the ground and threw him backward.

Skidding against the ground once more, Davyn twisted back to a crouch and brought his sword in a defensive stance. Catriona grabbed her weapon from the ground where it had fallen, flipping it easily in her hand to regain the balance of the blade.

"Sindri, do something!" she growled, slowly advancing.

"Like what?"

"Like—tell her I'm not a shapeshifter!" Davyn said urgently, readying himself for Catriona's next attack.

"How am I supposed to tell that?" Sindri cried as Catriona rushed forward again. Her sword struck against Davyn's blade, echoing through the tomb with a bitter ring. Davyn felt his entire arm shiver from the pure force. She struck from above with a flurry of blows, driving his blade down with each powerful attack.

"Don't listen to him, Sindri!" Catriona said

"If you're Davyn—if you're Davyn . . ." Sindri's face contorted in thought.

"Just hit him with a spell," Catriona urged, her sword striking again even as she spoke. Davyn dodged to the side, and felt the tip of Catriona's blade cut through the side of his tunic before it bit into the wall behind him.

"That was close." He tried to smile.

"Not close enough," she growled. "Sindri! Spell him!"

"Uh . . . I . . ." Sindri looked uncomfortable, as his friends fought. Their weapons chimed again. Catriona clearly had the advantage in strength, but Davyn's swiftness allowed him to dodge even her most powerful blows. "Hey! I've got it!" Sindri yelled. "If you're really Davyn—then you'll let Cat kill you!"

There was a shocked pause, as both Cat and Davyn stopped to stare at the kender. A long moment of silence passed, and Cat struggled to find the words. Sindri ran toward them and took hold of the sword blades. He stood between them, a blade clamped in each hand. "Don't you see? If it's really Davyn, then he'll do it. Ophion would never do it. But Davyn trusts you, Cat. He knows you won't kill him."

"It's . . . not . . . Davyn!" Catriona choked in anger.

"It is." The voice did not come from either of the combatants, and even Sindri jumped a bit, startled.

Fading out of the shadows, Elidor strode toward the group. "Davyn and I were trapped on the far side of the cave-in. We followed your light across the garden, to the tomb."

Catriona's sword wavered, and then slowly fell. "Elidor?" Her face lit up with joy at the sight. "We thought you were—I mean—the cave-in! But you're ok?"

As the elf nodded, Davyn let out a great sigh of relief. "Glad you showed up, my friend. She almost had me skewered for supper."

Panting, the ranger leaned back against the wall and saluted Catriona with his sword before lowering it to his side.

"I've been investigating the tomb," Elidor said in a quiet monotone. "We've got a problem."

"Another one?" Davyn said sardonically, and Cat smiled.

The elf nodded, his face dark. "Asvoria has Maddoc. While we've been trying to navigate these hallways, she's captured him and brought him into the tomb. I saw Ophion dragging him in. Without his magic, he was helpless to resist her.

"She wants him to tell her where her sword is," Elidor said. "And he's willing to make a deal."

They followed Elidor through the hallways, trusting the thief's instincts to lead them through the confusing tunnels of obsidian that laced the interior of Asvoria's tomb. At last, they turned a corner and saw a stark white light ahead of them, illuminating the central chamber of the building—a room hidden deep within the labyrinth.

Catriona gasped. Maddoc stood in a golden chamber, his hands folded into thick velvet sleeves. Asvoria's magic bound him: a thin golden leash ran from her fingers to a glittering glow that circled his neck.

She was seated on a golden throne, running her hands over the lacquered armrests and fingering the once-magnificent brocade. Though Asvoria's flesh was still that of a simple country girl, Catriona could not help but be struck by her movements—regal, supple, and powerful. Although it was Nearra's face, the humorless detachment belonged entirely to the sorceress. Asvoria did not speak at first, fingering the leash that bound Maddoc to her. A chill trickled down Catriona's spine.

The imposing throne, upon which Asvoria sat, stood at the far end of the room. The room was large, enclosed. Once the stone walls had been polished and glittering; now they were dull with age. In the dim light of Asvoria's floating illumination, the chamber glowed, but there was no warmth in its static, unflickering light. Treasures littered the floor, gold piled upon platinum higher than a person. Statues of unimaginable beauty and perfection stood as though guarding the room, in alcoves of obsidian around the edges of the room. In the center of the space, was a massive platinum seal. It was as wide as three people standing side by side, ringed with obsidian and sparkling jewels, and covered with etchings. Davyn could make out the symbols of manticores and hellbeasts and other ancient creatures. But one sign stood out, unique among all the others. A needle in a haystack.

"The key," Davyn breathed, staring at the glistening seal. "The key to the Obsidian Heart." There it was, simple and unadorned: the bronze dragon, the head raised in a fierce roar, claws extended as though to pierce an enemy's flesh, just as it had appeared on the portal wall.

"What?" Catriona whispered back, confused by Davyn's strange utterance. Davyn did not answer, his eyes drawn to Maddoc.

As Asvoria tightened her grip on the magical leash, the old wizard was forced to step toward her. Maddoc's robes brushed against the treasures heaped upon the floor at Asvoria's feet. He stepped among rings that sparkled, long scepters jeweled with rubies and diamonds, and overturned casks of glittering amethysts as bright as the eyes of the woman on the golden throne. Someone had torn through the room like a hurricane, overturning the stacks of gold and emptying chests of jewelry and gems onto the cold black floor.

But she had not found what she was looking for.

At last she looked up with a slow, appraising glance. Her lips curved into a sultry smile, and she tossed her blonde hair gently about her shoulders as though admiring the way it matched her royal seat.

"Tell me, old man," she breathed softly as she tugged the leash again, her voice filling the chamber. "Did you ever think to see me once more enthroned?"

"Perhaps," Maddoc admitted. "But not this way."

She laughed, and the sound was like crystal breaking upon steel. "It suits me, I think. When I have my castle rebuilt, I will move this throne there, and judge my populace from this seat. Ah, wizard, what gifts you have given me—and what opportunities. Although"—she ran her fingers through her hair—"you could have chosen a better vessel. This girl has some heathen beauty, but she is nothing compared to what I once was when I stood before nations and made them weep."

"You are an abomination, Asvoria." Maddoc's voice was harsh, uncompromising. "I took the risk of releasing you because I wanted your knowledge. I did not give your freedom to you; nor would I ever have done so."

"No. You would have made me a slave." Her purr belied the cold speculation in her eyes. "As I have now made you."

"Yes. But only long enough to take your power for my own."

She laughed. "You are bold, wizard."

"No," he replied. "I am practical."

"How lucky for me, then, that my shapeshifter found you and brought you here before you could steal my greatest weapon." Asvoria stood, and in her clenched fingers a ball of black lighting began to grow. She watched it with a smile, channeling the destructive power through her fingertips. "Now, Maddoc." She mocked him. "Shall we have a wizard's battle, or shall I simply torture you until you tell me where the Aegis is hidden?" Her eyes flickered down to the platinum seal upon the floor. "Is it there, Maddoc? That seal is enchanted with a power that rivals my own . . . many souls were tied to it, lashed with magic to power the spell which protects whatever lies beyond. That is where it lies, yes?" Asvoria coiled the leash around her fingers, drawing the old wizard closer. "And you know how to open it, I'm sure. Good Maddoc, always drawn to forbidden knowledge. If anyone knows how to open it, it is you."

"It would do you little good to duel me, Asvoria. You have the Daystar." Maddoc shrugged. "If you intend to kill me, then cease your prattle and have done. You have stolen my magic as I planned to steal yours; the rest is but a charade. We who wear the black robes have no use for pretty lies to cover dark truths."

"No," she hissed, raising her hand as the arcs of lightning grew. "I don't suppose that you do."

The lighting coursed through Maddoc's body, driving the wizard to his knees. Despite himself, Maddoc screamed in agony as Asvoria's spell took hold, and he fell to the ground before her. Her face lit with delight as the wizard buckled, writhing in the grip of her spell.

19   THE DARKNESS BEYOND

Catriona stepped forward as though to charge toward Asvoria. Davyn clutched her arm, preventing her movement as the strange magical light flickered on the walls around them.

"Cat, no," he hissed, keeping his voice pitched below the sounds of Maddoc's torture. "We have to think about this before we rush in. I don't see Ophion."

Through the archway, the throne room glittered. Maddoc's body was a black stain against a carpet of gold and jewels, the magical lightning emanating through his body. Asvoria stood at the base of the throne, completely engaged in her debilitating spell, enjoying every shriek of agony, every trembled shudder of the wizard's form.

"Tell me how to open the seal, Maddoc," she said sweetly, "And this can end. There will be darkness for you—sweet oblivion. Which is more than I gave to most of those who betrayed me, in my time. Even my beloved . . . the only man I trusted." Her face contorted with the memory, and the spell cut Maddoc more deeply. "The man who killed me, in the end." She snarled. "So much for love."

"She's killing him." Cat's muscles flexed, barely controlling **197** her urge to run Asvoria through—no matter what the cost. "We have to do something!"

"What you're going to do," said a cold voice behind them, "is lower your weapons, and step into the room." Catriona and Davyn turned in shock, and saw Elidor holding Sindri off the ground, a thick dagger biting into the kender's throat. The kender was limp, made unconscious by a blow to the back of his head. Elidor's features melted and shivered into blank emptiness.

Davyn clenched his teeth. "Ophion." The word, spoken in the sudden silence, echoed through the tomb and reverberated from the drum-like well at its center.

"At your service." The shapeshifter's tone was empty, absent of all emotion or intent. Still clutching the squirming kender, Ophion stepped around them and into the golden chamber. "Milady," Ophion said forcefully. "I have them."

Knowing that the shapeshifter's words were no bluff, Davyn and Catriona allowed their swords to slip from numb hands.

Asvoria's eyes flickered up from her amusement, and she laughed to see Ophion and the others at the arched door.

"Well done, Ophion," she beamed. "Do come in, my guests. My hospitality awaits you." To punctuate her words, she clenched her fist and Maddoc shuddered with a new wave of agony. Asvoria's laughter, so strangely reminiscent of Nearra's smiling joy, echoed through the corridors of the tomb and from the eerie darkness of the well. The shapeshifter carried Sindri easily. It walked toward Asvoria, placing the limp body of the kender at her feet.

"Reunited at last." Asvoria's eyes traveled from Catriona to Davyn down to the limp body of their small friend. "But where is the half-breed thief?"

"He was not with them, your Majesty," Ophion said tonelessly. "He may be doing further investigations of your tomb. I was able to duplicate him, and control the situation." With no other option,

Davyn and Catriona stepped into the room and left their weapons on the floor behind them. Ophion watched them carefully, ready to counter any defiance with Sindri's blood. When they reached the shuddering Maddoc, Ophion nodded, and sank to one knee at his mistress' side.

Asvoria's smile was victorious. "Well, Maddoc, it seems I am unexpectedly delivered with a means to elicit the knowledge I need *and* destroy my enemies at the same time. How efficient." She reached down and slid a gentle finger along the kender's face, and the flames that covered Maddoc slowly faded and died.

The wizard pushed himself to his elbows, gasping for breath. "Sindri." He looked up at Asvoria. "He means nothing to me. Kill him if you like." Catriona knelt beside Maddoc, helping him to sit up and face their captor.

"Nothing?" Asvoria purred. "That must be why you've spent the last several days teaching him the forbidden knowledge of the wizard's tower. Silly of you, Maddoc. Kender can't learn magic. You should know that, even if he is fool enough to believe that he might. It was a waste of your time, and his. Were you indulging in mindless charity, Maddoc? Or was it some other means of manipulating the poor, deluded creature?

"Oh, yes, Ophion told me everything. My loyal shapeshifter had plenty of time to discern your actions and develop a cama-raderie with your little team." She glanced at Davyn slyly. "A clever fellow, my shapeshifter, quite capable of sabotaging a few locks and encouraging a rockslide. It must have been so very easy to separate your party and get established among them as you, Davyn. All Ophion had to do was insult and intimidate Maddoc, and try to seize control. You're so very predictable. Even Nearra thought so." She laughed again as Davyn's face reddened at her cruel words. Catriona's heart sank.

"I know everything, you see. About all of you. And now I'm

going to destroy you, one by one." Her luminous smile held an evil delight. "Say farewell to your little companions, Maddoc. You're about to watch them all die." She stepped back toward the great golden throne, turning to run her fingers over the jewel-encrusted arms once more before taking a seat.

Catriona used the moment of Asvoria's distraction to speak to Maddoc. "Are you all right?" Catriona asked, keeping her head down so that only Maddoc and Davyn could hear her.

Maddoc shook his head to clear it, taking a quick survey of their position. "The injuries to my body are few; Asvoria is more interested in pain. She believes that she needs me alive. Regretfully, she does not."

"Maddoc," Catriona whispered in horror. "You don't know how to open the seal, do you?"

The old wizard shook his head, his salt-and-pepper hair falling before his eyes. "No. The Obsidian Heart was mentioned only vaguely in the texts—it is one of the best-kept secrets of Asvoria's tomb. I had hoped to have some time to study it, learn its magic, find the pattern . . . but no, Catriona. I cannot open it."

"I can." Davyn saw the stunned looks on their faces.

"So now it seems the tables are turned for us, Davyn," Maddoc murmured. He winced, gripping his ribs where the fire had seared his black velvet robes to charred rags. His fingers shook, the skin on his torso and face bruising in dark reddish contusions from Asvoria's torment. "Asvoria will torture me until she has what she wants, but she won't kill me—yet. She will not be as gentle with Sindri. Or with you."

"What are you going to do?" she whispered.

"I'm going to give her what she wants. If Davyn will help me." Maddoc's sober eyes took on a faint warmth. "Davyn, I must ask you to trust me again . . . and I hope that you will find it in yourself to do so."

"I'll never trust you, old man." Davyn's voice was hard.

Maddoc nodded, resigned. "Then there is only one other choice."

Aware that they were being watched, and that Asvoria would wait no longer, Maddoc lifted his eyes from the floor and stared toward the sorceress once more. "Very well, Asvoria. If for no other reason than to ensure that our deaths are swift, I will give you what you wish. Perhaps we can negotiate a trade—my life, and my magic restored, in exchange for the Aegis, and their lives." He gestured to the others, his face betraying no hint of feeling.

"Maddoc, no!" Catriona stared, stunned, as Asvoria laughed upon the throne. What was he doing?

"Well done! Oh, very well done, Maddoc." Asvoria clapped her hands with delight. "Their lives for yours, and my Aegis in exchange for your magic. Yes, very well done. If I didn't know better, I'd think this was your plan all along."

Davyn jumped forward, gripping the front of Maddoc's robes and dragging the injured wizard from the ground. Maddoc was too weak to resist, and Davyn gripped him tightly. "You played us for fools, Maddoc. We trusted you, and you only thought of your own power."

"Davyn," Catriona tried to intercede, much to Asvoria's delight. "It wasn't that way. You didn't see him in the palace." She stared at both men, unsure if the explosion between them was genuine. The fire in their eyes seemed all too real. Regardless, she had to play her part. "Davyn, stop it."

"No. This is the way it has to be, Catriona. I can't let her have the Aegis, and I won't let him give it to her." Davyn hurled the wizard to the floor once again and facing Catriona. "I was wrong to trust him. He doesn't care about us, Catriona. And if I get the chance again—I swear it—I'll see him dead."

"I'll take your deal, Maddoc," Asvoria said before Catriona could protest. Asvoria ran her fingers along her jaw, relishing her superiority. "But you will show me *now*, and I will return your power only after the Aegis is once more in my hand."

He did not flinch from Asvoria's eyes, struggling and failing to rise from his position on the floor. "Done."

She stepped from the golden throne once more, her honey-blonde hair swaying in a heavy cascade over her shoulders and down her back. She walked beyond the dark seal at her feet, stepping cautiously around its edges with her bare feet making soft sounds against the cold floor of the tomb. Her smile was arrogant, eager, as she gestured to Ophion. "Keep your blade on that one." She nodded to the still-limp Sindri. "And make sure that dear Davyn doesn't get any brave but foolish ideas."

"I cannot stand." Maddoc tried to rise, but his legs were too weak to hold him. He stared into Asvoria's eyes, refusing to bow before her. "The seal must be opened by touch. But it is trapped, and only I know how to unlock it safely. I will need to accompany you."

Asvoria's eyes narrowed. "You. Catriona. You are strong enough to lift him. Carry him to me." She swept across the gold-littered floor, her bare feet treading on the ransom of kings and nations.

Feeling Davyn's angry eyes upon her, Catriona bent and placed Maddoc's arm around her shoulder. Davyn had the key—Davyn, not her. But would he have helped Maddoc, even if given the chance? Catriona remembered Davyn's anger, the fire in his words. No. He would rather see Maddoc dead than Nearra free. Stumbling, Catriona helped the wizard stand, lifting him from the floor with gentle guidance. Each step was a slow agony, the wizard's tortured legs refusing to hold his weight.

"Maddoc," she hissed softly. "You can't do this, you can't give her the Aegis. You don't have the key."

"I know that very well, Catriona. Therefore, it should be obvious to you that I'm not going to." He kept his eyes down, his voice a mere murmur.

"What are you going to do?"

The wizard paused, very slightly, before answering. "Given that I have no other choice, we must draw the obvious conclusion. I intend to set off the trap that guards the Aegis."

The implications rocked Catriona, and she stumbled beneath his weight. She froze, trying to appear to be readjusting the wizard's arm around her neck. "That will kill you."

"And Asvoria," he said.

"You can't do this."

"I told you once that I cannot afford to take chances. I have the opportunity to destroy Asvoria. She is a danger to Krynn and to me, and I will end what I have begun."

"Catriona!" Asvoria's voice was sharp. She gestured from beside the alcove, pointing at Catriona and the wizard. "Don't dawdle or I will have Ophion begin his . . . carving."

Catriona shook her head. Her red hair brushing against the wizard's face as she began to shuffle forward under Maddoc's weight. "Maddoc, no. We can get out of this. I'll talk to Davyn, make him give you the key. You just have to trust—"

"Trust?" Maddoc began to laugh, but it rapidly degenerated into a bloodstained cough. His face was white and pained, and each plodding step toward Asvoria and the well seemed like an eternity. "No, Catriona. Trust is a two-bladed sword. If you cannot trust me, then I cannot trust you. That is the price. Davyn will never trust me. As, it seems, you will not. You knew the price of my assistance before we entered the tomb. It has not changed." He sighed. "No, Catriona. It is better that we live in the moment, as you do. Let this moment define me, then. Without trust, there is no other way."

Three more steps, and they would be at their destination. "You have it," Catriona whispered.

"What?" Maddoc said, surprised. He pretended to stumble, nearly falling from her grasp.

Catriona lifted him once more, holding tightly to his arm. Her words were serious. "There is another way, Maddoc, and I'm giving it to you. I swear to you, Maddoc. My sword, my duty, and my honor. If you would have them, then I give them to you freely. From this moment onward, I vow to serve as your protector." The words came easily, drawn from her soul by need and by—yes, conviction. "I shall continue to do so until you no longer need my service." She paused as they reached the well, and helped Maddoc sink down onto his knees beside the platinum doors against the chamber floor. While Asvoria was not looking, she whispered finally, "Find another way."

Maddoc's hand clenched Catriona's shoulder. He remained silent, aware of Asvoria's close attention upon them. Catriona stepped away slowly, unable to say more. Asvoria gripped Maddoc's arm, her hand searing him with magical force. The wizard gasped, struggling to remain standing.

"Enough, Maddoc. I've run out of patience. Now, open it." Asvoria gestured toward Ophion and the shapeshifter levered a bit more weight upon its knife. "Or else Sindri dies in agony, and you will get *nothing*."

Maddoc nodded, turning away from Catriona. "The keyhole is here." His hands touched the golden statue within the nearest alcove. He concentrated, feeling along its intricately engraved sides. As he did so, Catriona stepped back to Davyn's side, her eyes flickering from Sindri to Maddoc.

"What did you say to him?" Davyn hid his words behind a raised hand, pretending to rub his forehead.

"I told him that I trusted him." Catriona let her anger show, staring into Davyn's eyes. "He's going to kill himself, Davyn. Himself and Asvoria—Nearra," she corrected herself. "Because he has no other choice."

Davyn's face turned white. "He . . . he'd do that?"

"He doesn't know the key to the Obsidian Heart. You do. Without it, he has no other choice." Catriona gripped Davyn's shoulder hard enough to make the ranger wince. "He needs us, Davyn. If you care about Nearra—if you care about me—then show him the *key*."

Davyn stared past her at Maddoc as the old wizard's hand began to hover over the sigils inscribed on the platinum plate. Magic swirled up from beneath the metal. The closer Maddoc's hand drew to the platinum, the stronger the mist became. Anticipation ran like a chill up Catriona's spine. She squeezed Davyn's shoulder, her oath ringing in her ears. "Please, Davyn."

Maddoc glanced back at them, perhaps willing his last view to be of Catriona—but instead of pressing at random, Cat saw him pause. Beside her, Davyn lifted his hand an inch from his sword hilt— and pointed at the bronze dragon inscribed upon the tremendous platinum seal.

The wizard said nothing, gave no sign that he had seen Davyn's slight signal, but his hand slipped immediately to the mark.

He pressed lightly, and the howl that had been building around them changed tone, becoming a sigh of disappointment. The platinum shifted, slid to the side, and revealed a long chasm beneath.

"How appropriate," Asvoria murmured to herself. She stared at the sigil, recognizing it. "That is the mark of Captain Viranesh, the man who destroyed me on the eve of my ascension. The Aegis, which was once buried in his heart, should be protected with his mark. In a way, it still lies within him, an eternal blade within an eternal wound." Asvoria's tone was softer than Catriona would have believed possible . . . but when Asvoria saw the blade beneath, her eyes shone once more like amethyst fire.

The Aegis hung within the chasm, suspended by a silver thread so fine that Catriona could only see a faint, thin shimmer. One wrong move and the thread would snap—plunging the sword forever into the darkness below. Beneath the Aegis, an artesian well older than the Cataclysm, stretched down into oblivion.

But it was the sword that made Catriona gasp, her hand still clutching Davyn's shoulder. The hilt was magnificent, a single great malachite stone shimmering like a fourth moon in the glow of Asvoria's sterile, magical light. Thick emerald shards embedded within the upper inch of the sword's blade twinkled beneath the first light that had touched them in an aeon.

"My Aegis!" Cooing, Asvoria reached—but Maddoc caught her wrist in one hand.

"There may be a trap on the blade. If it is not handled properly, you will lose the Aegis forever. Let me withdraw it."

She nodded, sensing the wisdom in his words. Stepping back, Asvoria spread her arms and her hands began to glow. "Slowly, wizard . . . slowly. Remember that the blade you hold serves only me." Her threat was clear, and Maddoc nodded subserviently.

Catriona desperately tried to catch his eye, but he would not look toward her. What was he doing? Why had he twice stared toward the golden throne as though seeking knowledge in its glittering silence?

Cautiously, Maddoc began to slide the sword from its resting place within the well, trying not to stare past the blade into the unknowable depths below. Catriona saw him pause, closing his eyes to combat the vertigo, and then reach in once more, sliding his hand along the infinitely thin silver cord until he reached the hilt of the Aegis. This time, the sword came free.

It glittered and gleamed as he lifted it from the well, refracting the light into a thousand green shards that danced across the black walls of the tomb. Though the sword was both thick and broad, it seemed as light as a feather in the old wizard's hand. The malachite in the hilt twinkled, and then began to glow with a strange, crackling light.

"Mine, at last!" Asvoria laughed, reaching for the blade.

20   Echoes of Salvation, Shards of Pain

The rest happened so fast that Catriona could not remember which occurred first. Somewhere between Ophion's shriek and Asvoria's howl, she suddenly felt the weight of the Aegis landing solidly in her hand.

She saw Maddoc hurl the sword toward her, felt it land within her palm, and then a sudden charge of power rushed through her body like adrenalin.

The Aegis was blinding, its green light swelling to encompass Catriona's vision, her heart, and her mind. It was like nothing she had ever felt before—a perfect blending of mind and soul with the steel; every warrior's dream. Holding tightly to the hilt of the weapon, Catriona let the magic of the Aegis wrap around her. It felt for a moment as though she were of two minds, two convictions, one her own and one within the sword. So long as she held the blade, and knew her path, she would never be defeated.

Beside the tremendous darkness of the well, Asvoria screamed the words of a brief spell. Suddenly Maddoc was flung backward, slamming into the golden throne. The impact was tremendous, and Catriona heard something snap in Maddoc's body as the old 209 man struck the massive metal chair. He fell, and did not move again.

For a second a stab of fear pierced Catriona's heart. Conviction, she reminded herself as she stepped between Asvoria's anger and Maddoc's fallen form. "I won't let you hurt him," Catriona said bravely. "Any of them."

The sword glowed in her hand, its blade crackling with lightning the color of her eyes. Its heft and balance were perfect—unimaginably so. It was the most magnificent sword she had ever known. Yet even as her eyes beheld the Aegis in her hand, even as she heard Asvoria's vengeful howl, Catriona saw something more.

From the shadows behind the throne, the real Elidor emerged. In one swift movement, he stepped forward and plunged his knives into Ophion's back.

Ophion's body melded around the blades that pierced its skin, freeing the shapeshifter from the thief's sudden attack.

Sindri rolled to the side, awakened by Elidor's attack. The kender's swift foot connected with Ophion's knife, sending it hurtling toward the center of the wide room. The knife spun across the floor, slipping into the open well. It fell down the dark shaft, and vanished into the depths. Catriona never heard any sound of its landing. It seemed that the well was truly bottomless . . . empty and dark beyond words.

Stripped of its blade, the shapeshifter hissed angrily, and plunged its hand into one of the golden piles of treasure for another weapon. Catriona's heart leaped to see Elidor, and she grinned as Sindri winked, assuring her in a flash that he would be fine. Then she turned to face Asvoria's wrath.

"Cat!" She heard Davyn yell as he dived for his weapon. Out of the corner of her eye, Catriona saw him as he rolled across the floor. She stepped forward, ready to take on Asvoria, but suddenly her vision blurred, and a great, blinding light erupted from Asvoria's palm, engulfing Catriona in a pillar of white fire. Catriona was forced to look away, her eyes searing with the brilliance. The blast did not hurt her, and the fire of Asvoria's spell felt like only a faint warmth against her skin. Catriona grinned, knowing that the Aegis was protecting her.

When she could see again, Catriona strode forward, the Aegis held tightly in her grasp. Asvoria's face contorted with rage, and her shrill shriek split the air. Catriona turned toward Asvoria with fire in her eyes, only to see the sorceress hastily hurl a magical shield between them, distorting the air beyond. Catriona hesitated for an instant, allowing Asvoria to complete the shield—and Davyn understood. Behind the spell work raised by the terrible queen was Nearra's flesh, Nearra's face—but Asvoria's violet eyes.

"Davyn!" Cat shouted, squaring her shoulders and driving the Aegis against the magical wall. "Help Maddoc!" Davyn could hear the faint ring of uncertainty in her voice, but Catriona committed herself to each stroke.

The Aegis shivered in Catriona's hand, green lightning trickling up and down the stalwart blade. Asvoria's magical shield began to crumble, the framework of her magic splintered and at last destroyed by the strength of Catriona's arm. It was working! Catriona's mind reeled with the power of the weapon, and she struggled to control it. Was Maddoc alive? What if the Aegis wasn't enough? What if Asvoria's power was greater than that given by the sword?

Conviction, Catriona reminded herself, but the sword's fire dimmed and flickered for a moment. I have to have conviction.

"What's wrong, girl?" Asvoria hissed. "Having a little trouble with my sword? You're not ready for that kind of power. You never will be. You're a failure—a waste. You can't even protect yourself, much less your friends. Give up now, return my sword, and your death will be swift."

Serpents hissed from Asvoria's fingertips, striking out through the air toward Catriona. They came in great handfuls, and the air was filled with twisting, hissing snakes. Catriona cut through them with the Aegis, her blade spraying their blood through the air. Several reached her, but their fangs could not pierce Catriona's plate armor. Not to be denied, Asvoria caught one of the slithering serpents, whispering another spell as Catriona advanced past the well toward her.

Asvoria threw the final snake down, her fingers splayed. Before Catriona's eyes, the snake began to swell, doubling in size within a fraction of a second—and still growing. Catriona leaped forward—but Asvoria's next spell took far less time, and a rush of ice-cold frost sheered over Catriona's body, chilling her to the bone and causing her muscles to stiffen to a stop. Conviction, conviction . . . she felt herself failing, felt her own fear overcoming her as Asvoria laughed. Although the Aegis flared again, slowly casting off the petrification that threatened to freeze her muscles, Catriona could tell that the serpent would be larger than a man by the time she regained control over her body.

She could tell that Davyn saw it too. Ignoring Cat's plea for him to tend to the injured wizard, he slid down a mountain of jewels, hurling himself onto the serpent while it was still the size of a small pony. The beast was quick, and darted out from beneath him, rolling in the scattered rubies and sapphires and striking with fangs the size of thick fingers. He raised his sword. But the snake slipped through, and its fangs passed within inches of the ranger's throat.

Catriona's heart jumped in fear again, and the Aegis's flame fell farther along its blade.

"Davyn!" Catriona gasped, the ice's grip crushing air from her lungs. She struggled again, but Asvoria's frost spell held her still, and she was unable to do more than mutely stand and watch. She had failed him, as well . . .

She struggled as Davyn tried to wrap his arms around the now-giant serpent's neck, locking his hands at the limit of his reach. Catriona forced herself toward him, trying to free her body from the paralysis of Asvoria's spell. Step by step, she forced herself forward through a sheer act of will. She raised the crackling green lightning of the Aegis high above her head and prepared for combat against Asvoria's massive asp—no matter what the cost.

"I've got it covered," Davyn cried, hanging on to the thrashing serpent. "Stop Asvoria!"

Catriona nodded, worry in her eyes, but she followed his instructions. Asvoria stood beside the terrible, dark well that once held the Aegis, raising her hands in a complex motion to begin yet another debilitating blast of magic. Catriona's steps were slow, forced one at a time as though she were on parade march through the obsidian chamber, and Asvoria backed away as she chanted. Strange words of magic seared the air. Catriona raised the sword again, staring at the tremendous blade and willing it to protect her as it had before—but this time, the Aegis truly failed her. It did not shimmer against Asvoria's spell, though the greedy lightning still flickered up and down the blade.

I failed them . . . I failed them . . . The words echoed in Catriona's mind as Asvoria's laughter rang through the chamber. Nearra's laughter. She'd sworn to protect Nearra . . . and Maddoc. Now her friends were slaves to an evil sorceress—or dead by that hand.

Cat saw Davyn's hands slide around the neck of the still-thrashing serpent, gripping the flat of the blade in one palm and the pommel in the other. He hung on for dear life as the snake swelled and grew stronger under Asvoria's spell. Its fangs were

DRAGON SWORD

213

as long as daggers, dripping poison that pitted the gold baubles scattered on the ground where its body struggled for freedom. Davyn couldn't let go of the beast, or it would certainly strike faster than he could defend himself. As the serpent swelled ever larger, the sharp edge of Davyn's blade began to sink into its neck. He tightened his grasp, pushing the blade ever further into the asp's flesh. The beast flailed near the edge of the well, and Davyn's feet kicked out over dark nothingness. He gripped tighter, refusing to let go. If the serpent fell . . . he would go with it into the depths.

But he was still fighting, Catriona reminded herself.

Asvoria completed her spell, and the light of the Aegis flickered and died as it rushed over Catriona. The magic lashed out like a great white wave, curling through the air. It struck Catriona, and she was hurled ten feet backward into the air. Catriona flew toward the obsidian wall. There was a distinct crack as she struck it, and her head snapped back to meet with the wall. Davyn yelled her name, but Catriona did not hear him. She slumped inside an alcove, the golden statue of a long-dead warrior standing silent vigil over her fallen form.

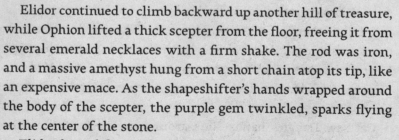

Elidor continued to climb backward up another hill of treasure, while Ophion lifted a thick scepter from the floor, freeing it from several emerald necklaces with a firm shake. The rod was iron, and a massive amethyst hung from a short chain atop its tip, like an expensive mace. As the shapeshifter's hands wrapped around the body of the scepter, the purple gem twinkled, sparks flying at the center of the stone.

Elidor leaped forward, a knife in each hand, dancing on the slope of gold. His knives would be of no use against the massive jeweled rod, but his swiftness allowed him to press the flat of his blade against Ophion's wrist, turning the blow aside so that it slammed into the ground near Sindri's head. The elf lashed out with a boot, pounding into Ophion's chest and sending gold flying in a glittering arc.

Sindri seemed to have extricated himself from their combat. He now stood on the seat of the throne and peered about the room. Ophion struck at a chest of jewels balanced in the pile, forcing Elidor to leap back as his footing avalanched away toward the bottom of the pile.

Elidor's knives flicked back and forth like claws, cutting at Ophion's arms each time the shapeshifter's heavy weapon swung past. Though Elidor couldn't get a good blow through Ophion's guard, the shapeshifter was already wounded and breathing heavily. Elidor only had to keep the mace from crushing his ribs, and eventually, weariness would work against Ophion. There would be an opening.

Ophion feinted, drawing the mace in a circle over its head and reversing the weapon's trajectory in a flash. Elidor grinned. Before he could extricate himself from the sliding rubble beneath his feet, there was a trail of purple smoke and a crackling sound from the amethyst in Ophion's hands. Both the shapeshifter and the elf started in surprise as a rainbow ray flew out of the heavy, jeweled scepter and scattered through the air like a prism. Elidor tried to leap out of its path, but his foot twisted on a pile of small statuary and he slid slightly into his jump. The imbalance caused Elidor's leap to be a half-second slower than he had intended, and the edge of one of the rays of the prism slid down across his leg.

A rush of drowsiness flooded through Elidor's veins as the purple light struck him. It became a massive struggle simply to land on his feet again. Each movement of his body felt like pins and needles lancing through his skin, ripping into him as though his entire body had fallen asleep. He tried to shake off the debilitating effects of the mace's ray, fighting to remain on his feet despite the wash of dizziness and the pain. Ophion smiled, seeing its opponent slow, and marched toward the staggering thief, the heavy mace still in hand. Elidor looked down, hoping to find Sindri nearby, but the kender was no longer by the throne. Instead, he knelt beside the crumpled form of Maddoc and seemed to be frantically listening for breath from the old man's lips.

Fighting to retain consciousness despite the terrible weariness that gripped him, Elidor dodged the mace's swing once more. He heard the stone wall beside his head crack as the mace connected. The lingering effect of the mace's strange ray prickled through Elidor's body, dulling his reflexes and making every move an agony. Ophion pounded again with the scepter. Elidor ducked and punched out, trying to drive his knives into the shapeshifter's chest. The pain that lanced through his arm made him slow, and Ophion dodged to the side, taking only a strike from the pommel of Elidor's steel, and not the cutting edge of the blade.

"You killed Baron Darghellen," Elidor rasped, his eyes narrow and glinting as yellow as the gold that surrounded them. It was a strange place to hear the Baron's name echoing—a name that Elidor had always connected with green grass, soft breezes, and tall mountains. "And you left your 'priest' behind to kill Vael."

Ophion responded tonelessly. "I sense from your words that the Baron's daughter still lives. A pity. I will have to return to Tarrent and correct that failure."

The threat to Vael enraged Elidor, and he lashed out with both knives despite the agony in his muscles. The blades slashed Ophion, forcing the shapeshifter to ripple its flesh in order to allow the knives to pass through. Not swiftly enough, and strange blackish-scarlet blood trickled down Ophion's arm in the wake of Elidor's wrath. "You won't touch her, you filthy, inhuman creature," Elidor panted. "I'll kill you first, I swear it."

"Only me?" Ophion taunted. "I am not important, Elidor. I am not the threat. I am only a servant, bound by the laws of my people and constrained by the command of my queen." The scepter pounded down again, and caught Elidor's wrist. There was a sharp cracking sound, and one of Elidor's knives fell to the ground. Elidor staggered back, rage still burning in his heart. He clutched his other knife firmly, weaving it in and out. He was not yet defeated.

"Asvoria has plans for Tarrent, Elidor, and those plans involve blood and pain." Ophion's too-blue eyes glowed faintly in the darkness. "You cannot stop her. You will not hurt her. When you look at her, you see Nearra, your friend. But I, and the people of Tarrent, we see a queen, reborn to bring a terrible and merciless death to those who defy her."

The taunt enraged Elidor, and he felt his face flush. He raged forward, picking up the shapeshifter and hurling it backward with strength beyond the limit of an elf. Ophion kept hold of the massive scepter, bringing it down onto Elidor's shoulder and forcing the elf to let go even as the two plunged down a golden hill and crashed into the golden throne. Ophion fell limp, the fight leaving the shapeshifter's body like the rattling breath of a dying man. Elidor stood over the creature, knives bared, his eyes shining in the reflected light of the steel.

21   Bitter Revenge

Asvoria's bare feet stepped lightly across her treasures, a victorious smile on her face.

"At last," she crooned, reaching down to take the Aegis from Catriona's fallen hand.

"No!" The scream took Asvoria by surprise, and a small form struck her broadside, knocking her to the ground before she could recover the sword. Sindri gripped Asvoria's arms, trying to pin them to her sides. "Nearra!" he yelled, "Nearra, wake up! I know you're in there! We need your help!"

Asvoria rolled aside, pushing Sindri's body off of her. Sindri fought bravely, but Nearra had been a worker in her life, not a pampered aristocrat. She lifted the kender with little effort, shoving him aside even though he clutched her shoulders and clung to her dress.

"Nearra!" Sindri called again, shaking her. "Nearra come out—"

Before he could finish his desperate plea, Asvoria struck him with the back of her fist. Her hand left an imprint on the kender's white face, reddening his already bruised cheek as he reeled away from her.

"You fool," she hissed. "Your friend is dead."

"She's not dead." Catriona forced the words from a dry, parched throat. She tried to rise, but fell back again, clutching the Aegis in white-knuckled fingers. Her ankle was badly sprained; the twisted tendon burned with every movement she made. "Not as long as we don't give up on her."

"Foolish girl," the sorceress spat, her violet eyes terrifying. "I am Asvoria. None can stand before me—especially not some brainless farm girl. Nearra has been erased from the face of this world, and only Asvoria remains!" But her hand shook as she began to cast another spell, and the magical energies would not coalesce.

"Perhaps Nearra is alive after all," Catriona said grimly.

Asvoria laughed, a crystalline, shattering sound. She batted the Aegis aside, and Catriona's hand fell weakly to the ground, still holding the sword in a forced, deadly grip. The warrior tried once again to stand, but the landing had taken too much out of her, and though she struggled, her legs were as feeble as a kitten's.

"Cat!" Sindri cried, leaping to her side. "I'll help you get up. We've got to stop her—"

"No, little kender," Asvoria preened, sensing that victory was near. "Give up all hope of stopping me. You do not have the ability, or the power." She turned back to the wounded Catriona. "You may have been told that I cannot take the Aegis from you until you surrender it. It is so. But there are many ways to make people do what you wish them to do. Especially"—she smiled wickedly, and her voice dropped into a threat— "if they have friends."

"I'll fight you!" Sindri raised his hands, structuring them as Maddoc taught him. He glanced back at the unconscious wizard, and then began an incantation. Asvoria only laughed. Sindri struggled, face reddening, fingers twisting in a mockery of Asvoria's powerful spell. He chanted, repeating the words that he had been given, and placing all of his will behind their form.

The only answer was silence.

Again, Asvoria laughed, an empty, hollow sound. "Kender can't do magic, Sindri. Anything else the old man told you was a lie." She walked toward Sindri, arms open, daring him to draw forth power from the air. "Oh, Maddoc, such excellent friends you've made. This one believes he can learn your secrets, another remembers a life as your child, and the girl . . . well, she has her own intentions, doesn't she?"

Sindri stood between the sorceress and her prey, refusing to step aside or be intimidated by Asvoria's powerful magic. Unlike the others, not even a faint hint of fear touched the kender's heart. Still, as Asvoria advanced, Sindri began to show doubt, and it nearly broke Catriona's heart.

Catriona struggled to rise again as a hopeless expression spread across Sindri's face. Her leg failed her, and she pitched forward, still keeping her tight grip on the Aegis in her right hand. Sindri redoubled his efforts, desperate to prove Asvoria wrong and produce a magical spell.

Nothing happened.

Catriona's legs shuddered, threatening to drop her once more to the floor. But she refused to give up her struggle so long as her friends were in danger. She pressed her back against the obsidian wall and gripped the arm of the golden statue at her side.

"Stop, Asvoria. Face me, or die." The threat felt weak, even to her, but the Aegis flickered dimly at her words. Conviction, Cat reminded herself, cursing her own weakness. The sword began to flare again, but the lightning was sporadic and uncontrolled. Asvoria scowled, realizing that her magic would not work on Catriona so long as the Aegis protected her.

The sorceress flexed her fingers as though choosing her next assault. She strode toward the kender, and he fell back into the center of the room. All the while, Sindri continued to shake his arms, trying to force the incantation to work as Asvoria approached him.

"Leave them ... alone ... ," Catriona repeated, staggering forward, only to fall once more to her knees as her legs collapsed beneath her weight. The impact of the wall had been considerable. Any normal person would have broken their back from the sheer force of the blow, but Catriona refused to give up, gritting her teeth and pushing up once more to her feet.

"What will you do, warrior? You have barely strength to swing a sword." The sorceress flicked her fingers as though brushing water from the tips, and Sindri rose into the air under her power. With a gesture, she hurled him across the tomb toward the dark well. Gasping, the kender caught himself just before he passed the edge of the well and hurtled into darkness. He hung from the edge of the well, his legs kicking gently above a vast nothingness below.

"I could kill him with a thought, plunge him into the darkness, and you would never see your little 'wizard' again." She smiled pleasantly at Catriona, as though she were suggesting a picnic or a day in the sun. "And I will do it ... unless you surrender *my* sword."

"No!" On the other side of the tomb, the mighty snake fell to the ground, head severed at last from its tremendous body. Davyn stood over the bloodstained corpse. He lifted his sword, shaking the blood from his blade and stepped forward. Though the battle with the snake had wearied him, determination shone in his eyes.

"One of us will stop you, Asvoria. You will fail." Davyn raised his sword to his shoulder and stepped between the sorceress and her prey. She did not fight him, spreading her arms as though to embrace him.

"Davyn, dear Davyn." The voice, soft and pleasant, sent a chill down Catriona's spine. She couldn't believe how much it sounded like Nearra. "Come to me, Davyn. Love me. Spend the rest of your days with me." Asvoria walked toward him, crossing the room with long, elegant strides.

"No, Davyn!" Cat yelled. "Don't listen to her!"

"I have need of a consort with your strength and determination. You could be general of my armies; master of my castles, second only to me in power beneath the three moons of Krynn." Asvoria's smile was bright and genuine, and she reached out to touch Davyn's face. For a moment, the ranger's face relaxed, his eyes seeking hers desperately, as though looking for something he'd lost. In that frozen instant, Cat felt certain that they had lost him, that he'd found something reflected in her eyes that called him home.

"Davyn!" she yelled again. "She's *not* Nearra!"

Catriona saw Sindri crawling out of the well, his quick kender reflexes allowing him to grasp small imperfections in the stone at the lip and drag himself upward. The kender was now on the far side of the opening, skittering across the floor to Maddoc's unmoving form.

Unaware, Asvoria focused her full attention on Davyn's frozen stare. She pressed her body against Davyn's, her smile holding his eyes. "What will you do?" She laughed again at Davyn's discomfort. "Destroy the woman you love?"

"Sometimes love means you can't hurt someone. And sometimes, it means that you *must* . . ." The voice wasn't Davyn's, and neither was the knife that spun in the air like a shooting star. Now weaponless, Elidor stood over the fallen Ophion, the shapeshifter's eyes following the knife with horror and dread. Catriona could tell that Elidor had meant to finish the shapeshifter with his final blow, but Asvoria's taunts had drawn the elf's attention away from the fight before him—his attention and his rage.

The knife sank into Asvoria's back, tearing through silk damask and skin alike and sinking to the hilt. She gasped, eyes opening wide, and her scream echoed through the chamber.

"Nearra!" Davyn caught her as she stumbled forward into his arms. "No! Nearra? Can you hear me?" Davyn tried to grasp her, but she slid through his arms to the floor. He clutched her to him, holding her body tenderly and feeling warm blood flowing over his fingertips. "Talk to me. Please. Nearra?" For a moment, Catriona thought she saw a flicker of Nearra's gentle soul within her wide, staring eyes, but there was no audible response. She lay limply in Davyn's arms, blood spreading from the knife that lodged between her shoulders.

22 THE PRICE

Elidor!" Davyn lifted his head, tears streaming down his eyes. He screamed in rage. "What have you done?!"

The elf stood by the golden throne, his face uncompromising, his features set with anger and unchanging conviction. "I did what had to be done. To save you."

"You're a hypocrite, Elidor." Davyn clutched Nearra against him, and Cat could see the shallow rise and fall of her breath against his shoulder. "You didn't do this for me. You did this for Vael."

Elidor's face was stricken as though cut to the quick, but he said nothing.

Before he could speak, Asvoria's violet eyes opened once more—and in them was a terrible hatred. From her position in Davyn's arms, she thrust out her hand to grip Davyn's chest. A blue light began to shine out from beneath her palm. Speaking a word of terrible power, Asvoria's fingers morphed into claws, piercing Davyn's chest. Davyn gasped. She uncurled herself from Davyn's embrace, her right hand still gripping his chest.

"You . . . will all . . . die . . ." She reached out her other hand, wounded as she was, and another shaft of blue light branched 225 out from her to strike Elidor. The elf fell to his knees, jaw falling open in sudden, overwhelming pain. His face turned white and pale, his weaponless hands shaking.

Asvoria hissed, "You do not have the power to kill me, halfbreed. You only condemn your beloved—and your friends—to an even more terrible fate."

Her power drew upon their life energy, sucking out their strength to fuel her body. As Catriona watched, the wound in Asvoria's back began to slowly close, and Elidor's blade slipped from between her shoulder blades to the ground. She was feeding on their strength, adding it to hers, using their life-force to heal her body. As the fleeting seconds flew past, Davyn's face, contorted by shock and betrayal, became gaunt. His body was riveted by her power, unable to do anything as Asvoria drained away the very essence of his being—to heal herself.

"Asvoria!" Catriona screamed. Tears streamed down her cheeks as she struggled to rise. "I'll kill you!"

"You can try, girl," Asvoria sneered, growing stronger with each passing second. "And you will fail, as you always have. If you had been able to wield my sword, none of this would have happened. But you were weak. Weak, and soon, you will be dead. And a dead body is as good as a willing one, for my purposes. I will have my Aegis either way."

By the throne, Elidor sagged, barely able to hold himself up. He pitched forward onto his hands, shuddering as Asvoria's dark magic consumed his soul. He was an elf, and his life-force was strong—but that only made it all the more horrible. As Davyn grew cadaverous and gaunt, Elidor became nearly ethereal, his skin losing its healthy color and turning to an almost ghostly pallor. As Catriona watched, Elidor's bright eyes closed, and blue veins began to show through the skin on his face and hands. In only moments, he had gone from strength to suffering.

"Give me the Aegis." Asvoria's eyes shone with pleasure. She grew stronger with each passing second. With a quick motion, she clenched her hand. Davyn moaned in pain. "Or I'll rip this one's heart out and throw it at your feet."

The blue energy flowing from Davyn and Elidor was healing her wound all too quickly, and any trace of Nearra's soft, gentle presence was long vanished from her smile.

Catriona shook her head. "No . . . I . . ." She wanted to fight, to charge, to plunge her sword into an enemy's flesh and feel the surge of victory—but were those thoughts her own, or did they belong to the weapon that pulsed in her hand? Everything seemed strange, almost too clear. Her friends were suffering. She had to save them . . . but the effort of moving was almost too much to bear.

Elidor shivered, his breath coming in sharp, shuddering gasps.

Asvoria sneered at the elf's fallen form. "Ophion," Asvoria called to her shapeshifter. "That one is of no more use to me."

The shapeshifter rose, wincing from the grievous wounds that Elidor had inflicted. The marks of Elidor's knives criss-crossed its flesh, wounds too deep to simply meld away. Its movements were slow and injured, but it staggered to Asvoria's side. Ophion stood over the elf's crouched, gaunt form, blue eyes reflecting the ethereal light of Asvoria's beam. "With pleasure."

"You should have killed me when you had the chance." Ophion's toneless menace roared like an undercurrent as it swung the mace upward.

Catriona screamed.

The mace descended, and Elidor, trapped by Asvoria's magic, could not evade the blow.

"Vael," Elidor whispered, his eyes closing as the heavy mace fell.

Catriona surged forward to her feet, ignoring the shooting pain through her injured leg. *"NO!"*

Catriona took three steps forward, her sprained ankle protesting each movement—but she had to see.

The elf's collapsed body was ravaged by Asvoria's spell. Blood dripped from the place on his skull where the mace had made contact. He wasn't breathing, and he lay where he had fallen as though he would never rise again.

"No . . . Elidor . . ." Catriona protested, the Aegis limp between her fingers.

"Still want to save your friends, my dear? Or is Nearra's death becoming more and more attractive?" The blue light faded and died from Elidor's chest. "Or do I kill Davyn next? And then the kender . . ." Her eyes wandered to Sindri, a purple-cloaked lump still bent over Maddoc's broken body as if attempting to protect the fallen wizard.

"Stop it." Catriona sank to her knees beside Elidor's body. Ophion stood above her still holding the jeweled mace.

"Leave them alone, Asvoria. You want your sword? Then fight me." Despite the agony of her twisted leg, Catriona was serious, and she raised the Aegis in a warrior's pose.

"And give you a martyr's death? No, Catriona. I don't want to kill you. I want you to *fail*. Either in keeping my sword, or in saving your friends. Either way, I want you to live with that failure for a very, very long time." She relished Catriona's pain. "Give me the sword."

Her face hardened as Catriona paused. "No?" Asvoria's fingers sank deeper into Davyn's chest. "Then he is next . . ."

23 SPLINTERED NIGHTMARE

Maddoc." Sindri shook the wizard. Asvoria's spell had seriously wounded the wizard, and he seemed barely able to hold onto consciousness. "It didn't work. The magic that you taught me—it didn't work." Maddoc lay in the kender's arms. Sindri shook him again, willing Maddoc to stay awake.

"Wake up. Get up. Fight her," Sindri pleaded. "You don't give up, Maddoc. You're not that kind. No matter what happens to you, you keep fighting."

"Sindri." Maddoc's eyes fluttered. The sounds of fighting around them were dying, but Sindri couldn't afford to look up. Each shuddering breath was more ragged than the first, but Sindri kept calling to him, forcing him to listen.

"Asvoria's here. Do you hear me, Maddoc? You were right. She's here. And she's more powerful than ever. You have to wake up." Exasperated, Sindri shook the wizard roughly. "Maddoc!"

"Asvoria—Asvoria . . ." Maddoc's eyes blinked. "Yes. I hear you, Sindri." The wizard looked around. "What's happening?"

"She's winning. You have to get up. The spell you taught me—I tried it, just like you said, but it didn't work. I don't have magic." **229**

"Foolish kender," the wizard replied, placing his hand on Sindri's shoulder. Maddoc tried to sit up, winced, and then lay still once more. "Of course the spell didn't work," Maddoc rasped, his voice hoarse. "You only have half of the incantation, Sindri. I was going to walk you through the rest of it after we reached the tomb. There wasn't time to teach you all of it." He coughed. "I never expected you to face her alone."

"I knew it!" Sindri's eyes grew wide. "I knew it!" He grabbed Maddoc, half-embracing and half-crushing him. "Get up. Show me the rest." The kender tried to push Maddoc into a sitting position. Frantically, he laced his fingers within Maddoc's weathered hands. "Now."

"Sindri." Maddoc took his hand and pulled the kender close. "I don't want you to cast this spell. I thought I did, but with everything we've been through—now that I know you—I think that I was wrong to have taught you as I did."

"Why?"

"The spell is powerful. It is too powerful for such an inexperienced caster. And the only way for me to ensure that it will work is to summon the power of Nuitari. The black moon, Sindri." His words drew the kender's entire attention, and Sindri stared at Maddoc for a long moment. The two seemed to be in a world alone, and Sindri felt his mind reeling with the implications of Maddoc's words.

The kender blanched. "A . . . dark spell? I can't—I can't do a dark spell. I'm going to be a purple wizard, Maddoc. Not a black robe."

Maddoc coughed violently, the pain in his body rippling through his muscles as he tried again to sit up. A faint trickle of blood appeared at the corner of his mouth, and Sindri used the hem of his purple cloak to wipe it away. "There are only two ways to stop Asvoria now, Sindri. The Aegis must be used against her, or it must be destroyed."

Catriona's yell split the air, and the warrior staggered across the tomb on her twisted leg, collapsing beside the fallen form of Elidor. Over her, Ophion raised his bloody scepter once more. Sindri couldn't see Elidor's fallen form, but the tears streaking Catriona's face told the story he had been so afraid to see. "Oh, Paladine! Not Elidor," Sindri whispered. The fallen elf did not move, and blood trickled from behind the throne, spilling down the dais like the scarlet hem of a royal cloak.

Asvoria knelt over Davyn's pained body, her fingers buried in the ranger's bloody chest. Sindri heard her words as clear as the bell ringing in his village. " . . . he is next . . ." Catriona's face hardened, as though she knew that she had no more options.

She surged to her feet, her sprained ankle twisting beneath her weight and her face turning as white as a ghost from the massive pain. She had pushed her broken body too far. Sindri knew she had made her choice to die in battle, fighting Asvoria until her last breath rather than giving up either her friends or the blade.

"Tell me what to do." Sindri's usually cheerful voice was serious.

"Sindri, it isn't that easy."

"No, it's exactly that easy. I asked for this, Maddoc. I asked you to show me magic. Now I'm asking you again: teach me the spell, and let me save my friends." He stared into the wizard's eyes, unflinching. Sindri had made his decision, and Maddoc could tell that nothing would change the kender's mind now.

"They will hold it against you, Sindri. You'll become as mistrusted as I am, in their eyes. Even if you save them, they will blame you." Maddoc could see that his words of warning fell on deaf ears.

Behind the kender, Catriona's blade flickered as Catriona fought. Sindri knew that she was losing hope. There was no escape from her situation. She couldn't defeat Asvoria; she couldn't save her friends. She believed that she would fail, one way or the other, and that alone had destroyed her ability to master the sword. Sindri watched, and he could tell that without the weapon's magical protections, Catriona would soon be defeated. And when that happened—they would all die.

She'd given up.

"Maddoc. Show me." Sindri was serious. Everyone was depending on him, and if he didn't do something, Asvoria would win. He pulled Maddoc up, helping the wizard to his knees. They were nearly eye level. "I'll do whatever it takes—but I have to do something. If this is the way to save them, then I choose it. She killed Elidor . . . I can't . . . I won't watch them all die."

Something changed in Maddoc then, and he offered no more argument. He wrapped one arm around the kender's shoulders. Taking the young kender's hands, Maddoc laced his own fingers over them and began guiding Sindri through the complex motions of the spell.

"*Astrath nevar tonnai Nuitari . . .*" Maddoc began, and Sindri repeated every word exactly as the wizard spoke them.

Catriona wielded the Aegis with desperate intent. Ophion had tried to take advantage of her, striking from behind. But Catriona knew the shapeshifter, and guessed its intention. With a deft twist of her blade, she sent the mace crashing to the ground. Even on only one good leg, Catriona's reflexes were as quick as a lion, tearing into the shapeshifter with the full force of her anger and desperation.

"Kill her! Get my sword!" Asvoria hissed, but the shapeshifter was unable to comply. It lashed out again and again with the mace, only to be driven back from the red-haired warrior by her skill with the blade. Yet despite Catriona's desperate rage, it was obvious that her passion would only carry her so far—and she could do nothing about Davyn's predicament.

" . . . *meditrai deveranis Nuitari* . . ." Sindri's chant continued, guided by Maddoc's ashen-faced whisper. The spell was far more complex than Sindri could have imagined, and he felt powers rising around him that nearly blinded him in their intensity. When Sindri felt his strength fading, Maddoc's whisper offered a tie to the material world that reassured the kender. Each motion was more difficult than the last, and the magic surrounding them prickled Sindri's flesh, bursting the blood vessels within the kender's eyes and hands so that his vision was dim and red-shrouded.

"Maddoc, I can't . . . "

Without breaking the chant of the spell, the wizard murmured, *"You will."*

Only Asvoria's complete obsession with the Aegis prevented her from noticing the shift in the magical currents of the room, the glow that began around Sindri and Maddoc's combined hands, culminating in the final incantation of the destructive spell. " . . . *encantari votae nihils!"*

There was a rush of power that knocked Sindri from his feet. He held his arms out, landing roughly on his knees but maintaining eye contact with his target. In an instant, the Aegis began to glow—first green, with lightning bursting from the steel, then white, like fire released from an inferno. Catriona's scream was muffled by the detonation of the spell, ricocheting through the tomb with the sharp crack of shattering steel.

The Aegis's light flashed once more, and then went out. Steel shards exploded from Catriona's hands, leaving them cut and torn. Catriona's scream echoed through the chamber, and the broken fragments of the Aegis fell to the ground.

24   FALLING INTO DARKNESS

N o!" Asvoria howled, and she staggered backward. Catriona seemed equally shocked, her bleeding hands still grasping the pommel of the now-shattered sword.

The sorceress sank to her knees, touching the shards upon the ground as one might caress the face of a lost child. "My Aegis . . ." she screamed again. "Ruined!"

Released at last, Davyn hobbled to Catriona's side and sank to his knees against her. He held her raw hands in his. "I would have died, Davyn," she whispered, the hilt of the Aegis falling from her bloodied fingers. "I would rather have died than give up the sword."

Nearby, Asvoria moaned. Davyn readied himself for the blast of magic that was certain to come. Without the Aegis, they could not protect themselves from the sorceress' spells—but even as he watched, something changed in Asvoria's face.

Her voice shifted from cold impassivity to desperate loss. "I can't—I can't—" She tried to pull herself together, but in this moment of weakness, something else fought from within. She took a great, shuddering breath, and the Aegis shards fell through her hands. 235

"Davyn . . ." The girl's voice was soft, and her eyes were quiet, calm—and as blue as a summer ocean. Davyn suddenly understood.

"Nearra."

Ophion stepped forward past Elidor's fallen body. "Milady! My queen!" Ophion said urgently. "Return to us!" The shapeshifter pushed past Davyn and Catriona before they could react. Before the shapeshifter reached her, the young girl stood and took a step backward. Behind her were piles of gold and jewels, the strong monument of the golden throne—and the opening to the chasm that had once held the Aegis.

She looked over her shoulder, across the gaping well, and caught Sindri's eye. The kender clutched burn-scarred hands to his chest, still stunned by the power of the spell that had broken the Aegis. "Take care of them, Sindri," Nearra said softly, and the kender in the purple cloak stared in hollow shock. "Don't try to save me. Save yourselves."

"Nearra," Catriona burst out, "don't go!"

"I have to, Cat. I can't hold her back for long. The loss of the Aegis weakened her—but she'll return." Nearra took another step backward, her white foot balanced precariously over the edge of the echoing depths of the well. "When she does, nothing will stop her. She'll take vengeance on you all."

"Stop," Ophion called. Its hand grasped only air as she stepped backward once more.

"Run, Davyn," Nearra said softly. "Run." Her eyes, soft and blue, caught his, and something that could not be spoken passed between them. She stepped back once more. And she fell.

The well was wide and dark and bottomless. Ophion froze, pausing at the edge of the well in rigid horror. Nearra screamed as she plunged into the bottomless pit, her eyes flashing from pale blue to bright violet before she vanished into the darkness.

Without hesitation, Ophion dived after her. Sindri had a fleeting glimpse of wings sprouting from the shapeshifter's shoulders in the instant before the darkness swallowed him as well.

"Paladine," Sindri whispered.

Catriona was the first to recover from her shock. "It won't stop Asvoria for long. Ophion will catch her and draw her up again, and she'll be as strong as ever. Nearra's right. We have to get out of here before she returns. Get me a rope out of our packs." In a few seconds, she had tied two long scroll-tubes to her leg, the gold and jewels twinkling pleasantly. It would serve to brace her sprained ankle—for now.

"That's the most expensive splint I've ever seen." Davyn's humor came flatly, his smile weak and faded. His hand gripped the marks on his chest, and his half-laugh became a hoarse and painful cough.

"You're badly hurt, Davyn." Catriona turned to Sindri. "Sindri, I need your cloak to bind his wounds."

Sindri removed it, bundling the purple material gently. Despite the fact that he was still shaking, he carried it to Catriona and placed it in her hands. "Here, Cat. Take it. I don't need it anymore, anyway."

Catriona reached out and hugged the kender. "You did it, Sindri. You really did." She began binding the ranger's chest, trying to staunch the blood flow before it became critical.

Sindri glanced back at Maddoc, who still sat near the golden throne. "Maybe I did, Cat." His eyes traveled to the fallen body of Elidor. "But not nearly soon enough."

Davyn winced as Cat bound his wounds, his eyes occasionally becoming dull and unfocused. "That's not your fault, Sindri." The pain in his tone was clear, and Davyn did not seem to be able to bring himself to look at Elidor's silent form of the elf.

"He's dead, isn't he?" Sindri whispered.

Catriona paused, her eyes flickering to their fallen companion. From his seat beside Elidor's body, Maddoc answered, "He's not breathing. He has no pulse. I've already checked. Nothing." Catriona turned back to Davyn, tightening his bindings and ignoring the tears that ran down her cheeks.

Sindri ran back to Maddoc. "You have to get up now. Didn't you hear Nearra? Asvoria's coming back. We have to get out of here. Get up. Hold onto my shoulders, I'll help carry you. I'm not going to let her kill anyone else."

Maddoc pushed the kender away, gently. "No, Sindri." he sighed gently. "I'm not going with you."

"What?" Catriona's head snapped around. "You can't be serious. Maddoc, you can't fight her. We have to leave, get out of here. Davyn needs a healer, and there's no way we can defeat Asvoria right now."

"I'm not going to fight her." Maddoc's twisted smile was a shadow of its former mocking sneer. "She won't care about me, Catriona. She has other things to concern her now that the Aegis is gone. If I go with you now, I will only slow you down. My wounds are severe."

"Maddoc, I have to protect you. I swore—"

He cut her off before she could continue. "You swore to obey me, and you will do so, Catriona. Go. Now. Before she returns." He was serious, allowing no argument, and Catriona paled. She nodded, once, sharply, and then turned back to Davyn.

"No." Sindri protested. "Catriona, we can't leave him!"

Catriona pushed to her feet, testing her splint before reaching to help Davyn stand. Davyn stumbled, holding tight to her shoulders as he slipped in and out of consciousness. "Sindri, help me. I can't carry him by myself, not with my leg like this."

"Nearra?" Davyn whispered. Catriona looked at Davyn, and his eyes closed.

"Hurry, Sindri. We don't have much time."

"But what about Elidor? We can't leave him!"

"Sindri." Maddoc took the kender's shoulders and stared into his eyes. "You can't take Elidor with you. He's gone. Carrying his body will only slow you and make it that much easier for Asvoria to find you. As for me, I am an old man, but I am not a weak man. I will follow you, if I can. You aren't leaving me here. You're saving my son's life."

Gently, the wizard removed Elidor's knife belt, his pack, his lockpicks, and his traveling cloak. "Now, take these. Some day you may find you'll need them." He wrapped everything in the cloak and handed it to Sindri.

Sindri nodded. Then, spontaneously, he threw his arms around Maddoc's shoulders and hugged him. After a moment, the kender grabbed hold of Elidor's things, and hurried to Catriona's side. He wrapped his arm around Davyn's waist. "All right," he said roughly. "I'm ready."

"Take care of him, Maddoc," Catriona said from the entrance to the main chamber of the tomb. Her eyes paused, taking in the image of Elidor, collapsed at the base of the golden throne. It burned into her mind, and a lump rose in her throat, but she forced the tears away and concentrated on Davyn's shallow breathing.

"Goodbye, Catriona," was all that the wizard replied.

The sun shone brilliantly on Catriona's face, like the rise of a new dawn after a long and nightmarish night. She helped Sindri onto Davyn's horse, trusting him to hold the ranger steady while they traveled. Palanthas was too far away, but there was a small village along the main road back to the city. There would certainly be healers there, and Davyn was still strong. He wove in and out of consciousness, dreaming of Nearra, dark tombs, and someone named Ayudar. Once, he called out to Elidor, but then fell silent.

Catriona tied his steed's reins to her saddle, wincing as her sprained ankle bounced against the horse's side. She looked back at the mountainside, the rough scar of the collapsed area barely hiding the opening to Asvoria's palace. Somewhere deep beneath the earth was Asvoria rising? Had she killed Maddoc, or had she left him to die in the darkness of Navarre?

"What are you thinking, Cat?" Sindri asked softly.

"All of this death and pain that we've gone through, and Asvoria still won. She may have lost the Aegis, but she still has the Daystar."

"Oh. You mean this?" Sindri held up the medallion in the sunlight, and it glistened like fire in his hand.

"Sindri!" Catriona gaped in shock. When she recovered her voice, she stammered, "Where did you get that?"

"It . . . uh . . . fell out of her pocket during the fight, when I jumped on her. It's not my fault people don't have stronger dress pockets, you know. A queen really ought to get a better tailor." A hint of Sindri's old humor surfaced in the kender's bruised face. "Now, come on, Cat." Sindri tucked the Daystar into his pocket and urged his horse forward. "We have to make sure Davyn's all right. It's two days to the healer's, and he's not getting any stronger." The kender's voice held a new solemnity, and Cat felt a smile rising to her lips.

He was right.

But that didn't stop her mind from lingering on the past.

CHAPTER

25   MADDOC'S LIE

The illumination of the tomb's main chamber flickered, casting dancing shadows on the walls behind the golden statues. Asvoria was far away now, borne on the wings of her shapeshifter. She would return . . . but not yet.

The light that illuminated the tomb's golden throne would fade away long before she came back, constrained to a limited existence by the very nature of the spell. When that happened, the vast gardens would be dark once more, and the tomb would no longer be a beacon of light among the twisted iron and decayed plants. The cavern would again be as it had existed for an aeon: dark, cold, and silent as the grave.

Maddoc listened, closing his eyes and letting the darkness encompass him. The sliding step of Catriona's footfalls had long ago died away into the great cavern around the obsidian tomb, and even the chatter of Sindri's constant questions was gone. He was alone in the tomb.

Although he was surrounded by all the wealth of Asvoria's kingdom, Maddoc did not care. He looked beyond it, his eyes drawn neither by platinum, nor sapphires, nor crowns made of 241 the ransom of nations. The twinkle of gold—treasures beyond compare—did not interest Maddoc. Had he wanted only wealth, he would not have chosen the black robes.

At last, the time was right. Maddoc slowly unfolded, using the throne as a crutch until he could stand on his own. The pain was great, but no more than he could bear. He walked silently through the main chamber of the tomb, reaching into a sleeve of his black velvet robe and drawing forth a square of red fabric. Kneeling gingerly, he scooped the shards of the Aegis into the makeshift bag. Three times, he checked and counted, searched to be certain he had not lost even a sliver of the ancient sword's remains, then he stood once more and folded the fabric around the pommel. Maddoc looked down at the hilt of the sword, his fingers sliding across the malachite pommel. Shaking himself out of the reverie, he folded the fabric again and covered the hilt with its length, hiding it from view.

Placing the fabric-wrapped shards within his voluminous sleeve, Maddoc walked to the throne and stared for a moment at Elidor's body. For a brief moment, the elf's chest seemed to rise and fall, almost imperceptibly.

Maddoc frowned, his hands folded within his sleeves. Then, as though he had made some critical decision, he bent down and placed his hand upon Elidor's shoulder. Maddoc spoke a few quick words, and made a passing gesture with his free hand.

The wizard's chant echoed in the empty tomb and light sprang through the obsidian corridors, glinting in soft indigo and royal red hues. It engulfed both Maddoc and Elidor. There was a rush of air.

Then, they were gone.

The adventure continues in

DRAGON DAY

by Stan Brown

Shocked by the tragic outcome of the battle with Asvoria, the companions go their separate ways. Sindri enrolls in a legendary school of magic, while Catriona meets a dashing young cleric who helps her make peace with her failures.

But as Dragon Day draws near, peace gives way to new conflict. And this time, the two friends stand as enemies in a feud between the most powerful wizards and clerics in Solamnia. Spells fly. Loyalties shatter. All the while, someone is watching, preparing for the final battle that could bring doom to them all . . .

Available March 2005

THE NEW ADVENTURES

JOIN A GROUP OF FRIENDS AS THEY UNLOCK MYSTERIES OF THE DRAGONLANCE WORLD!

TEMPLE OF THE DRAGONSLAYER
Tim Waggoner

Nearra has lost all memory of who she is. With newfound friends, she ventures to an ancient temple where she may uncover her past. Visions of magic haunt her thoughts. And someone is watching.

THE DYING KINGDOM
Stephen D. Sullivan

In a near-forgotten kingdom, an ancient evil lurks. As Nearra's dark visions grow stronger, her friends must fight for their lives.

THE DRAGON WELL
Dan Willis

Battling a group of bandits, the heroes unleash the mystic power of a dragon well. And none of them will ever be the same.

RETURN OF THE SORCERESS
Tim Waggoner

When Nearra and her friends confront the wizard who stole her memory, their faith in each other is put to the ultimate test.

For ages 10 and up

KNIGHTS OF THE SILVER DRAGON™

A YOUNG THIEF.
A WIZARD'S APPRENTICE.
A 12 YEAR-OLD BOY.
MEET THE KNIGHTS OF THE SILVER DRAGON!

SECRET OF THE SPIRITKEEPER
Matt Forbeck

Can Moyra, Kellach, and Driskoll unlock the secret of the
spiritkeeper in time to rescue their beloved wizard friend?

RIDDLE IN STONE
Ree Soesbee

Will the knights unravel the statue's riddle
before more people turn to stone?

SIGN OF THE SHAPESHIFTER
Dale Donovan

Can Kellach and Driskoll find the shapeshifter
before he ruins their father?

EYE OF FORTUNE
Denise Graham

Does the fortuneteller's prophecy spell doom
for the knights? Or unheard-of treasure?

For ages 8 to 12

Enter a World of Adventure

Do you want to learn more about the world of Krynn?
Look for these and other DRAGONLANCE® books in the fantasy section
of your local bookstore or library.

Titles by Margaret Weis and Tracy Hickman

Legends Trilogy

TIME OF THE TWINS, WAR OF THE TWINS,

AND TEST OF THE TWINS

A wizard weaves a plan to conquer darkness—
and bring it under his control.

THE SECOND GENERATION

The sword passes to a new generation of heroes—
the children of the Heroes of the Lance.

DRAGONS OF SUMMER FLAME

A young mage seeks to enter the Abyss in search of his lost uncle,
the infamous Raistlin.

The War of Souls Trilogy

DRAGONS OF A FALLEN STAR, DRAGONS OF A LOST STAR,

DRAGONS OF A VANISHED MOON

A new war begins, one more terrible than any in Krynn have ever known.

Want to know how it all began?

Want to know more about the DRAGONLANCE® world?

Find out in this new boxed set of the first DRAGONLANCE titles!

A Rumor of Dragons
Volume 1

Night of the Dragons
Volume 2

The Nightmare Lands
Volume 3

To the Gates of Palanthas
Volume 4

Hope's Flame
Volume 5

A Dawn of Dragons
Volume 6

Gift Set Available
By Margaret Weis & Tracy Hickman
For ages 10 and up